PAT ROSIER is a former editor of *Broadsheet*, New Zealand's leading feminist magazine, a former school teacher, and currently earns her living as an organisational consultant. She shares a house at the beach with her partner, Prue Hyman, in Paekakariki on the North Island's Kapiti Coast. Her previous publications include contributions to two poetry collections and, with Myra Hauschild, *Get Used To It! Children of lesbian and gay parents*, and *Poppy's Progress*, also available from Spinifex.

Other books by Pat Rosier

Fiction
Poppy's Progress

Non-fiction
Women's Studies: A New Zealand Handbook with Candis Craven,
    Claire-Louise McCurdy and Margot Roth
No Body's Perfect with Jasbindar Singh
Workwise: A guide to managing workplace relationships

Anthologies
Been Around For Quite A While: Twenty years of writing from
    Broadsheet Magazine.
Get Used To It! Children of gay and lesbian parents, with Myra
    Hauschild

PAT ROSIER

POPPY'S RETURN

Spinifex Press Pty Ltd
504 Queensberry Street
North Melbourne Vic. 3051

women@spinifexpress.com.au
http://www.spinifexpress.com.au

First published 2004

Cover design by Deb Snibson
Typeset by Palmer Higgs
Printed and bound by McPherson's Printing Group

National Library of Australia
cataloguing-in-publication data:

Rosier, Pat, 1942– .
    Poppy's return.

ISBN 1 876756 44 6.

1. Lesbianism – Fiction. 2. Life change events – Fiction.
3. Interpersonal relationships – Fiction. I. Title.

NZ823.3

*For Prue for love and support
and, once again, a title.*

Chapter One

'Your father is dying,' the letter began. It was handwritten on thin blue airmail paper, folded in thirds to fit the envelope exactly.

Poppy made herself read the rest of the single page. George had been unwell for some time, his appetite had gone, he'd lost weight, and had less energy every day. He'd been to the doctor several times without finding out what was wrong, finally agreeing to see a specialist and have some tests when the pain got bad. The verdict was that he had liver cancer – inoperable – and the prognosis was bad; he could expect to live not much more than three months. She, Susanna, couldn't cope, with her arthritis made worse by the stress and George insisting he could manage more than he could, and she had decided it was time his family in New Zealand knew.

'Shit! Shit! Shit! Bugger! God-dammit!' Poppy didn't know who she was angrier with: George for not telling her right away, Susanna for taking it on herself to write… and for directing the letter to her and not Stefan, he was George's son as much as Poppy was his daughter… Why her? Why not her brother? Susanna wanted her to go and look after George, that was clear.

Mrs Mudgely appeared, rubbing against her leg, rumbling with her usual purr. Poppy picked up the cat, stroking and cuddling and

1

wiping tears on her fur. 'Oh, Mrs M, this means I'm going to go, doesn't it? I'm not going to decide whether to go to Yorkshire and see Jane, I'll go because of George and Jane's there, and… Oh, George, poor, stupid George, why didn't you tell me?' Anger and distress were hopelessly mixed, overwhelming her. Stefan, she must talk to Stefan. Ten-past-five, he wouldn't be home from work yet. But May-Yun would be home… No. George was Stefan's father, not May-Yun's. He'd be only too ready to let his wife deal with this; she'd wait until Stefan was home before she rang. Better still, she'd go around there. Poppy jumped up, startling Mrs Mudgely. Then stood still. Then sat down again.

'Think,' she said to herself. Then, 'Talk to someone. Martia.' Martia was her closest friend. The phone rang. It was May-Yun, who often rang when Poppy had been thinking of her. 'Are you all right?' May-Yun asked after a few minutes. She had rung to tell Poppy that Chan, her middle child, had heard back from a distant cousin they had located in southern China. Chan was planning a trip to southern China to visit the area his great-grandfather had emigrated from.

'Poppy, what is it? Say something to me.'

'I've had some word of George, I need to speak to Stefan about it, I'd like to come around this evening.'

'You know you are welcome any time.' Poppy could tell from her tone that she had hurt May-Yun's feelings by not telling her right away what the word from George was.

'Oh hell, please don't be offended, I was just wanting Stefan to, you know, take responsibility, not leave it to you, so I was going to tell him first…'

'I am offended that after twenty-five years in this family I am not allowed to know something until after my husband, that is all.' Poppy could feel ten years of friendship dribbling away through the phone line.

'No, no May-Yun.' She was trying desperately to keep the tears out of her voice. 'Look, I've done this all wrong, I'm terribly sorry. I've had a letter from Susanna, just a minute, I'll get it.' She read the letter over the phone.

'I am very sorry, Poppy, that George is ill, we must all talk about it. Would you like me to come and get you, or for us to come to your place? Yes, that's it, we will come to your place, I will catch Stefan before he leaves work and we will come right over. I'll tell Ivan and he can decide for himself.' Ivan was fifteen, her and Stefan's youngest child.'

'But I don't…'

'Never mind about dinner, we can go out, or get something in. We will be there very soon.'

Once again, May-Yun had done the right thing. Her brother seldom came to her house, she usually went to his. This time they would be on her patch. 'I know,' she scratched Mrs Mudgely between the ears, 'you don't need to look disapproving, this is no time for sibling rivalry, this is George and he's really ill.'

Poppy started thinking how little information there was in Susanna's letter. She saw George's face – her kind, loving father, taking a quiet place in the world, studying his trichoptera, happiest often in a world of insects – and could not imagine his absence. Even though he'd lived in Yorkshire for thirty years he'd stayed part of her life, working hard to keep in touch, sending her little parcels, phoning and emailing regularly, always encouraging her to visit and coming back to New Zealand himself occasionally. What did it mean, Susanna saying he was dying? Wasn't everyone dying? 'Don't growl at me Mrs M, you know what I mean.'

Three months. That would be mid-August. And didn't the doctors often get it wrong? It could be much longer. Or shorter. Poppy walked around, picking things up, putting them down, staring at the photo of George and herself at Windermere that Susanna had taken – how many years ago? He was laughing, they both were, he looked so young, he couldn't be dying. He was younger than

Katrina and she was perfectly healthy. 'I know, my mother's age and health is irrelevant, I'm having random thoughts.' This to the cat who was following her around the house.

She should be doing something. Ringing Susanna, no George, what was the time difference? Was it eleven or twelve or thirteen hours at this time of year? Where's the phone book, that would tell her. Never mind, the latest it could be was six in the morning, and that was too early. Oh heavens, she'd said she'd meet that new woman, Joy, at the movies tonight, where was her number?

If Joy didn't go home after work she wouldn't get the answer-phone message. 'Sorry, a family emergency, I can't make the movie so I hope you get this,' she said to the machine. Biscuits, did she have any biscuits? There were crackers and cheese and olives so she busied herself setting them out on a plate, filled the jug, and checked that there was still some dry white in the cask in the fridge.

'Early dinner for you,' she said to the cat at her feet, crumbling left-over cooked fish from the night before into one side of the cat bowl and scooping jellimeat into the other. There was nothing else to do, so she opened the front door and sat on the steps looking across the city at the western hills. The sun was low, casting its twilight colours onto the few clouds. She saw an image of George, leaning over her beside a stream, his hand over hers on the handle of the net, making her wait for exactly the right moment to scoop up the insect. His delight was equal to hers when she succeeded and palpable every time she agreed to go caddis-fly hunting. She didn't dwell on his equally obvious disappointments when she was older and preferred going out with her friends, or her own irritation when he was – she thought – over-friendly with them. Especially after one had described him as 'nice, but a bit drippy.'

But none of that mattered because George had loved Kate. Kate, Poppy's soul mate, lover, partner for thirteen years until her death in a yachting accident, 14 February 1990. Ten years ago this year. On the anniversary, Valentine's Day, Poppy had invited her closest friends to dinner. Martia, Rina, Eve, Shirley, Bessie, Alexa – they had all been there at that terrible time. She had wanted to invite May-Yun, the other person who had held her together, but in the end didn't know how to without including her brother, so had lunch with her on the day. Katrina had rung, she hadn't forgotten, but her mother and Kate had not really gotten on. George had sent her an email card with music, and then rung and cried with her. Now George himself was dying, and she was here on the other side of the world, knowing practically nothing of how he was, what was happening to him, what she should do…

'The Internet!' She jumped up and ran down the hall to her 'office', the small third bedroom of the house, jiggling impatiently while her imac connected, then typed 'liver cancer' into the Google search field, opening and scanning quickly down the first of the thousands of sites it brought up almost immediately. 'Generally not diagnosed until advanced stage,' she read. 'Cirrhosis of the liver a major disposing factor of primary liver cancer – patients with cirrhosis forty times more likely to…' then, 'Men are twice as likely as women…' She stared at the screen, trying to make sense out of what she was reading. George didn't have cirrhosis, surely, he drank very little alcohol… but then non-smokers did sometimes get lung cancer…

'Hellooo.' Stefan was in the hallway. He hesitated in front of Poppy, then hugged her briefly, patting her shoulder and saying, 'Well, Dad's in a pickle, then.' May-Yun said nothing at first, her hug long and close, then stood back and said, 'It is a big thing, a parent being sick, very sick, dying sick,' and Poppy nodded, unable to speak.

'I've come straight from work, I'll put the jug on, shall I?' Stefan was heading for the kitchen.

'No, I'll do that, you sit down and talk to your sister.'

Stefan and Poppy sat at opposite sides of the dining table. She pushed Susanna's letter across to him and sat silently while he read

5

it. Twice. Then he looked up and said, 'I don't…' at the same time as she said, 'We must …' They both stopped.

'You go,' said Poppy.

'I was just going to say I don't know what we should do.' Stefan was looking towards the kitchen. Hoping for help from May-Yun, thought Poppy.

'Neither do I,' she said, 'except that as soon as it's a reasonable time over there I'm going to ring George. He's sick, not incapable,' she added at the look on her brother's face, 'he'll be able to talk to m… us. We don't know anything really, well, not much. I started looking up liver cancer on the internet…' Her voice trailed off. Brother and sister looked at each other across the table, then looked away.

May-Yun came in with tea and the plate of food Poppy had prepared. She smiled at them. 'I don't think you two are making much progress,' she said, as she sat down and started pouring tea, 'so I'll make a suggestion. But first of all does either of you know when England goes on to summer time?'

They both shook their heads. 'I could fi…', Poppy began, and stopped as May-Yun continued, 'It seems likely that they are by now, so it will be,' she looked at her watch, 'about 7.00 a.m. there. 'So if we go out and get some dinner, when we get back it will be late enough to ring.'

Poppy didn't feel like eating, though Stefan was making an impact on the cheese and olives. But what other way was there to spend the hour or so until they could ring? It would be easier if it were just May-Yun and I, she thought, we're both holding back because Stefan is here. The table was vibrating slightly, and she looked down to see her hands, around her mug, shaking. Hot tea spilled, stinging her fingers, and she cried out and jumped up.

'I'm sorry,' she said, then wished she hadn't. She wasn't sorry about being upset because George was ill. 'I can't go out to dinner just like this isn't happening.'

It was Stefan who stood up and put an arm around her shoulders and led her into the living room where they sat side by side on the sofa. The three of them talked about George, and his trips to New Zealand, and theirs to visit him in Middlesbrough, and Stefan read Susanna's letter again and commented that he had 'never taken to her, though he never said so because she and George seemed happy with each other.' That was the most personal remark Poppy could remember him having made about any member of their family for years. 'Should we think about what she wants from us before we ring?' he continued.

'No.' Poppy was definite. 'Let's just talk to George first, and see what – I dunno – how he is, or something.' The time had crept around to half-past-seven, which they had decided would be half-past-eight in the morning in England. They all looked at each other and nodded, so she went and got the cordless phone and George's phone number. When she was about to press the first number, she suddenly gave them both to Stefan, who hesitated for a moment then dialled. 'George, please answer the phone yourself,' Poppy muttered under her breath. Mrs Mudgely was settling herself in Stefan's spot on the sofa, so he perched on the arm.

'Hello? Dad? It's Stefan. Yes, that's right, Stefan. How are… I'm at Poppy's, I hope we didn't wake you. Good. Dad, Poppy had a letter from Susanna today, and well, we're all a bit worried…' He made writing gestures in the air. 'Hang on a minute Dad, I'll take a note of all this.' Not so sure it had been a good idea to have her brother speak to him first, Poppy passed him a pen and moved closer until she could just hear her father's voice, but she couldn't make out enough words.

'That's good Dad, gives us a better idea… yes, Poppy's right here and she's dying – sorry, wrong word – to talk to you herself. You take care and I'll talk to you again soon,' and he held out the phone.

'Oh George, why didn't you tell me?' They were both crying within seconds. He'd been feeling unwell for some months and put it down to getting older until his loss of appetite and the pain began to bother him. The doctor had had some tests done and eventually, after several weeks, referred him to a specialist.

'According to Susanna's letter the doctor had to insist on a specialist,' commented Stefan, when Poppy was off the phone and they were sharing information.

The specialist had ordered a CT scan, the results of which came through about a week ago. That would be when Susanna wrote, Poppy thought. The results showed that there was one large tumor and several smaller ones, with evidence of affected lymph nodes. Surgery was not an option. George was refusing any of the other possible treatments, all of which had severe side effects.

'It looks pretty grim,' Stefan said. 'He seems to think that various treatments might slow it – the cancer – down but they make you sick anyway and, as he put it, he's "had a pretty good innings".'

'I asked him about the three months' prognosis that Susanna referred to,' said Poppy, 'and I didn't get a proper answer. I think that was probably what the specialist had said – but they're never definite, they usually say this to that range of weeks or months so maybe that was the longest…' she struggled to go on. 'I'm going to go, really soon.'

'We must all go.' May-Yun had not spoken for a long time. She looked at her husband. 'You have a few week's leave owing…'

'Four, but …'

'I think you and I should go as soon as we can and we can report back to Poppy who will probably want to go for longer,' – Poppy nodded – 'even until… I'm sorry, my dear.' Poppy reached out a hand and May-Yun clasped it, 'until the end.'

There wasn't a lot more they could discuss, but it was still after nine o'clock when May-Yun and Stefan left. May-Yun had looked at Poppy very closely, 'Will you be all right on your own?' Poppy nodded. 'Perhaps I could ring Martia and ask to her come? Or I could stay myself? Stefan and Ivan can manage.'

'I'll be fine,' Poppy insisted. 'Truly, I'll be fine.'

What will I do, she thought after they had gone, whatever will I do? Mrs Mudgely was at her ankles, so she gathered up the cat and returned to the sofa. 'I need to talk to people,' she nuzzled into the fur, 'who will it be first, Katrina or Martia?' She decided on her mother, who had after all been married to George for over twenty years.

'I am sorry, George doesn't deserve that,' Katrina said to a still-tearful Poppy, 'but our marriage ended nearly thirty years ago and I'm not emotionally attached any more. Now don't go telling me I'm brittle or hard or something again, dear, it's just a fact.' Well yes, thought Poppy, there had been three significant men in that thirty years, though it did seem that Don Smart had been the last.

'Don't write me off yet!' came the voice down the phone, as though she had said it out loud. 'Not that I'm looking. But, seriously, I imagine you will want to go and see him, and soon. So if money is a problem…'

'Thank you, Katrina but no, I'm fine for money.' Which was more or less true; Poppy had never been much of a saver, though she did have government super, had started it when she began teaching, and the mortgage on the house would be paid off in four more years. She told her mother all she knew about the nature of the illness and read her Susanna's letter.

'Don't let her take advantage of your good nature, now, will you?' Funny, until now, Poppy had never picked that her New Zealand family didn't like Susanna, never thought about whether or not she did herself, just accepted that as her father's wife Susanna must be all right. She and George seemed to suit each other.

'Do keep me in touch, and you know I will help in any way,' Katrina had said once more before she bustled off the phone, no doubt to ring Stefan and offer him money as well, Poppy thought. Once she had resented Katrina's tendency to 'wave her cheque-book in the face of any crisis', as Stefan had put it once, but she had learnt to appreciate having a generous parent who was, after many years as a successful bureaucrat, rather well off.

Martia's phone was engaged, so she left a message asking her to ring back if she got the message before too late. Martia and Poppy knew each others' 'too lates' and much more besides; they had been close friends since their first year at secondary school. Late last year Martia had been low and sick with a vague debilitating sickness, and Poppy had helped her get away on holiday for three months. When Jane was here.

Chapter Two

Martia rang back within minutes. 'I'm doing okay, now tell me what's up with you,' she said to Poppy's inquiry about her health, 'You sound dreadful.'

Poppy told her about Susanna's letter.

'Oh, Poppy, poor George. And poor you. When will you go?'

'Soon,' she replied and went on to tell her friend about May-Yun and Stefan's plans. 'And Martia,' she continued, her voice rising to a wail, 'what am I going to do about Jane?' After a few seconds silence, she said, 'You're not laughing, tell me you're not laughing.'

'I'm not laughing, not quite, honestly. It's the irony. George might well love that, he brought you together now he's forcing your hand, so to speak.' Another silence. 'I haven't offended you, have I. I don't mean to, really, it's just…'

'No, I'm not offended. More like bewildered. Jane would have had everything with her and Héloise sorted by the time I got over there at the end of the year, for sure, as it is…'

'She'll just have to get on with it. It's what, three months since she went back.'

'Yes, but…'

'Come on Poppy, you had a lovely few weeks travelling around

11

New Zealand together, now if she wants you she has to front up to her partner. For heaven's sake, she doesn't want a baby and Héloïse does, that's enough in itself, never mind her falling in love with you.'

'Yes, but I don't know…'

'How you feel, because you won't let yourself find out until she's dis-entangled.'

'Yeah, right, but George matters more than any of that now.'

'Of course he does, poor George, he doesn't deserve this. It's tough for you being so far away. This is stupid,' she interrupted herself, 'sit tight, I'm coming over.'

'But you're…' still not that well, Poppy was going to say, you shouldn't come out so late. When Martia arrived she hugged Poppy for a long time, and sat them down together on the sofa.

'I have to just think about George,' Poppy said. Martia nodded, and kept nodding as Poppy continued. 'I'll talk to Moana about taking leave for the rest of the term, from about two weeks' time. Then I'll have had some news from Stefan and May-Yun if they go right away.

'Why wait?' Martia asked.

'To be fair to school, so I can say as clearly as possible how long I am likely to be away, I think. And maybe to get used to the idea of seeing Jane so soon, as well as having George… you know. It's turning out very differently from how I'd planned.'

'Uh huh. Trust yourself, Poppy, do it – all of it, George *and* Jane – the best you can, as you always do. What's Jane said to her partner about you, anyway?'

There was a pause. 'I don't know,' Poppy answered, quietly. 'I didn't want to ask, and she never said. I guess I'd better ask now.'

'You sure had. Otherwise who knows what you'd be walking into… They're still living together, right?'

'Uh huh, and Héloïse still wants to have a baby, and Jane still wants out but she doesn't say much about how she's going to do that, except that she promised it would be before I go over in December. And that seemed all right – kind of – until now.'

'Sounds to me like she's faltering…' Martia hesitated. 'Which is not fair on you, she's got to make up her mind… so it might as well be now!'

Poppy smiled weakly. 'Just what I would say to someone else,' she admitted, 'but when she says she needs to pick her times for talking about it to avoid major upsets and arguments, well, it sort of seems fair enough.'

'Hurumph!' Martia laughed as she grumbled, which barely hid her concern.

'I've been happy enough to let her take her own time,' Poppy said, more defensively than she intended, 'My life's going along fine.'

'And this year was the tenth anniversary of Kate's death.' Martha spoke gently this time, 'and as you said then, you've been on your own for a long time.'

'Apart from R…'

'Rose, who you yourself have often described as "a mistake".'

'Are we nearly arguing about Jane?' Poppy's tears were starting again.

'If we are, we'll stop now. You going over to see George will change things, though.'

'I know. And I do have to tell you,' Poppy looked at her friend, 'I get a real, excited shiver when I see her name in my in-box and I do, um, sometimes go to sleep picturing us together in situations being, ah, significantly more than friendly…' By the end she was blushing. 'And I kind of like that!'

'You know there's nothing I'd like more than you to be…'

'Happy. Yes, I know. Dear Martia.' They hugged again and Martia suggested a cuppa.

'Yes,' said Poppy, 'But golly, it's after eleven, I'm sorry Martia, I shouldn't be keeping you up this late…'

'It doesn't matter, not at all. And hey, the new tests apparently show that I've had some kind of low grade virus, something that usually doesn't matter except when you are run down, you know the sort of thing. Anyway, it's a relief to know I had something and I do feel as though I am getting over it. Truly. I've got much more energy. I've even got enough energy to feel a bit sad at Barb's leaving, how about that?'

'That's great news! That you're feeling better, that is.' The jug was boiling but they decided they both needed to go to bed more than they needed tea.

'One last question,' said Poppy as she opened the front door, 'how are you managing the rent without Barb?'

'Just. I've got a rent subsidy from social welfare, that helps. And I'll think about moving somewhere cheaper in another month or so, I'm all right until then, honestly.'

They said their goodbyes with a final hug, and 'Trust yourself Poppy, you'll do the right thing by George,' from Martia.

Poppy dropped her clothes on the floor and fell into bed, exhausted. She lay there for a while, comforted by Mrs Mudgely's purring and thought about talking to George earlier in the evening, how he had sounded, how unconcerned he'd been that Susanna had written before he had told her – them – himself. Why hadn't he written or rung earlier? Was it really that he didn't want to worry her? Or did he not want to admit to himself how ill he was?

Then she was cross with herself for trying to work out things she couldn't possibly know. Two weeks, she thought, that's definitely when she'd go, regardless of what Stefan and May-Yun did. It was about six weeks until the end of June when term finished, and then two weeks' school holidays. Would that be long enough? She had better talk to Moana about being away for the third term, too. That would mean over four months without any salary, could she manage that and surely she wouldn't have to resign from her job and what about Mrs Mudgely and the house? The answer to the latter came immediately. Dear Martia. 'Now go to sleep,' she told herself firmly.

The purring had stopped, suggesting Mrs Mudgely had already set a good example.

The phone woke her in the morning at seven o'clock. She had forgotten to set her alarm. May-Yun was apologetic about waking her, but Poppy insisted she was grateful – who knows how late she would have slept otherwise. When they had got home last night, May-Yun told her, Chan had just come in and he got on the internet and had them booked for London and on a fast train to York – Stefan had decided on the spot they would rent a car from there – by eleven o'clock. Stefan had been impressed. 'Finally, Chan can please his father,' Poppy thought. They were leaving on Saturday which was a rush. Chan and Ivan insisted they would be fine in the house together but she wasn't sure about that, what did Poppy think?

'Don't know, straight off,' said Poppy, 'but probably fine. I can keep an eye out and I know you have some good neighbours…'

'We told them we'd think about it for twenty-four hours and then decide, so I'm going to talk to two of the neighbours today. I want to trust them…'

'Then do.' Poppy decided not to rush for school. As long as she was there by half-past-eight she'd be fine. Thank goodness her class routines were well bedded in, and the last hour was sports. Unless that was rain on the window. Usually she was at school before eight preparing for the day but, for once, she thought, she wouldn't be. And she must make a chance to talk to Moana.

The chance came near the end of lunch hour so she gabbled out the details as fast as she could. Moana made some notes and said, 'Of course, you must go. There's that young man, Stephen…' Poppy nodded, he'd relieved for her colleague, Amelia, a few times this year. 'I think he'd jump at the chance of some regular work. Leave that with me. Oh, I will have to get the Board of Trustee's approval, but that won't be a problem.'

'Thank you, Moana, for being so understanding.' How lucky she was to have such a great principal. No fuss. Do what needs doing. Let teachers teach – as much as possible in the current environment. Poppy smiled her thanks again as she left the office.

At two o'clock Moana came to her classroom and sent her off to 'book air travel, or whatever you need to do', while she took Poppy's class for sports.

The first travel agent in Takapuna took an age to understand what she needed. Surely a return trip with an open return date was straightforward enough? Then she had to go off and ask someone and after several minutes' waiting for her to return Poppy walked out.

The next one was better. 'You're lucky,' said Nigel, 'travel consultant' according to his badge, 'it's not the summer season – over there – yet.' No, she wouldn't stop over anywhere, via Singapore or Los Angeles it didn't matter, but through to London as quickly as possible. Two hours in Los Angeles would be fine. She winced when he told her what it would cost and handed over her credit card. Picking up the tickets would be no problem she told him, she'd come after school. He gave her a traveller's check-list, which would be useful. When *did* her passport expire?

'I wondered how long it would take you to ask. I thought of it when we were talking last night. And yes, I'd love to and you must let me pay at least expenses, your mortgage and phone and all that.' Poppy had called in at Martia's on her way home. 'And don't worry about when you get back, I have a plan.'

'Go on.'

'My ex-sister-in-law, you know, Gloria, in Matapouri…' Indeed, Poppy did know, she had taken Martia there for a holiday in January when she was so unwell. 'Well, she wants to open a craft shop on the edge of their place, by the main road, and I'm going to go there and run it. But not until spring, September or so. And I can send any of my stuff – she waved her hand around to indicate the modest contents of the flat – whenever I want to, there's plenty of room. So you see, it's perfect!'

'Perfect!' Poppy responded. Now wasn't the time to tell her friend how much she would miss her; this was the most energy and excitement Martia had shown for many months and Poppy shared it as well as she could.

By the weekend Poppy had found out that it was remarkably easy to re-arrange your life if you had to. The young man, Stephen, was delighted to relieve in her class and Moana had even found some money to have him come in a couple of half-days next week so they could do a proper transition with the children. As long as he… no, expecting him to run her class exactly as she did was silly, he would have his own ways, but she did hope he would keep up what she knew were her very good routines and classroom organisation.

When she had rung George to tell him she was coming Susanna had answered the phone. Poppy asked how she was and listened to a long reply and then asked for George. Stefan had already rung and said they would be there by the end of the weekend. 'I hope they find the spare room big enough,' George worried, 'and we've been living very simply, with us both being unwell. Susanna's son doesn't come by so often now his children are older.' After she had reassured him, confident herself that whatever the situation May-Yun would make the best of it and Stefan would be practical, she asked again about treatment for his cancer and whether he would have any and got another answer that didn't really tell her anything. While she was still on the phone she added to her 'to do' list, 'tell Stefan to go to the doctor with George and get some real information.'

Now she couldn't put off emailing Jane any longer. At no time since she got Susanna's letter had she allowed herself to really think for more than a few seconds about what it would be like, being in Middlesbrough for George, with Jane and Héloise still living in their joint house a few miles away. Never get involved with someone in a relationship had been one of the principle rules of her life. And she hadn't got involved with Jane. At least they hadn't been sexual, or even kissed, except on the cheek. But it felt as though they were involved, as though there was something between them, attraction and more than that, something they had to work out, but not until the situation with Héloise was resolved. And would it ever be resolved? Would they go on living together for ages, for ever, with or without Héloise having a child? Would Jane ever have the gumption to leave? In January before she went back to England it had seemed as though she would, but since she got home she'd lost some of the sense of an independent self that Poppy had seen grow in her while she was in New Zealand.

'Okay, Mrs M,' Poppy said when the cat jumped on the computer desk, making a line of zzzzzzzzs. 'I'll get on with it.'

Dear Jane,
This is a hard message to write.

She looked at screen. 'No, that's hopeless, she'll think I'm about to do a 'Dear Jane' letter.' She thought about that as an idea for a moment. Mrs Mudgely raised her head from the papers she had settled on and looked at her. 'Okay, okay, that's not a goer, I never thought it was, really, I didn't'. She deleted and started again.

This week everything changed. On Tuesday I got a letter from Susanna saying…

That was better. By the time she had finished it was a long message, but it had everything in it, including Poppy's concerns about forcing whatever it was between them and her subsequent thought that maybe that wasn't such a bad idea, and her need now to know more about what exactly the present circumstances were with Jane and Héloise. She read it through and was pleased with what she had written. One click on 'send' and she imagined her message flying through the air at the speed of light, or whatever it was in cyberspace, and sliding into the password-protected mailbox Jane had told her she'd set up on their computer at home. 'Their' computer, 'their' home, it was all too much for Poppy, she didn't want a bar of it, she just wanted – something – with an untram-melled Jane. Waiting until the end of the year, exchanging weekly emails and getting occasional phone calls from Jane when she was in the house on her own – and even that felt sneaky to Poppy – had seemed okay until the news of George. Now she was impatient and cross with Jane.

She checked her inwards mail again just before she logged off, as she usually did, and there was a single message and it was from Jane and that was odd, because she didn't usually write until Sunday.

'We crossed out there in the ether, I guess,' she said to Mrs Mudgely and clicked on the subject line, 'which is weird because it's only…

six in the morning and I can't sleep, she read.

I hope you'll be pleased, I have taken another step towards extricating myself from Héloise. Last night I moved into the spare room and it was fairly amicable, though H went out while I did it. I know you don't want to know too much about what happens between us, so I'll leave it at that.

'Surely, surely, I'm sure I remember her saying that ages ago, when she first got back.' Mrs Mudgely opened one eye. 'Have they been in the same bed all this time? No, no, I know there's something…' Poppy was scanning through Jane's earlier emails, one a week since the beginning of February. Nothing. 'That's odd. Nothing. Did I imagine it?' She stared at the cat then looked quickly away. 'Okay, okay, that's how I wanted it to be so I thought it was'. She looked back. 'And I know you were very taken with Ms Blackie and it's no good expecting you to criticise her.'

It is very difficult at the museum. Skimming the next few para-graphs, Poppy learned that the information Jane had brought back from her time at the Auckland and Wellington museums had everyone very excited about how they could spend the legacy that had been the reason for her visit; and there was also a lot of politicking about what exactly to do and it had started to get personal and nasty and she was trying to stay right out of that.

By the way, have you heard from George lately? He's been coming in less and less over the last month and looking quite poorly. I meant to say something last week and forgot. This was followed by the usual 'missing you' and 'love, Jane,' as always.

'How could I have been so certain she had moved out of their bedroom when she never said?' The computer was shut down and Poppy was pacing the living room with the cat on her shoulder. She stopped. 'Have they been…?' She flopped onto the sofa. 'Oh, what does it matter anyway?' she directed at the departing cat. 'It's George that matters for now, not my love life or whatever.' The ache in her stomach told her that wasn't true, so she sighed heavily, stood up and headed for the kitchen where Mrs Mudgely jumped down and sat by her bowl.

The next week dragged by, even though it was busy. She never actually got over to Howick to see Chan and Ivan, but Katrina had cooked for them on two days and stayed the night once. 'Checking up on us,' Ivan had reported on the phone, 'but she's a pretty good cook and actually she can be good fun.' And various neighbours were popping in with food and ringing and generally leaving no chance to, 'cut loose, even if we had wanted to. And I haven't been late for school once.' Poppy had smiled at the pride in his voice.

By Thursday Martia had arranged for her furniture to go up north to Gloria's and agreed with the flat owner that if he got a new tenant to move in Martia's rent would stop immediately, otherwise she would pay out the three weeks' notice she was supposed to give.

Shared mornings in her classroom with Stefan had gone smoothly. Moana reported that the Board of Trustees chairperson had approved her leave. (She didn't tell Poppy how hard she had had to argue to retain 'an experienced and excellent teacher' in the face of his opinion that it would be more efficient to find a permanent replacement.)

The only thing Poppy hadn't sorted was what to do about her car. It was the newest she had ever owned, a 1996 Honda Civic, and leaving it parked on the road for weeks seemed like a big risk in a city where car vandalism and theft was rife. When Katrina came up with a solution – 'I've got half a double garage I don't use, drive your car over here on Monday and I'll take you to the airport,' she wanted to have remembered that herself; she was so edgy that one patronising comment from Katrina would be one too many.

The following day there was a letter from Katrina in her mail. It contained a cheque for $10,000 and a note that read, '*You can't argue with a letter. I gave Stefan a little more because there are two of them going. Indulge me, I can easily afford it and you and Stefan will have it one day, anyway. xxK.*' 'Never mind pride, Poppy,' she said to herself and put the cheque in her bag to bank the next day when she went to get English money then rang Katrina and thanked her. 'I might just have surprised my mother for once,' she told the cat when she got off the phone.

Suddenly it was Sunday and she was leaving the next day. Her email to Jane had been brief, saying that Stefan and May-Yun would meet her train at York, then she could get the latest about George from them on the drive. The two of them had stayed at George's for the first week, then moved to a bed-and-breakfast nearby. Word from the specialist was that radiography and chemotherapy would slow down the progress of the tumours; they would also make George ill. The specialist's opinion was that, although she always encouraged patients to have treatment, at seventy, George was entitled to make the decision for himself.

There was a final email from Jane, sorry of course about George, *and everyone at the museum is concerned about him, one or two have been to visit and say he looks thin and not well, but is the same old George to talk to. It didn't seem right, for me to go.*

And, dear, dear, Poppy I cannot pretend that I am not excited, no, thrilled, that you will be here soon.

'Am I thrilled, Mrs Mudgely?' There was no answer. 'Well, I am something, pleased maybe, to be seeing her again soon. Oh, all right, very pleased, maybe even excited! When I can stop thinking about George.' She was crying again. Often during the days since Susanna's letter she had cried; once, half-watching a television programme, she had noticed a scene set in the English countryside with a man of indeterminate age walking along a stream, and had suddenly been sobbing. By the time the paroxysm had subsided into quiet tears the scene was long gone and she switched off the television and went to bed, thankful for the comforting presence of Mrs Mudgely.

'That is good, Poppy, very good,' May-Yun had said when Poppy told her about the tears during the next phone call from Middlesbrough. 'You are getting used to the truth that your father is dying, and he is, Poppy dear. He is not going to die before you arrive, but you must be prepared, he is very sick and has got weaker even since we arrived. And he has pain, and the medicine is dealing with that.' She also reported that Stefan had spent a couple of hours each day sitting with him and talking, something she was *very* pleased about. When Poppy asked her about Susanna it was clear from her reply that it was not possible to say anything at that moment.

On the Sunday afternoon Martia moved in. She would use the spare bedroom, she had decided, the one with the outlook up Maungawhau, not Poppy's room. 'The room Jane had,' Poppy thought and didn't say.

'I want to come to the airport with you. Shall I ring Katrina and see if it's okay for her to drop me here on her way back to Herne Bay?' Poppy was staring into space and didn't answer. Her friend watched her for a moment and then went to phone.

During the last minute rush Poppy remembered that she had never got back to the woman Joy and explained leaving her in the lurch regarding the movie, and that had been over a week ago. She asked Martia to ring Joy when she got back from the airport, following the request with a tearful farewell of Mrs Mudgely, glad she did not have to leave her at Moggy Manor for an indefinite period. 'We'll do just fine together,' Martia reassured her, and joined Katrina in bustling her out the door.

On the drive Poppy worried out loud about not having let other friends know what she was doing and Martia reassured her that she would bring them up to date. 'Rina especially,' Poppy insisted, 'And Alexa and Bessie. And Eve.'

'All of them,' Martia promised, 'and very soon. Please don't worry.'

As she and Martia walked back to the car after waving Poppy down the air bridge, Katrina said, 'Well, I'm relieved the flight wasn't delayed, or we'd have had two of her.'

'Two…?'

'Two Poppys. She'd have been beside herself.' Katrina explained.

'Oh, yes, I see.' Martha quickened her step to keep up with Katrina's brisk stride.

Chapter Three

When Poppy arrived at York railway station she had been travelling for over forty hours and had never been more pleased to see her brother. It was five o'clock in the afternoon and there was still the drive to Middlesbrough and seeing her father before she could go to bed.

'Where's…?'

'At a hotel on the way out of town, we're staying overnight.'

Relief swept through her so fast she stumbled. Stefan dropped a bag and grabbed her arm. 'Steady on.'

She leant on her brother's shoulder. 'I am so grateful, and so desperate to lie down, and to have a shower, and to eat something that's not airline food. Not necessarily in that order. Before I see George. Is that awful?'

'No, it's human. Come on, it's only five minutes in the car. Sometimes even your brother can have a good idea.' All Poppy could manage was a nod.

The warmth of May-Yun's greeting when she opened the door, being taken care of, her absolute weariness from travelling, all combined to undo her completely. She fell into an armchair and let the tears flow. 'Sorry,' she managed after a few minutes. 'It's the tiredness, and you both being so kind.'

'What else would we be?' Stefan asked.

There was salad, just made, freshly baked bread, ham off-the-bone, strawberries, melon, mandarins, all beautifully arranged on the few plates in the room. 'There is no kitchen, so this is very simple; we thought you would not want to go out again once you were here,' May-Yun explained and Poppy ate, grateful for fresh food.

When Poppy looked around she could see that there were two rooms, the one they were in containing a double bed, a television, the necessaries for making hot drinks, a tiny fridge, and a built-in corner that was, no doubt, a shower and toilet. And the other room would be a bedroom. How sensible. She smiled at them both. 'It just didn't occur to me that we wouldn't have to drive to Middlesbrough today; this is so good.' She paused for a moment then asked, 'You haven't said, how is George?'

'He is ill, and he is not going to die yet,' May-Yun answered. 'And he's very excited to be seeing you tomorrow.' She looked at Stefan, who continued, 'We're staying on for three more days, at Mrs Jacob's B & B, so there'll be plenty of time to talk. Just now, you need to get rested, you look dreadful.'

'I'll bet. But… this,' Poppy gestured around the room, 'and where you are staying, it must all be costing a fortune!'

'Okay, just one thing now, then May-Yun and I are going out for a meal and a movie and you will stay here and wash and eat or whatever you have to do and then rest, sleep even.' Stefan went to a zip bag in the corner of the room, took out a thickish envelope and handed it to Poppy. All that was in it were one hundred pound notes. 'Twenty of them,' Stefan told her. 'From George.' She was shaking her head. 'He gave me an envelope just like it.'

Stefan explained that George had had him drive him to the bank two days in a row and on the second day had collected four thousand pounds cash. The way George had told it to him, after his death there would be little enough for the two of them, he would leave everything to Susanna, of course, and it would, in due course, no doubt, go to her children. So he didn't want any discussion or argument, it was little enough.

Poppy couldn't help herself, she laughed. 'Katrina and now George, throwing money at us… I feel a bit funny about it. Do you think they believe we couldn't manage without their help?'

'I think they're both doing their best to be decent,' said Stefan. 'When I got Katrina's cheque and rang her she said she wouldn't argue, if I didn't want the money give it to charity, she didn't need to know what I did with it, she needed to give it to me. And I didn't. Give it to charity, that is. But I – we – are thinking about giving some to the kids.'

'When I think how hard it is for Martia to manage…' Poppy was struggling with heavy eyelids, 'I can't think just now.' She stuffed the envelope in her bag and stood up. 'You're right, everything else can wait until tomorrow, I'm heading for the shower.' The other two had left when she came out, so she picked at some more food then collapsed into one of the twin beds in the other room.

As she started to drift off she thought of Jane. Should she ring her? Jane hadn't answered her email question about what Héloise had been told; *a little* was not informative. No phone in this room. How to do toll calls from a hotel phone? Too hard. She went to sleep. When she finally woke fully after a night of restless dreams it was 6.00 a.m. and she had to creep out through the other room to go to the toilet. She couldn't remember another time when she had seen her brother in bed as an adult. Ring Jane, there was urgency to that now, she wanted to ring Jane. But not at this time. A walk in a couple of hours, a public phone box. What would she say? 'Hi Jane, here I am, are you still living with Héloise?' What if H answered the phone? Back in bed she started planning what to say to Jane, but before she got much further than deciding to say 'hello' rather than 'hi' she fell asleep again.

By eight-thirty they were on the road to Middlesbrough and Poppy had not found or made an opportunity to ring Jane. Over breakfast of instant coffee and the remains of the food from the night before, Stefan had reported in detail on his visit to the oncologist with George. The oncologist, Stefan thought, generally agreed with George's decision to forgo treatment but was obliged to encourage people towards various options in case he was seen to be failing in his medical duty. The local doctor was pretty good, he thought, and could probably be relied on to make sure they knew what support services were available as they were needed. George absolutely refused to go to any 'living with cancer' or 'facing death' groups. He, Stefan, was glad to have come – here he nodded an acknowledgement at his wife – and had spent some good times with his father; they had even talked a little about some sore spots from the past.

'Will you come back for his funeral?' Poppy was as startled as anyone when the question came out.

'I don't know. Probably. I think. That's the best answer I can give at the moment. Do you want me to?'

'I don't know. I might. I don't know why I asked that right now.' Poppy was slightly embarrassed. 'I guess I'm scared of, you know, the next bit, whatever it is going to be.' And she busied herself with closing her bag, not willing to say out loud that she was just as scared of talking to – seeing – Jane and the two mixed up together was just about more than she could deal with.

They took the A19 to Middlesbrough, skirting the Yorkshire Moors, talking very little on the way. George was expecting them by lunch-time. Poppy sat in the back seat, reasonably refreshed from her arduous journey, watching the English countryside go by without really seeing it, oblivious for once to the intrusions of industry and the big white power stations. Separating her fears and feelings about George from those relating to Jane was suddenly imperative; how to manage time and attention for each, how much or little to tell George, whether to tell May-Yun and Stefan about – exactly what about? – her and Jane? There were so many questions and she didn't have answers for any of them.

During a stop in Thirsk for 'some decent coffee' at May-Yun's insistence, she found herself talking about how she and Jane had been continuing to keep in touch, how she had planned to come over at the end of the year when Jane's present circumstances were more sorted and see whether they had anything to, 'you know…' she stopped, flustered, unused to talking to her brother in this way, looking at May-Yun for help. It was Stefan who responded first.

'That's good to know,' he said, meeting her eyes briefly, 'it sounds pretty difficult to me.' Then he looked at his wife for assistance. She took her time.

'Thank you for telling us,' she began, 'now we can help a little while we are still here. Perhaps you could take some time – this evening or tomorrow evening – to spend with Jane. And do tell George.' She smiled a little. 'It will be good for him to have some-thing outside himself and Susanna to think about – although his interest may be a little trying for you sometimes.' Poppy felt a weight fall off her. Of course, it was simple really, why ever was she even beginning to think about not telling, she couldn't separate them, there was no need to, they were both difficult and she had to do them both at the same time, that was how it had worked out, and of course she would manage. Over the years she had expected support and encouragement and sympathy from her friends and got it in large measure, and from May-Yun too around that dreadful time when Kate had died. It was new, though, to have a sense of positive interest in what he called her 'lifestyle' from her brother. She felt a renewed warmth towards him.

'There are some other things you should know about,' began Stefan, and went on to tell Poppy about the cleaner who was coming in twice a week and the home nursing that would be available when it was needed. George had cancelled the cleaner for this week, not wanting a stranger about, 'and it has given May-Yun and me some things to do,' he concluded.

May-Yun turned from the front seat and said, 'It is good to be able to do some practical things.' Poppy nodded in agreement; she hoped there would be more for her to do than sit with George, though she certainly wanted to do that.

Stop it, she told herself, stop trying to work it out in advance, you'll just do the best you can, making it up as you go along and she began to pay more attention to the countryside they were passing through, enjoying the English green-ness of it under the grey cloud. Shortly she dozed off yet again and woke with a start as Stefan turned the car into the driveway at George's Middlesbrough house; modest, two-level, brick, semi-detached. Her father appeared in the doorway and she jumped out of the car and ran to him. They hugged closely for a long time, then stood back and looked at each other, both tearful.

'You are a grand sight, a grand, grand sight.' He gripped her lower arms with both hands, his mouth trembling, his eyes wet.

'You're not looking so bad, yourself,' Poppy managed, glad he was in fact better than her worst fears, but thin, terribly thin, the skin around his jaw seemed too big for him. Susanna was hovering the hallway and Poppy released both arms from George's grip, putting one around his shoulders for a moment, then went forward to greet her – no, not step-mother, Poppy had been grown-up when she married George thirty years ago – father's wife. She was shocked when she got close, to see how drawn the other woman was, how tired looking, how slowly she moved and how claw-like her hands had become. Poppy hugged her carefully.

'I am glad to see you too, my dear, as I was to see your brother. This is very, very hard for me,' Susanna waved her hands helplessly. 'Come along in, all of you,' she raised her voice and the whining tone diminished, 'there's some dinner ready.' And she led the way to a table with cold-cuts and bread and honey and jam and a large pot of tea under a brightly-coloured tea cosy.

Everyone did their best to keep a conversation going, commenting on the grey day, the general warmth of the month, the trip from York, whether Stefan and May-Yun would dally a day or two in the old city on their way home; they would leave in three days and were planning to spend a week, or even ten days holidaying in London and Singapore. Stefan had been in touch with his work and the deputy-manager insisted she had everything under control and head office had agreed to the extra time so long as he was back at least a week before the end of June sale.

'So,' he said, obviously pleased with himself, 'we'll have our first real holiday without any children for twenty-five years. It will be like…' he stopped suddenly, embarrassed. 'I'm sorry Dad, that must sound awful, we really didn't come over to make an excuse for a holiday.' George reassured him and went on to talk about what they must do in London, until Poppy pointed out that it had taken her all of her year in London after Kate had died to do everything on his 'must-see' list, and sure, she was working as well, but she doubted they could all be done in three days. And everyone laughed and it became almost an ordinary family get-together over lunch.

Susanna was quiet until May-Yun asked after her children and grandchildren; she became animated while she spoke of her older son, Oliver, now deputy principal of a secondary school in Harrogate and how well his children were doing. 'Still married to Jean,' she added with a small laugh, 'not like my Sylvia, twice-divorced'. There's that edge in her voice again thought Poppy. Sylvia, it transpired, lived not far away in a 'pokey flat' and had a job with the council, her mother said, 'administrating. Well, that's what she calls it, sounds like nowt more than clerking to me. She's had all the chances and pines for what she can't get, I'm right fed up with her.'

George took his wife's hand. 'Don't upset yourself about Sylvia, she's all right,' he said. 'Plays a good game of backgammon,' he added to the others. 'And there's Gavin,' he went on, 'who lives in the States, we don't hear much from him.' Susanna pushed back her chair and the New Zealand three jumped up and insisted on clearing away and doing the dishes.

'Tell me, please, what's with Susanna?' Both she and George had gone for an after-lunch rest, but Poppy asked quietly nonetheless as they all busied themselves in the kitchen, Stefan washing, she drying and May-Yun putting away. 'She's never been like this before.'

'I think she finds it hard, George being ill, she's always been the one to need care, and you can see how bad her arthritis is now. None of her children come around much, and she's gushy with Oliver and picky with Sylvia so it's pretty unpleasant if they are both here at once.' Stefan scrubbed vigorously at a clean plate. 'Makes me appreciate my own family.' He smiled over his shoulder at Poppy.

'That's a little harsh,' intervened May-Yun. 'She's scared of what will happen, to her and to George.'

'Who's that taking my name in vain?' He was standing in the doorway. 'I couldn't sleep. Come and sit with your old father,' he said to Poppy, who handed her tea towel to May-Yun and followed him down the hallway to the sitting room. He sat on the sofa and patted the space beside him.

'How much have they told you?' he asked and gave her no time to answer, 'I'm not having treatment, you know, good innings and all that, rather go out quicker and cleaner. I'll take all the pain relief the medicos will give me but I'm not going through losing my hair and nausea and burns, would if I was a young chap, but not now.' He slumped back into the sofa. 'Get tired easily.'

'Perhaps you should…'

'One more thing, one more thing.' Thin fingers gripped her hand. 'You will stay, won't you?' His voice was pleading, his eyes moist. 'You will stay until the end, please?' Irritation, followed quickly by guilt, welled up in her. Of course she would stay, she wanted to stay,

31

there was no way she could leave while he was still alive. Yet she did not want him to cling and plead like this, she wanted him to be the father she remembered, a bit distracted maybe but interested and caring and fun and – above all – grown up. She wanted the father she experienced as a child, the father she was beginning to think had been an illusion, a fantasy, someone she had created for herself. And yet, and yet, he *had* been caring and interested and fun *and* grown up. It was now that he was something else, something less, diminished by the illness, child-like and dependent as she had been back then. And she could, she realised, be the grown up he wanted, now, at the end of his life, without giving up her early memories of him. It was so obvious once she had thought it, so obvious and so all right.

'Of course.' She turned her hand and squeezed his gently. 'Of course I will stay. For as long as… as long as you are here.' The next hurdle, she thought, is for one of us to actually say he is dying. For me to say, 'When you die,' not 'when you have gone,' and for him to say, 'I am dying,' instead of 'the end' or letting a sentence trail off. May-Yun and Mrs Mudgely were both nodding in her head. 'Okay you two, if you are so wise, why does it matter to say dead, dying, die, what's wrong with a little euphemism here and there?'

'Uh,' George jerked out of a doze. 'What did you say, Poppy dear?'

'Nothing George, just thinking out loud.'

'Mmm,' and he smiled a little and drifted off again, so she took his elbow and steered him up the stairs and to the door of the bedroom he shared with Susanna, who she could hear gently snoring. George patted her hand and moved slowly to the bed, easing himself on to it. Once she was sure he was safely lying down, Poppy closed the door quietly and went to phone Jane. She wanted to talk to George about herself and Jane, but clearly he needed to sleep first. She met Stefan at the bottom of the stairs.

'Oh good, I wanted to see you,' he said, 'I just thought of something.'

She was impatient to ring Jane now so she hovered, one foot on the bottom step, the other in the air.

'Gregory,' said Stefan, 'the mysterious and absent older brother in Sydney. We should contact him.'

Poppy hadn't thought of Gregory for years. According to George he had visited once, when she was a baby and Stefan a toddler, on his way to a 'gay lifestyle' in Sydney and they had lost touch.

'Yes. Yes, I guess we should. Let's ask George when he wakes up. I'm just going to use the phone in the kitchen.'

'Of course.' He stood aside. 'I hope, you know…'

'Thanks.' Don't try too hard, brother dear, Poppy said to herself, and then felt churlish; he was a good brother.

Chapter Four

The receptionist at the museum wanted to know who was asking to speak to Jane Blackie.

'You'll be George's girl. He'll be right chuffed you're here.'

'Yes.' She just wanted to talk to Jane.

'Putting you through.'

A few rings of the phone, then, 'Jane Blackie speaking'. So the woman on the phones hadn't needed to know who she was!

'Hello?'

'Hello, Jane, it's Poppy.'

'Oh my, oh, wonderful, just a mo.' There was the sound of a door closing. 'Hello again, oh goodness, you're here, really here!'

'I am indeed here, and pleased to be talking to you at last.'

'When can I see you? And where?' The silence that followed reminded them both that neither question had an easy answer. Poppy explained that she would be telling George what there was to tell as soon as he was up from his afternoon rest, so 'when' wouldn't be too difficult but she had no idea about 'where'. She wanted to know what Jane had told Héloise but didn't ask again; she wanted Jane to say, she wanted to not be disappointed that she didn't. And yet, this conversation was simply to make an arrangement, that was all.

'It's near the centre of Middlesbrough so it should be easy for you to find,' Jane was saying, and Poppy had to ask her to repeat the name of the bar. Eight o'clock would be a good time because by then the Friday after-work drinkers would have dispersed, 'at least from the small bar out the back, which is usually quiet,' Jane worried. 'I've got some news,' she continued, 'some good news, I'd love to tell you now, but…'

'I can look forward to hearing it.' Suddenly Poppy could not bear to hear it just then in case it wasn't what she wanted to hear. Three-and-a-half hours, she had worked it out instantly, three-and-a-half hours and she would see Jane and… Poppy didn't know, but she did know that she badly, desperately even, wanted to see Jane, talk face-to-face. Now that she had seen how George was, she added hurriedly to herself.

'Sorry, what was that?"

'Is there a car you can use? Should I swing by and pick you up?'

'No, I'm sure I'll be able to use George's, I don't know that anyone is driving it at the moment.' She was certainly not ready for these two elements of her life to come face to face, not yet.

'Tar-ra then, see you at eight.'

'Bye.' The handset was moist, so she wiped it with her sleeve, feeling flustered, confused by a busy muddle of emotions.

'Earth to Poppy, come in Poppy.' Her father was looking around the kitchen door, smiling, pleased with himself for remembering a joke from Poppy's childhood. She started.

'I was asking if you'd like a cuppa.'

Nodding, she moved towards him. 'Shall I…'

'No, no, my dear, I can still make cups of tea and other things besides.' But she saw him wince as he turned and noticed for the first time an uneven lump in his lower abdomen.

Making tea involved loose leaves, a warmed teapot and cups and saucers on a tray with a plate of wine biscuits. Poppy observed the routine closely and insisted on carrying the tray into the sitting room where May-Yun and Stefan were looking at a London guide and Susanna was placing a small table in the centre of the room. Getting her father on his own would be difficult and really, did it matter? Poppy sat down on a stool beside George's armchair while Susanna poured tea and gestured to each of them to take a cup.

'I've something to tell you, George.' Poppy kept her attention on her father, the others could listen in or not, she decided. 'It's about me and Jane, you know, from the museum.' At least that had him sitting up and looking interested, so she told him – and the others, she supposed, in more detail than she had on the way here – about her and Jane getting 'kind of close' as they travelled in the South Island, and Jane's dilemma about her partner Héloise wanting to have a baby, and her own unwillingness to get involved at all until that was settled, and their agreement to wait until the end of the year to see if there was anything to pursue further...

'Well, I interfered in that didn't I?' George interrupted. And he was positively smug. 'What about that?' he said, looking at Susanna, 'I'm a bit old for a cupid, I suppose, but not too old to want to see my girl happy. She's a splendid person, Jane, I'm sure it will all work out beautifully. It doesn't make this...' he gestured towards his stomach, 'worthwhile, but I'm surely happy to bring the two of you together – again.' He laughed, the first real laugh Poppy had heard since her arrival. 'This is the most fun for a long time. You must go and see her – today, tonight, take my car.'

'Hold on, George.' She had held up her hand before he finished speaking. 'Yes, I'm seeing her tonight, and I'd love to use your car.' This last glancing at Susanna for confirmation, catching a glimpse of something, something angry, or disapproving perhaps, before the smile and nod of agreement. Then, to her relief, George started talking about going to the museum together next week so he could show her the work he had done in the last couple of years, he was proud of how comprehensive the trichoptera collection was, there had been two post-graduate students this year, come especially to study it.

'Will you come?' Poppy asked Susanna, wanting to include her.

'Oh no, George has tried umpteen times to show me his insects but I can't be having them or that old museum. It's best I stay away. George understands.' The smiles they exchanged looked genuine to Poppy.

May-Yun talked about where they were going in York and London and thanked George for making it possible. That earned another look from Susanna that Poppy didn't understand; there was a great deal about Susanna she didn't know. Then May-Yun suggested a 'ladies lunch out' the next day, Saturday, her last full day at George's, leaving the men at home to fend for themselves, 'unless, of course,' she looked at Poppy, 'you have other plans.'

'No, and I won't make any, I think that's a terrific idea. What about you Susanna?'

'Yes, dear, that would be lovely.' Take that at face value, Poppy said to herself, don't go imagining an under-tone, and thought she saw a quick glimpse of a nodding Mrs Mudgely. May-Yun was cooking for them all that evening and refused her offers of help, so Poppy left George to a programme on television and went upstairs to her room.

Lying on the bed, hands behind her head, eyes closed, Poppy thought back over the thirty-odd hours since she had arrived in England. Something was different with Susanna, that was certain, the pleasant, casual, straight-forward woman she remembered had been replaced, or at least overlaid, with a more edgy, tight, watchful, hard-done-by person who had not been at all evident in earlier visits. Then here was the bad feeling towards the daughter, Sylvia, and Poppy struggled to remember what she was like. Ten years ago Sylvia had been here on Christmas day, with her second husband and his twin boys, teenagers; all Poppy could recall was a tallish

woman who made witty comments that were almost always
followed by an indulgent (or so Poppy thought at the time) 'Oh
Sylvia!' from her mother. What a boon to have May-Yun around,
who else would have thought of the three of them going out to
lunch together?

She would be okay with George. They did love each other, and
that wasn't affected by her irritations at him; he would sometimes
be too interested, sometimes treat her like a child, sometimes be
clingy and he was always George, her father, who had loved her and
made time for her through a secure childhood.

Half-past-six. No point in thinking about Jane. Seeing her soon,
seeing her soon, ran through her mind like a song. Only an hour-
and-a-half and 'supper' would take up most of that. What a relief to
have told everyone. What did Susanna think, really?

There was a knock on her door. 'Grub's up, sis.'

The car hadn't been driven since Stefan arrived with the rental.
'Waste of money renting one when there's a perfectly good car here,'
George had muttered once or twice. When Poppy asked Stefan why
he hadn't just used George's car he had said, 'An old grudge between
Dad and I, cars. Got it out of my system now, along with a lot of
other things.'

For an anxious moment Poppy thought George's Mazda wouldn't
start. She had memorised the route to the café; two rights and a left,
parking in the second block.

They met at the entrance, both a few minutes early, and stood,
looking at each other for a moment before they hugged long enough
to attract the attention of passers-by. The bar was full and noisy.

'There's a small one, at the back, that might be…' Jane began,
then grabbed Poppy's hand and started walking them both down the
street. 'My car's down here, I'll drop you back to yours later.'

Poppy was laughing, a little in relief at not going in to the
crowded room, 'Where are you taking me?'

'Somewhere, anywhere, somewhere we can look at the sea.'

While they drove out of town the last of the twilight faded, and the lights and steam from Teesside industries added a weird beauty to the landscape. Poppy talked about George, then Susanna and how her brother was rising to the occasion better than she would have ever anticipated. When they passed the turnoff to Redcar she wondered how far they were going.

'Not far now,' was all the reply she got and soon she recognised the cable car to the beach at Saltburn and they were driving down a short, steep road and stopping, at the opposite end of the parking area from two other cars, close enough to hear the sea and pick out the white-tops of the low waves.

'That's better.' Jane let out a big sigh. 'I couldn't face all those people, the noise.'

'Me neither.' They turned to look at each other at the same time and were hugging again, awkwardly around the steering wheel until Jane set the driver's seat back and showed Poppy how to move hers; laughing and crying, and nuzzling into each others' necks and holding so tight it was hard to breathe. Then they were kissing, slow, assuaging kissing, hands in each others' hair at first, then backs. When Poppy felt her nipple respond to Jane's touch through her shirt she pulled back, holding Jane's arms, shaking her head to dislodge Mrs Mudgely's smiling face.

'Go away, you Cheshire cat,' wasn't what she had planned to say. She blushed, still shaking her head.

'And how is Mrs Mudgely?' Jane was laughing at her.

'Interfering. Sorry.'

'Don't be. Do you want to stop?'

'No. Yes. In a car!?'

'Mmm.' Jane's face was in her neck again and she was sorry when she sat back. 'But no, perhaps not a car. Too, too teenage. But soon, soon, with grapes and champagne and sweet music and low lights.' Suddenly Jane was out of the car and on the sand, whooping and circling. After a startled moment Poppy joined her, kicking off her shoes, getting the bottom of her jeans wet and not caring. The headlights of one of the other cars flicked on-and-off, on-and-off and they stopped abruptly and hurried back into the car, Poppy scrabbling on the sand for her shoes.

'Maybe they wanted to share the fun,' Poppy suggested as Jane started the engine.

'Perhaps.' She was clearly not convinced, but she turned off the engine again. 'Shall we talk here, or elsewhere.'

'Elsewhere, so we don't get caught out here in fragrante delecto by some passer-by, or worse.' And yet, and yet. That other insistent, miserable voice wanting to say and wanting to not say, 'What about her? What have you told her?'

'Right. We'll try the pub again.' Then, anxiously, 'Are you sorry I brought you here?'

'No, definitely not. It's lovely.' Tell me. Tell me. Don't make me ask.

'Shall I tell you my news?' They were going back by a different, faster route. 'Museum news, real life news, you decide.'

Poppy opted for the museum news while they were driving. 'I've backed right off,' Jane began and went on to talk about the factions that had developed and how even the staff were lining up behind one board member or another and their pet project and much of the material she had brought back from New Zealand was being side-lined. 'I even drew up a development plan that actually incorporates most of what they want, but they're not interested, they want to fight their little battles and I'm right sluffed!!'

'Sluffed?'

'Fed up, tired of it all. And it's trivial enough, compared to what you're dealing with.' She put her hand on Poppy's knee for a moment then turned into the street they had left earlier. There was one noisy group remaining in the front bar, but they found a spot out back in an area almost surrounded by empty tables; two men were at one, engaged in a low-voiced discussion about some papers in front of them.

Jane bought them each a glass of white wine which they held up and clinked before they drank.

'Now, my news,' said Jane firmly. She was looking pleased with herself. 'Don't you want to know?"

'Of course.' What Poppy wanted to know was that Jane had left the house she shared with Héloise and would run away to New Zealand with her when… well, when she, Poppy, could leave England.

'I've got a flat!' excitement enlivened Jane's usually watchful expression. 'Well, a bed-sit really. I sign up on Monday and can move in next Friday. A week today!' She was jiggling, ebullient.

Poppy did her best to match Jane's mood, not wanting to dampen it with her questions. Questions like, 'Have you told Héloise about me?' and 'When did you stop having a sexual relationship?' and 'What took you so long?'

'I'm going to tell Héloise in the morning,' Jane went on, 'we've agreed to have a talk.'

'What have you been doing all these months since January?' Poppy didn't ask out loud, was distressed by her own reactions. She wanted to be happy, happy that she and Jane were on the verge of something, something she hoped – believed – would be wonderful, and here she was, full of resentment.

'I'm not coping with this!' she blurted. Instantly Jane was concerned, anxious.

'Oh! Have I done something wrong, I thought…'

'No, it's me.' Poppy did her best to explain her ambivalence, her head down so she wouldn't see Jane's pleasure fade.

'The waiting,' she said to her glass, 'then the travelling, and coming to grips with what's happening with George – He's going to die – and all the emotion of seeing him and now seeing you…' she looked up finally, into Jane's teary eyes, and ploughed on, 'and I've really wanted to know what you've said… about me… us… to her and there was something about those flashing headlights…' She looked at the tissue Jane had handed her then blew her nose on it. 'Sorry. Wet blanket.'

'Nothing will put out my fire!' and Jane giggled. 'Sorry. And I do understand, really, as well as understanding, now – at last – that you want what I want. I think.'

'Yes. Yes I do.' They were holding hands, tightly, on the table between them.

'I haven't talked to Héloise about how I feel about you, I thought you wanted to stay out of…'

'Yes I did,' Poppy said. And didn't say that everything changed when she had to come over so soon, surely Jane realised…

'But I told her you were coming to see George. She wasn't very interested. And you're exhausted.' Poppy was so tired suddenly all her limbs felt leaden. Jane stood up. 'Come on, I'll walk you back to your car.' Neither had finished their wine. The two men watched them leave then glanced at each other, shrugged, and went back to their papers.

Of all the times to take a wrong turning! By the time she had found George's house, Poppy could hardly keep her eyes open, and was relieved to see there were no lights on inside the house. May-Yun and Stefan would be back at their B & B by now. She answered, George's, 'Goodnight, Poppy dear,' as she passed his bedroom door, closed hers quietly behind her, took off her shoes and jeans and fell into bed. They had agreed that Jane would ring Poppy the next afternoon, Saturday, after she had talked with Héloise about moving out of their house and Poppy had been out to lunch with Susanna and May-Yun.

Poppy woke late and lay thinking of Jane, more happy at the memory of last night than anxious about 'the Héloise thing'. Just stay out of that, she reminded herself, let it take its course whatever that is, never mind planning the rest of your – and Jane's – life.

When she went downstairs she found a note on the kitchen table.
> *9.20 Taken George shopping for slippers. Susanna a bad night and sleeping. S & M-Y'.*

So they had come around straight after breakfast. She wondered whether Susanna's bad night would mean cancelling the lunch arrangement and hoped it wouldn't; she needed to get a better idea of what was going on with her.

Chapter Five

By the time Stefan and May-Yun arrived at the house on Saturday morning, Susanna had made a booking for the ladies' lunch. Taking advantage of the early sun, Poppy and George sat in the back garden, Poppy squirming a little under her father's close questioning about what had transpired between her and Jane. Finally she told him he'd have to be satisfied with general reports, she wasn't doing blow-by-blow accounts. They both laughed, she to soften her words, he acknowledging his over-eagerness for detail.

As the morning wore on Poppy tried not speculate about what might be happening in the talk Jane was having with Héloise and not to listen out for the phone. The men left first, for George to show his son the local transporter bridge – 'Why?' Susanna had asked, and no-one had answered – and their own lunch out at the pub nearby.

Susanna took a long time to get ready and came down at exactly time to leave in a mauve linen dress, with her hair and make-up carefully done. Poppy and May-Yun looked at each other in their more casual trousers and tops, and simultaneously decided they would do as they were.

It soon became apparent that Susanna saw this lunch as an

opportunity. As soon as they were seated she began, looking at
Poppy and May-Yun in turn. George and she had been very happy
she told them, even after arthritis began to limit what she could do.
In fact he was always willing to do whatever was needed, including
cutting her toenails (which was getting close to more than Poppy
wanted to know), even while he was going to 'that museum' nearly
every day.

Over the last few months though, she continued, not waiting for
any response, he had been so tired, and she had been so worried,
and he'd cut right back on the museum and suddenly wasn't even
interested in going there, 'and it had been his life'. She had been on
at him for weeks to go to the doctor and had finally insisted when
she noticed him wincing with pain while he got dressed. The doctor
had found the swollen 'sore spot' and then it had taken 'an age' for
the tests. At this point the National Health Service got a severe
drubbing that included a long story about two local gynaecologists
who had 'got away with it' for years. Neither of her listeners
enquired into what it was they had got away with, nor the relevance
to George.

The recital turned into a catalogue of the difficulties that she,
Susanna, had to deal with, not only her own pain and diminishing
strength, but worrying about George and what would become of
her when he had gone and having to deal with cleaners and the
doctor coming to call, and nurses in time no doubt, it was all a
terrible strain. Then she gave a big sigh and said, 'Well I'm right
pleased to have that off my chest,' and set to eating her luke warm
pasta.

May-Yun broke the ensuing silence first. 'Yes, I can see it is
difficult.'

'I'm going to stay,' Poppy added, 'as long as… well, until George
dies actually.'

'I thought you would, dear. And it's George you'll be concerned
about, as you should. You'll not need to be worrying about me.'

'Well, no, but...' Poppy was now less certain that Susanna was being unkind or selfish when she talked about George.

May-Yun was looking from one to the other. 'I think you will do very well together,' she pronounced. 'No bullshit, either of you.' She laughed at the look on Poppy's face. 'Maybe I'm not quite as proper as you think when I am not setting an example to my children,' she said. The tension was eased, and Susanna and Poppy could talk about practical things like when the cleaner came, and what days would be best for Poppy to drive whoever felt up to going to the supermarket, and how she could help generally.

May-Yun watched, making a suggestion now and then. They decided in George's absence that Poppy would go with him on his next visit to the GP and quiz her in more detail about what they could expect in the next weeks and what nursing and other assistance would be available and whether it would be possible for George to get the care he needed at home as the pain got worse. No-one's even considering the idea of him getting better, Poppy thought.

A walk in the Central Gardens was Susanna's suggestion; she should walk a little every day, she said, and struggled to make herself do it if there wasn't something pretty to look at. Wanting to get back for when Jane rang, Poppy did her best to show enthusiasm. The other two walked together, commenting on the formal gardens and sharing stories about their children.

Dawdling behind, Poppy tried to distract herself from Jane by thinking about Susanna. She couldn't work her out. In the past she had been pleasant, welcoming, showing about as much interest in Poppy's life as Poppy did in hers; it had been easy to get along with her father's undemanding wife who had never shown any resentment of Poppy and George's closeness. There were undercurrents this time, that whiny voice – but not over lunch – an apparent indifference to George's fate, a degree of self-focus that Poppy found slightly shocking, but perhaps, as May-Yun seemed to think, Susanna was realistic rather than heartless.

They had turned back towards her; Susanna with her hand through May-Yun's arm and leaning heavily. As they made their way slowly to the car Poppy chatted brightly to cover her impatience, which earned her some 'what's going on' looks from her sister-in-law. It was a relief to concentrate on driving on the way home while May-Yun responded to a more cheerful Susanna's comments about the gardens over the years and the Middlesbrough of her childhood.

The men had already returned and George had gone upstairs for a nap right away, Stefan was reading the paper. Yes, the bridge was very interesting, he told the women, there was nothing like it in New Zealand, cars drove on and were winched across the river on a pad suspended from the 'bridge' part, which of course was high enough to not impede shipping, and earned it the name 'transporter bridge'… he cut short his explanation as the two women smiled at each other. 'We had a good lunch,' he went on, 'but George tired dreadfully very quickly. He could barely speak by the time we got back.' Stefan shook his head. Grave, thought Poppy, my brother is looking grave. Too appropriate.

'A bed downstairs might be a good idea fairly soon,' Stefan was continuing, 'I had to practically carry him up, and there was one dreadful moment when I obviously pressed on something painful.'

'It gets worse every day.' Susanna was pale, and her voice shook. May-Yun helped her upstairs to rest.

'I've been looking around,' Stefan continued to Poppy, 'and I think the living room – come with me – which is hardly ever used, would make a downstairs bedroom, maybe for them both. I think you could all manage with the kitchen and dining room.' They stood in the doorway, Stefan talking about various items of furniture that would 'have to go,' or maybe, with an almost boyish 'bright idea' look, 'you could set yourself up a sitting room upstairs.' With an arm around his sister's shoulder, he apologised for going off on holiday and leaving her with two ailing 'olds'.

'It's okay,' she felt herself rising to it as she spoke, 'I can manage whatever needs doing, Jane will have some local knowledge, and there's the doctor, and I am a competent adult, you know. Oh. Has there been a phone message?'

'Oops, I forgot.' Her heart raced. 'Katrina rang.' She tried not to let her disappointment show. 'We had a long chat. She sends love and says she'll ring every week to see how you are going, and you must let her ring you because it's cheaper from that end.' He went on before she had time to say anything. 'And I asked Dad about his brother.'

'Oh Yes. The uncle we never knew…'

'Apparently he died, quite a few years ago, in Sydney. AIDS probably.'

'Oh.' How was it she such could have a surge of loss for a stranger long dead? 'Did he say anything else?'

'Not really. He cried a bit, made a comment about past mistakes and changed the subject.'

'Oh. 'I'll ask him sometime maybe…'

'Or leave it be,' Stefan suggested. 'Apparently Gregory had no family. Is that the phone?'

Poppy raced off, leaving her brother to measure up items of furniture with his eye and speculate on the possibility of moving them up the stairs.

A distraught Jane on the other end of the phone was making very little sense.

'Hey, slow down, what's happened? Are you all right?'

'No, I am not all right I am absolutely, totally, completely angry, no enraged, I've been… I've been cheated and I can't bear it! Can you come over, now, right now, please!'

'But…' They had agreed that she wouldn't go to the house, she didn't want to go to the house, she had no right to go there, as far as she was concerned it was off-limits. She did not want to come face to face with Héloise.

'I'll come to you then, I've got to see you, I can't tell you this on the phone.'

It was her brother's last night, Poppy must be in for dinner with them all. And she must find out what was going on with Jane. Now was not the time to bring everyone together, anyway Jane was in no state… and George and Susanna… no, it was impossible.

'Pick me up here, fifteen minutes, I'll be out the front,' she said.

'Yes. Okay. See you soon.' And Jane had put the phone down before Poppy could say, 'Drive carefully.'

Poppy explained as best she could to May-Yun and promised to be back by six-thirty. Two hours. She glanced out the window. Grey. They could walk. Maybe Central Gardens again!

Once she was herself in the driving seat, on the way to the gardens with a slightly subdued Jane beside her, Poppy insisted on some information; she hadn't wanted to dally, holding each other, on the footpath with possibly George, or anyone else, watching.

'I've done this all wrong! I should have rung my friend Rachel first and got myself a bit better sorted…'

'For heaven's sake, just tell me what happened! There'll be four of us in this car soon.'

'Uh?'

'You and me, both beside ourselves. Katrina's joke. Now tell!!'

After a restless night Jane had got up early, thinking to make a nice breakfast and set things up for the two of them to have a reasonable talk.

'Cut to the chase, woman!' Poppy parked the car and turned to face a bleary Jane in the passenger seat, who gulped and blurted out that before she could tell Héloise about the bed-sit and moving out, Héloise had told her that she was moving out, tomorrow, Sunday, to stay with the two gay men in Guisborough one of whom would father her child. And then she had presented her with lists, of things in the house, and who should have what and a price for the sale of the house, or Jane to buy her out.

'Everything!! All sorted, according to her!! No discussion!! Nothing!! I've never been so angry!! And she said now I could do what I liked with my New Zealand fl... – how could she know?'

'Come on, let's walk,' said Poppy. Apparently the talk had turned into more of a shouting match, Jane couldn't remember exactly what she had said but thought she was probably nasty, as was Héloise, who finally stormed out with a 'You'll be hearing from my lawyer'. What a cliché! and Benjy, she just called him and he jumped in the car and she went. 'We didn't even talk about Benjy,' Jane ended with a wail.

Their walking pace was considerably faster than had been possible earlier in the day and eventually Jane ran out of outrage, for the moment at least.

'Well, what do you think?'

Poppy shrugged. 'I don't know. Splitting up is difficult, it gets nasty, people behave badly.'

'I thought you'd be on my...'

'Side? Well, I guess I am, but hell, Jane, Héloise probably sees this as at least partly my fault...'

'Well it's not! She had no right to bring you into it!' Poppy was not sure about that, but said nothing, and Jane went on, 'I just want... I don't know... to feel that you're supporting me, I suppose.' She took Poppy's hand and got a squeeze in return. They kept walking.

'I do, I do, really. I suppose I thought... well, that I'd come along at the end of the year when these messy bits were all over. Bit of a cheek I suppose.' Back and forth, they talked while they walked, not looking at each other much, both being as careful and honest as they could with their words.

They were sitting side-by-side on a bench, knees touching, facing, holding both of each others' hands, when Poppy said after a few moment's silence.

'I'll have to go, it's my brother's last night.'

'Perhaps now she's gone you could come to the h…?' Jane squirmed and pulled a face at the pleading tone that had crept in to her voice. 'If you want.'

'This teenagerish meeting in public places is certainly not my first choice.' Feeble humour. Didn't work. 'Maybe – what I don't want is to come face to face with her on the doorstep.'

'Why not? Get it over with – or something. Anyway she's gone.'

'Conquer by confrontation. Look at my arm, just the thought of it brings me out in goose bumps.' The whole conversation felt forced to Poppy, the situation was exactly what she had wanted to avoid. Héloise had clearly worked out something close to the truth for herself and Poppy wished Jane had…

'That or the cold wind. Come on.' It was Jane who stood. 'Tomorrow?'

'I don't know, really, I need to work my way into, you know, a place in the house with George and Susanna, it doesn't feel right to keep sloping off and I don't think I can be much help with… your stuff… not really, it's not my business.'

Jane's short, tearful laugh was hard to bear. 'I know,' she gulped, 'you want me unencumbered. As I do you.' And at the look on Poppy's face Jane turned abruptly and set off towards the car.

They separated miserably outside George's house. As she crossed to the driver's seat Jane said, 'I'm not going home, I'll go to Rachel's, stay the night even, if she'll have me.'

Everyone worked hard over dinner and they more or less succeeded in making it a pleasant evening. Even after a long afternoon sleep George looked tired and grey, and he clearly flagged from time to time but would rally himself and rejoin the conversation. When he went up to bed soon after nine, insisting that he needed no help with the stairs, Susanna followed him, making a comment as she left that George was, 'right fortunate' in his family.

'There's not been a sign of her daughter or son since I got here.' Poppy hadn't thought of that before and it seemed odd. The son from Harrogate had called in one afternoon since they had arrived Stefan reported, but that was so he would miss the rush-hour traffic on his way home after a deputy principal's meeting at Middlesbrough Secondary. May-Yun thought Susanna was very pleased to see him and he was a bit off-hand with her, spending most of the time telling them all about his 'brilliant, twenty-something children'.

'What about the daughter?

'Yes, Sylvia, she lives around here somewhere but apparently they don't get on,' Stefan offered.

'We suggested asking her over for a meal when we first got here,' added May-Yun, 'but it never happened.'

When she had waved them off to their B&B, promising to be back first thing for breakfast together before they left for York and London, Poppy found some paper in the printer with George's computer and sat at the kitchen table writing a list.

Ask George

> *using his computer – password?*
> *S's relations*
> *(& S) downstairs bedroom*
> *doctor/medications*
> ~~*how would she know what to do and when to do it?*~~

Don't be silly, she told herself, talk to him.

> *his idea of routines – nurse visits? shopping, washing*
> *cooking – should she simply do it all?*

Would there be enough for her to do, she wondered. How would she fill her days? What did Susanna do all day; did she have friends? How would she fit Jane in? She almost wished Jane lived somewhere else. She *did* wish Jane lived somewhere else, so there'd be a tidy separation of this and that; no, no, not really, people dealt with much more, all the time.

A picture floated into her mind, her Mt Eden house, Mrs Mudgely, Jane a hope, a dream, something to look forward to, in the meantime a life she was in charge of. That was it, that was what was unsettling her so badly, she wasn't in charge, life events were happening *to* her. But surely she could cope with that? How feeble, hankering for her orderly, predictable, plannable life and she'd been here only a few days.

What if George got better? Or stopped getting worse? What if it went on for months and months, and she had promised to stay? What if she were bored? Lonely? Ah, lonely struck a chord. She couldn't expect too much of Jane, there had to be other people. George didn't want support groups, maybe she did. No, that wasn't it, there was something about being lonely. Jane had only ever mentioned one friend, Rachel, and Poppy wasn't even sure if she was a lesbian. She had no idea who Jane hung out with. A check in the phone book under 'l' found her a lesbian line number and she added ringing that to her list of things to do.

Starting Monday, she resolved, there would be a plan. Several plans. George (lots of time with him). Jane. Susanna and her family (maybe). Herself – lesbian company, exercise, reading (local library?), some supply teaching (maybe). Check out lesbian places and groups. This felt better; familiar territory, planning. She chuckled at herself, she must be a teacher!

An hour later she was lying in bed unable to sleep. There was so much swirling around in her brain that after a restless hour she turned on the light and went back to her list. Several minutes of doodles later she flung paper and pen on the floor but remained sitting up in the bed, a blanket around her shoulders, hugging her knees, acutely missing Mrs Mudgely, her silky fur, soothing purr and 'wise counsel.'

Poppy knew there was a core in herself that would handle her father's dying and death, both the practical and the emotional aspects; if she had to clean and wash him, she would. This slow, creeping death was very different from her only other experience of losing someone she loved deeply, the sudden ripping from her of her beloved Kate by a silly boating accident. It was, after all, in a very basic way, ordinary to have a parent die, though the actual happening of it was particular, enveloping, she could feel herself – just the beginnings so far – sliding into his – what? orbit? arena? ambience? She would increasingly align herself with his state of being, his needs, his rhythm, she would, she realised, be grieving for her loss of him as he – diminished? became less, less what? less the father she remembered, wanted to remember afterwards, the loving, sometimes annoyingly sentimental, always caring father she had been blessed with. This time was such a small portion of their knowing of each other, ending, not negating what had gone before, not a wrenching so much as a gradual withdrawal, fading into memories. Do not, she told herself, do not let all the other memories be extinguished by these painful and difficult ones.

Afraid that in the morning she would have forgotten these insights – and they were important, and she'd bet she wasn't by any means the first to have them, though they were new to her – she scribbled words and phrases on the back of her list. Another idea – a notebook for her lists and thoughts; she couldn't risk leaving scraps of paper lying about and she might from time to time need to remind herself. Yes, a notebook. She turned the page and added it to her list.

But – and it was a big but – could she immerse herself in her father's dying *and* in whatever it was – a love affair? a relationship? – with Jane. Had Jane *really* expected Héloise not to notice that Poppy's arrival, was, at least, significant?

Suddenly there was a stern Mrs Mudgely perched on the end of the bed. 'Of course you can handle it all! Don't get grandiose about George, you're not the only person involved! And don't expect 'happy ever after' with Jane in two weeks!'

'Gosh, that was a…' the image was disappearing as she spoke… 'long speech for you, Mrs M.'

Poppy started writing thoughts as they came into her head.

*One day at a time – small steps – give love a chance – letting go
– time will tell – live in the present – it takes two people – look
after yourself – a trouble shared – that's what friends are for – go
with the flow –*

Omigod! Clichés every one! She scribbled over them, then wrote:

*Martia – email
Katrina – phone
S & M-Y – email
Mrs M – who knows?
lesbian line – ?*

and felt much better. Like the hungry caterpillar in the children's
picture book, she thought, and added, *Don't take myself too seriously*
to her list. Then she noticed she had also written: *Jane – weekend
away.* Where had that come from? It would certainly give them an
opportunity to spend some time together away from everything else
that was going on for them both. And a place to – talk – whatever –
'make love' – she forced herself to say under her breath.

Chapter Six

They were sitting around the breakfast table. No-one wanted to initiate Stefan and May-Yun's departure. George kept the conversation going, putting off the inevitable, Poppy thought, on the verge of making a move herself when Susanna stood up and said she must go and have a cuppa with her friend Glory next-door-but-one, she hadn't seen her all week. So she said her goodbyes, and there was no reason for the rest of them to dally any longer.

May-Yun went to George first, and they held each other in a long hug, talking quietly. Stefan opened his arms to Poppy; she was certain his eyes were wet.

'Go well, Sis,' he said. 'phone, write, anything, any time. I'm not sure I could do what you are… but I do want to know…' he nodded towards George.

'Of course.' Poppy pulled back and looked at him. 'You came, that's the main thing. I can do this,' she went on, 'and I want to. You have a really, really good time on the way home.'

And there was nothing more to delay father and son from making their farewells. George was openly weeping. Poppy and May-Yun moved away.

'I can do this, and I want to.' Poppy repeated her statement to her sister-in-law.

'I know you can. This is a good family, I am fortunate to have married into it.' And May-Yun was wiping away tears. Poppy thought of the dead or dispersed relatives that May-Yun and her brother were trying to uncover for Chan, her Chinese-looking son, and said, 'I think we're the lucky ones.' And they both laughed, neither knowing why and hugged warmly.

Poppy and a still-weeping George, arms around each others' shoulders, waved them off in their rental car, then Poppy led him inside and they sat side-by-side on the dining room couch.

George was entitled to his emotion, he would not see his son again, Poppy told herself. So she sat, still and silent, keeping her arm around his shoulder, increasing the hold slightly until he sat up and blew his nose on a damp handkerchief.

'According to the book on grief I've just read…' he began.

'But I thought you didn't, weren't going to…'

'This isn't about me, I wanted to know what it would be like for the rest of you.' He paused for a moment and Poppy nodded. 'Well, you and Stefan really, Susanna has her own ways.'

'Yes,' Poppy saw a chance, 'I wanted…'

George held up a hand. 'In a moment. What the book said was it's easier for people when a parent dies if old wounds have been attended to.' He was silent for a moment, then went on. 'And I think Stefan and I have done that, attended to our old wounds.' He smiled at his daughter, 'And they weren't all the same, his wounds and mine. That was very interesting.'

'Do you think we…'

'Have old wounds? No. Do you?'

Poppy shook her head. 'Should I read the book do you think?'

'If you like.' He wiped his eyes again. One thing about her father, Poppy thought, he had never been ashamed of showing his emotions.

'No, don't get up,' she said, 'tell me where and I'll get it, I want to get something else.'

The book was, as he said, beside his bed. While she was there she looked around at the twin beds, the dressing-table, two sets of drawers, the wardrobe, the two bedside cabinets, the lamps on them, sizing them up for the room downstairs. Then she went into her room to collect her list and pen and returned to the dining room. Susanna was back, putting on the jug. It was eleven-thirty and Poppy already felt like it had been a long day. What was Jane up to, she wondered, was she staying at home while Héloise moved out? She'd never had to do that herself, separate belongings after living in a shared house for a long time, she'd seen friends do it, some did it easy, some hard.

'Cuppa?' Susanna was holding up the teapot.

Poppy shook her head, and brandished her list, 'But I would like to talk to you both,' and sat down at the table.

An hour later she had a much clearer idea of how the coming days might work out. She'd drawn up a daily calendar for the week and it was on the fridge door (held by two New Zealand magnets: one a sheep, one a kiwi) with the trip to the doctor and the cleaner's times blocked out. Also, a note in the Friday night slot said, ?Poppy away weekend? an idea George had endorsed enthusiastically. Poppy couldn't tell what Susanna's reaction was and couldn't think what Susanna had been like with her and Kate, and supposed it had been all right or she would have remembered.

George took her through the basics of using his computer, which sat on a small desk in a corner of the dining room, covered with a flowery table cloth. 'I hardly use it now,' he had said, 'I've unsubscribed from most things, can't seem to get interested any more.'

'Why's that, you always…'

'Can't see the point. Conserving energy for the important things, you know. Don't look like that, Poppy dear, your old father's dying, and he knows it. Do you know what they say in these parts?'

'No.' So she'd had that wrong. He wasn't avoiding the idea of death.

'Goin' dahn t'nick,' he said, with a fair imitation of a Yorkshire accent, 'ill and not going to get better.' He smiled at the doubtful look on her face. 'It's all right you know, I don't mind, really, I've done enough for one average kind of chap. Come on, give us a smile.' So she did and he went off to 'grapple with the *Observer*' as he said.

The internet-based email account she had set up before she left home, had only one message in it and that was from Martia. Pleased, she opened it, as usual in Martia's idiosyncratic email-writing style. 'I gave up on Mavis Beacon's keyboarding programme before I got to capitals', had been her explanation.

> *dear pops,*
> *all fine here*
> *nothing to report except mrs m misses you and so do i*
> *oh yes, one thing, i got the woman joy and she had waited outside the movie theatre for you but said she didn't mind in the circumstances*
> *she came round for a coffee. nice woman, finding auckland hard to break into*
> *she liked your house a lot*
> *so do i, just as well i've got plans for when you get home or you might not get rid of me*
> *how's it going over there, hard i imagine*
> *how's george*
> *how's jane*
> *and, most important, how are you*
> *write soon*
> *lots of love and hugs*

59

martia
ps nearly forgot
got a job, temporary, two hours a day mon-fri at the local fruit
and veg, it's okay, like the walk there and back specially when it's
not raining

Poppy started replying right away; thoughts and feelings from the night before pouring out fingertips onto the keyboard. Then Susanna came in and started making lunch and George was putting things on the table, asking who she was writing to… Anyway it was time for lunch; though she wasn't hungry she could hardly keep writing while they ate, so she joined them at the table.

'What do you think about Stefan's idea of making a downstairs bedroom?' Poppy addressed the question to them both. George thought it was a good idea but a bit soon. Susanna said he should do it while he was still reasonably well and that she would prefer to stay upstairs, she didn't like the downstairs lavatory, it was narrow and awkward and she worried about falling there and then the door wouldn't open and if she couldn't get up… And she did like her bath and that was upstairs, and Glory had just had a special thing put on the wall by the bath that helped her get out, one of those would be good, she could find out where Glory got hers. George paid close attention while she was speaking and Poppy started another list.

'What else needs doing?' She had her pen poised, 'I know, see if that lavatory door can be changed to open outwards,' then to Susanna's 'Huh!', 'not to make you move bedrooms, it's just that it might be dangerous for George, too, when…' He was nodding at her, so was Susanna now. Poppy told herself to get over her reluctance to say out loud anything about George getting more ill.

'That computer,' George said, 'might just fit in your room, Poppy, you're the one that'll be using it.' He turned to his wife, 'Now where was the extra phone jack put in that time, it was somewhere upstairs, I'm sure.

'But – what do you think about that, Susanna, putting the computer in my room?'

'It's nowt to me, dear, I've not used it and I'd be pleased enough to have it away from here. The phone jack, that's in the hallway, directly under my mother's picture.'

And so, another plan developed. Both Susanna and George were pessimistic about having furniture moved and grumbled about tradesmen. Spurred on by George saying it was a shame they hadn't managed to get onto all this while Stefan was here, after all it was in his line, Poppy undertook to make sure everything got done; she started by looking up the classified ads in the *Evening Gazette*.

When George went off for a sleep, Susanna and Poppy cleared up together, and for the first time since she had arrived they were alone together. 'I hope you don't think I'm taking over too much,' said Poppy. Susanna was washing dishes slowly and probably painfully. She turned and faced the younger women, holding her dripping hands over the sink.

'Don't you be worrying about that,' she said. 'I'll not hold back if it's too much you're doing and I've no complaints yet,' and turned back to her task. Poppy, drying every dish unnecessarily thoroughly so she didn't catch up with the washing, was about to ask about Sylvia when Susanna, not turning around this time, started telling her about how she had been thinking for some time about how to get them sleeping in different rooms. She didn't think George realised, she went on, how much he grunted and groaned at night and she had her own troubles with getting asleep and staying there when she did, but she hadn't wanted to hurt his feelings. She suggested it would be a good idea to leave the sofa and maybe an armchair in the sitting room, then when he couldn't get up much they could sit with him; and the television could go in there, there were a few programmes they liked to watch together. He could lie down then, and even drift off, but it would be companionable.

Poppy decided to leave Sylvia for another time; quit while we're

ahead she said to herself, noting yet another cliché. With Susanna
gone for a rest, she decided to grasp the nettle – jump in with both
feet – take the bull by the horns – there was a laugh in her voice
when she replied to Jane's 'Hello.'

'Hi, Poppy here, cliché queen, how's it going?'

'Awful! I thought you weren't going to ring here… not that I
mind, it's wonderful to hear you, it's been a dreadful day, they've just
gone a few minutes ago. You sound cheerful.' She probably hadn't
meant that to sound like an accusation, Poppy thought.

'Yeah, I am rather, all things considered it's going well and I seem
to be drowning in clichés. Weird.'

The conversation couldn't get going; Jane was stuck in misery and
Poppy was stuck in cheerful platitudes. After an awkward silence,
Poppy said, as neutrally as she could manage,

'What are you doing next weekend?'

'I don't know… why?'

'It's not a trick question. What are you doing next weekend
because I had an idea that we could go away together on Friday
night and not come back until Sunday and actually have some time
together away from our respective, um, goings on.' There was
silence for a moment, then a sniff.

'Really? Where?'

'I don't know, far enough to be away and not so far we're driving
for hours. Hartlepoole?'

'No. Not far enough.' The possibilities were finally sinking in.
'What about Whitby?'

'Sure. But that's where you grew up, won't there be ghosts?'

'No ghosts, not in old Whitby. Let me arrange a place to stay.'
Now Jane was sounding excited. 'Friday and Saturday nights?'

'Yep.'

'What about George?'

'He's almost too keen, and no more "what abouts", please, let's just
do it.'

'All right. Let's.' And Poppy held the phone away from her ear as Jane whooped.

When they'd arranged to talk again the next night and said their goodbyes, Poppy went back to writing to Martia and finished a long email before anyone re-appeared. That evening Katrina rang, saying she was lying in bed having a lazy Sunday morning and how was everything? She was amused by Poppy's attack of platitudes, and told her that the thing about clichés was that in difficult times they did have some meaning, the human condition was universal wasn't it, at the same time as being extremely particular, and the sayings must have started from someone's experience.

The week went by fast.

Jane was mysterious about exactly where she had booked them to stay, other than saying it was in the old town near the river.

After a number of unproductive phone calls, Poppy found someone to come and install a handrail by the bath and turn the downstairs lavatory door around. The 'handyman' – his self-description – who came talked in a broad accent that Poppy could barely follow. It took most of the day to change the door, and involved going out to buy new facing boards and Poppy balancing the door while the hinges were re-set. When it was open the door blocked the hallway but it certainly improved access to the tiny room and there was no danger of anyone getting stuck inside. Jock ('Of course,' Poppy thought when he told her his name) offered to come back and paint the new wood, but Poppy had decided to do that herself. He was keen to get a couple of 't'lads' who could 'do wi' a few quid' to come another day and move furniture. When he had gone she realised she had not thought to ask how much that would cost. Still, his charge for a day's work had been reasonable and really, she didn't care. (Don't ever forget that you are fortunate that you don't have to care, she reminded herself.)

When Poppy did mention Susanna's daughter to her the older woman would say nothing more than that they didn't get on and as

far as daughters went Sylvia was a 'feckless ninny'. A further suggestion that she, Poppy, would like to meet her got a sharp glance then
silence. 'Would you mind if I invited her here?'

'What for?'

'A visit, cuppa, anything really.'

'No, what for?'

'Oh, to meet her I suppose.'

'She'll have nowt good to say about her ma, mark you that.'

'I don't mean to upset – anything, anyone – I just thought I'd like
to meet her.' The only response was a shrug. Poppy struggled on.
'Would you mind if I rang her, maybe met her somewhere else?'

'You do what you like, it's nowt to me.' Getting stubborn, Poppy
managed to glean that Sylvia's phone number was in the back of the
phone book. When she had talked to a startled Sylvia and arranged
to meet her in town in her lunch hour the following week, she
passed this information on to Susanna and got no response. Otherwise Poppy and her father's wife were doing well together.

One thing a day, especially if it involved going out, was all George
could manage and he pronounced himself unfit to drive. Susanna
did, a little, locally; there were more friends beside Glory. She played
cards on Wednesday afternoons and would need the car for that,
otherwise would fit in with Poppy's use of it; the weekly shopping
she could still manage, especially if Poppy helped bring it in from
the car.

The day Poppy and George went to his GP he had woken feeling
particularly unwell, not so much in pain, he insisted, as unwell. Dr
Jasmine Owens turned out to be fortyish, plump, and kind. After
giving George a 'push and a poke' as he called it, she sat at her desk
and looked from one to the other.

'Tell me everything ab…'

'Just as much as…'

Poppy and George started talking together, then both stopped.
The doctor said there was nothing new, just more of the same and

George decided to wait outside so Poppy could ask as many questions as she liked.

'Call me Jasmine,' said the doctor when he had gone. 'George has made it very clear that he doesn't want anything other than palliative care and only wants to know about medications and anything he has to do.' Poppy was nodding. 'I take it you would like to know more.' Poppy explained that she would be staying on and it seemed as though she would be somewhat 'in charge' of things, so, yes, she would like to know as much as she could understand without being a medical person.

The best news for Poppy was that the GP could access nursing services as and when they were needed, she herself would not have to find out how. Macmillan nurses, Jasmine explained, were especially trained to deal with cancer patients and could be used as well as the district nurse, who could come up to three times a day. George should come in to the surgery once a week while he could, then she would visit at home. At the moment he was doing all right on oral pain medication, though there would come a time when he needed more. No, Poppy would never be expected to give injections! As he would not have any more diagnostic procedures she couldn't tell how the primary tumour was advancing except by external examination and it seemed to her today to be much the same as a week ago. And, of course, there was no knowing about any secondary growths, they could be anywhere, though the bowel, lungs and brain were the most likely.

To Poppy's questions about how quickly he would get worse and how would she know, the reply was that he had plateaued over the last couple of weeks, probably because his family came – there were smiles of approval at this – and it was possible that there would be a sudden deterioration in the next week or ten days, but really, it was all speculation. Guiltily, Poppy said she was planning to go away over the weekend, should she perhaps not?

'Not at all! Splendid idea! This is as good as it will be, you know, and Mrs Sinclair will be at home no doubt.' Poppy let out her breath in relief. And thought, for the first time, that maybe Susanna could do with a few days away some time soon.

Chapter Seven

Poppy woke early on Friday morning as was becoming her habit. Being awake, alert and ready to get up soon after six was a new phenomenon, one she thought she would appreciate more at home. The problem was there was nothing to stay up for in the evenings, with television failing to attract her interest, so she went to bed early, intending to read from the pile of science fiction novels that sat by her bed since a trip to the local library with Susanna's membership card. She had not yet had managed more than a few pages before drooping eyelids and flagging concentration wiped out her usual pleasure in escaping to other worlds.

Resisting the urge to get up, Poppy hugged herself with a wriggle of pleasure at the thought of the coming weekend away. The weather was predicted fine and the idea of a respite from the hot-house atmosphere she was living in – only a week and I'm hanging out for a break, she thought with dismay – was most appealing. And, of course, two nights and days with Jane. Of course. When they had met mid-week for a meal out, Poppy had been aware of them touching, a hand on a knee as they were driving, hands across a restaurant table, a foot underneath, shoulders, arms as they walked along the street.

She welcomed the touching but continued to be troubled by Jane's emotional unfinished-ness with Héloise and, even more, her lack of awareness of the importance for Poppy of frankness about the situation between them. Poppy herself found it hard to describe that situation – interest in each other? love? lust? She always assumed that a sexual relationship would become a full partnership, and was assuming this was the same for Jane. Yet Jane, who made it quite clear that she wanted herself and Poppy to be sexual together, had been surprised – and outraged – that Héloise had worked out that possibility and taken action. Had she really expected that Héloise wouldn't notice, or if she did, wouldn't do anything until Jane was ready to talk about it?

When Jane had called at the house one lunch-time with messages for George from his colleagues and an invitation for him to a special afternoon tea at the museum, Poppy felt awkward at first, but George had been so delighted to see Jane and so keen to hear news of the museum that she soon relaxed. He said near the end of the visit, that he thought his days of working at the museum were over and Jane responded, genuinely, that he would be missed and the work he had done had increased the reputation of 'the Cleveland' throughout the museum world.

'Yes,' he said, 'it is satisfying to know that there is a small piece of work of mine that contributes to our knowledge of the world.'

'It is small,' he had been firm when Poppy objected, 'in the overall scheme of things, and I am proud of it.'

Today, Jane was leaving work early and picking Poppy up at three. 'Don't think about anything except what clothes to bring,' she had been told and was happy to have her idea so thoroughly organised for her.

Picking up the notebook she'd bought to replace her initial sheets of paper, Poppy skimmed down the two pages she had written, mainly about George and being here in his house and realising she had to get out regularly, out in the open; walking on the moors a couple of times a week, perhaps. She had written 'Jane' a couple of nights ago and doodled around the name for some time but not written anything. She put the notebook with her pile of things to take away for the weekend, got out of bed and stretched, humming to herself.

Removing her night-shirt she examined her nearly-fifty-year-old body; some flabby bits under the upper arms, a little drooping of the breasts, inhibited by the roll of flesh underneath, solid thighs; she was happy enough to show all this to Jane and was blessed, she thought, with a good, well-functioning physical self, wondering briefly whether it held any frights in store for her.

Friday was one of the days the cleaner came. The other one was Tuesday. Poppy felt awkward while she was there. Susanna would make a list of things for her to do once the basic vacuuming and bathroom and toilet cleaning was finished. The cleaner was small, wiry, energetic and ageless and told everyone to call her Mrs Madge. She called Poppy, and everyone else, Pet. There was a form to sign, 'for the social', confirming that she had worked three hours on a particular day. Apart from fifteen minutes when she sat at the kitchen table with a cup of strong sweet tea and read a romance novel she carried in the large pocket of her apron, Mrs Madge worked steadily, starting and finishing promptly. Poppy was to leave her bed unmade for the sheets to be changed on Fridays, though she thought there was no reason why she couldn't do that herself. Mrs Madge, Susanna had told her, took the sheets and towels away to the laundry on Friday and brought them back Tuesday, so she started fifteen minutes after the hour on Tuesday. They had to pay the laundry themselves, on a monthly bill, but it was worth it, Susanna said, because she couldn't lift wet towels or sheets out of the machine, never mind hanging them on the washing line.

'Washing! What am I doing thinking about washing?' Her weekend bag was packed. It was only seven o'clock, three hours until she was taking George to get a haircut and eight hours until Jane was collecting her at three.

In fact, the day passed quickly. George wanted to take advantage of the weather and visit the moors so Poppy drove after the hairdresser's to a spot near Guisborough, and they walked a tiny portion of the Cleveland Way very slowly. They both enjoyed the warm, clear day and the smells of early summer. The heather was not yet in flower, but the tawny browns and greens, even golds where the sun struck shiny leaves or damp grasses had their own beauty. George was delighted to spot a grouse and they talked about the very particular beauties of both England and New Zealand and whether it would be possible for George to make a last visit to the Lake District.

'Would you consider a wheel chair?' Poppy asked as they turned back towards the car. 'We could go a lot of places with a folding wheelchair in the car…'

'As long as you don't put a hand-knitted blanket over my knees.' George said immediately. 'My grandfather,' he explained with a laugh. 'Actually it wasn't the blanket so much as the way he dribbled.'

'Okay, let's get you a wheelchair. I noticed a mohair blanket in the back of the car, would that do?'

'Yes, indeed it would.' The pressure on Poppy's arm increased and her father stopped walking. 'And seriously,' he said when she turned to look at him, 'do stop taking me out if I dribble, there's something so diminishing about an old man dribbling in public.' She promised and didn't argue with 'old'.

When Jane arrived at ten-to-three Poppy had been ready for some time. Susanna was saying, 'Of course I can manage, I did until you arrived, didn't I?' so Poppy apologised for fussing, then George came in from his sleep and he and Susanna were bustling her out the door.

'I'm driving.' Jane was definite. Poppy thought she looked tired. 'Yet another bad day at the museum,' she explained as they pulled away, Poppy waving her hand out the window until they turned the corner. 'Plus a letter from Héloise's lawyer'.

They would talk out their respective pre-occupations during the drive, they decided, then do their best to put them aside for the rest of the weekend. Jane took the quicker, more inland road, telling Poppy how she planned to reply to the unreasonable demands in the lawyer's letter for her to meet all the house expenses. She went on to say that the museum staff, were a big disappointment to her, aligning themselves with various factions in the board and being entirely unprofessional.

'How are you doing?' she finally asked Poppy, and Poppy told her about feeling helpful in practical ways as well as needing to be there emotionally for herself and for George.

'I'm going to ring the local Lesbian Line next week, have you ever...'

'Not really, no. It never seemed necessary I suppose. Why...?'

'I guess I'm used to lesbian company, I miss it.'

'Oh. Don't I coun...?'

'Of course you do.' Perhaps she should never have raised it. 'I just thought, if I end up being here for more than a couple of months...' They turned into the road down to Whitby town centre and Jane waved a hand towards the coast, 'That's where we lived while I was growing up', she said. 'A bit in from Sandsend really, a newish – then – flat suburb, nothing like where we're going.'

Many of the houses they passed had Bed & Breakfast signs with 'vacancy' in most windows but Jane wasn't stopping for any of them. 'Where...?'

'Wait and see.'

Seagulls, big and noisy, were circling overhead. People poured out of the railway station from a recently-arrived train, and they were driving right down to the river, over the narrow bridge and turning left up an even narrower street, barely one car wide, leading to the abbey steps and the old lighthouse. Jane stopped outside a tea-room. She was looking very pleased with herself.

'I'll have to leave you here with our bags while I park the car.' Her grin became a giggle at the look on Poppy's face. On both sides of the street were tiny shops, on the river side interspersed with doorways into pubs. Buildings, mostly two-level, huddled up to each other and the narrow footpaths.

'Ah-ha.' Poppy had spotted a 'rooms' sign and pointed to it.

'Nope.' Jane's giggled again and jumped back into the driver's seat, leaving Poppy standing on the footpath with two bags and a very large chilly bin.

'No peeping,' Jane called out the car window, nodding towards the chilly bin, 'back in five minutes.'

It was early in the summer and there were not many people about. The Duke of York hotel, a bit further along the road was the busiest spot. Poppy sat carefully on the chilly bin, testing to see if it would take her weight. Soon she saw Jane running towards her with a skip and a wave. She stood up, saying 'okay, where to now?'

Jane picked up the bin and one bag, 'Follow me,' she said with a forward sweep of her arm and set off down a cobbled alley leading to… tea-rooms. She spoke to the woman at the counter. Were they stopping for afternoon tea? Another woman came out and led them to a door and handed Jane a key. 'Breakfast is seven-thirty to nine,' she told them brusquely and walked off.

The room was charming, with a double and a single bed, the double a wooden four-poster with curtains on the back corners. Blue and white walls and fittings with a shower and toilet under what must be a stairway. Lacy curtains filtered the light, and drapes hung beside each window, ready to shut out the world completely. Poppy put down her bag and took a moment before she turned to Jane; she had been thinking open space, looking out at the sea…

'Do you like it?' Anxiously.

And it didn't matter where they were, they were alone, and in private. Poppy forced a smile, felt it spread through her. 'Mmm,' she said, 'romantic.' Jane held her gaze. Poppy took a step backwards and flopped onto the big bed. 'Take me!' she said melodramatically, flinging open her arms and her legs, wanting suddenly to be swept out of herself, to be alive in her body, carried away from thoughts and disappointments, cautions and caveats.

Jane moved slowly towards her, touching her first on the face and neck with a cool hand, running light fingers down her arm, bending into a kiss. They did not hurry. Not like the first time with Kate… 'Stop it!!' Poppy told herself. Then there was nothing, no-one else, just her and Jane, touching, kissing, stroking, exploring each other, eyes holding contact for long moments, hearts pounding, moving around each other, tasting, licking, kissing, stroking, always stroking, all in a timeless blend. They discovered dimples and bumps and bones, freckles in unusual places, ticklish spots and erotic places, giving and receiving pleasure in a series of sexual eruptions that left them both, finally, damp, limp and laughing in languorous satisfaction. The room was dark.

Jane stood up to pull the drapes, trailing a hand along Poppy's back. Poppy raised her head, kissing each naked buttock in turn, mmmmmmm.

'I'm starv…'

'I could eat a h…' They spoke at once and collapsed into laughter again, biting at each others' arms, elbows, noses, until Jane jumped up and shrugged on a dark blue satin bathrobe, without bothering to close it.

'Yum, sexy.' Poppy was reclining on an elbow.

Jane lifted the chilly bin lid and held up, one at a time, a smoked chicken, French bread broken into pieces, a bottle of champagne, glasses, a lidded container of salad, a jar of dressing…

'I know this is not exactly camping but I thought' – she indicated the chicken – 'as a first night of its own sort…'

Poppy had made much of her tradition of taking a smoked

chicken for the first meal of a camping trip when they had travelled in New Zealand in January. 'And I suppose you have bacon and… oh, hang on, this is a B & B, they'll do it.'

'Right. As long as we're up and dressed in time.'

They ate and drank hungrily, talking with 'do you remembers?' of the time Jane was in New Zealand, laughing, shying away from anything difficult or painful, wanting to stay wrapped in a cocoon of each other.

'Who's going to sleep in the single bed?' Poppy asked as they cleared the remnants of food back into the chilly bin, each holding a glass with the last of the champagne. They both collapsed in help-less laughter, spilling their drinks on each other, giggling at the tickle of the bubbles, licking the liquid off, and not stopping, making love again, noisy and laughing and moaning, and, finally, sleeping. Sleep was fitful for them both, stirring to touch and confirm the presence of the other, to murmur and make small throaty noises and sleep again. They made love again in the early morning and lay dozing in the warmth and smells of each other until the faint sounds of crockery mingling with the raucous noise of the inevitable seagulls woke them fully, thinking of breakfast.

Over the bacon and eggs (poached these days) that Poppy insisted on for the first morning, they reminisced some more about camping together earlier in the year, laughing at their separate tents, and over second coffees planned the day. 'Out-doors, open spaces, sea air, walking,' were Poppy's requirements and Jane concurred happily, requiring herself that they lunch on scampi and dressed crab and have a fish dinner that night. 'After all, that's what Whitby is famous for.' Poppy had promised to get kippers from a certain place made famous by the Two Fat Ladies of television cooking, for George and Susanna, so she needed to check that it would be open the next day, it being Sunday.

Jane bought their lunch items from two separate shops and they found bread rolls at a third. 'No chips, oh well, times change,' Jane said. There were certainly plenty of places that sold hot chips and numbers of people sitting on benches along the breakwaters that guided the river into the sea eating them, seagulls, always the seagulls, squawking, circling, large and black and white, demanding, intrusive, and necessary to the English seaside.

They climbed the one hundred and ninety-nine steps to the church and the ruined abbey that dominated the cliff-top over the town. The old graveyard fascinated Poppy, weathered grey and black headstones, many unreadable, meandering up a green slope. Markers of people's lives, she thought, whole lives, names eroded by the salt wind. Mrs Mudgely hovered over the nearest grey slab, shaking her head; Poppy shook hers, 'None of that today,' she told herself, and hurried to catch up to Jane.

The church was lovely, homely rather than grand, ramshackle, with the usual box for donations to assist restoration plans, so she dropped her change into it. The Abbey ruins, on the other hand, were grand, imposing. A new visitor centre was promised, work underway, opening in March 2002. They wandered around, Poppy taking photos of the sky through empty windows, a passing Swedish tourist offering to take a picture of 'you and your friend together'. Jane had binoculars out, scanning for the sea birds she loved. It took a while to find the path along this coast that was the Cleveland Way and when they did they set off striding along the top of the cliff. Jane stretched out her arms, whooping and running along making gull-wing movements.

'Remember you can't fly!' Poppy's voice disappeared into the wind.

There was no-one else in sight except for tiny figures far away. She revelled in the air, the height, the wide sky and sea disappearing beyond the horizon, discoloured where the river flowed into it. This was what she missed in Middlesbrough, this sense of natural vastness, unencumbered by needs or emotions, untamable, unmanageable, demanding nothing but due care. Suddenly she became aware of Jane at the next headland, waving, so she hurried towards her. Holding hands they danced around and around together, throwing yells and whoops into the wind, exhilarated, stopping only when they became aware of a party of five on the path ahead.

They turned back towards the town, finding a spot looking over the town to the sandy beach on the far side of the river to have lunch. Swimming in the North Sea this early in the summer was for those more intrepid than themselves, they decided.

'Yum,' Jane licked her fingers as they gathered the remnants of their feast. Poppy passed her the water bottle. 'Nectar!' she proclaimed as she passed it back. 'Let's do the shops on our way to the other pier and stand out at the end, gazing at the north sea…'

'Okay.' Poppy was looking about for a rubbish bin. She took great lungsful of the air. Making their way down the steps, taking care on the narrow treads, they saw the two piers, curved in breakwaters out into the sea, feeding the river waters out and moderating the inwards tides. Directly across the river were stone and brick houses, roofed mostly in tiles, occasionally painted white, filling every space. Poppy supposed there were roads among them but from this angle none were visible, nor was any pattern that might indicate where they ran. Huddled, as though for warmth or comfort, she thought, houses cuddling up together on the low hillside.

They walked in narrow cobbled lanes, among tiny shops selling fish or crafts or teas, with entrances to hostelries or accommodation of various kinds. Jewellery made from local jet, and ammonites and other fossils attracted them both. Poppy thought of buying them both a jet ring, but decided it was not yet time for that, so bought an exquisite ammonite, its perfect curves set in a tiny piece of rock forever and gave it to Jane right away, there in the shop. Jane blushed fiercely under the interested gaze of the artisan-shopkeeper and hustled them both out onto the footpath.

'Sorry, I should have waited and given it to you later…'

'No, no it's fine, it was all I could do not to kiss you in front of him. Maybe we could go back for a… rest? Oh dear, I feel like a gauche school-girl.' Jane was blushing.

'Soon. I want more sea air, come on.' And they raced through the Saturday afternoon crowd, along a couple more lanes, paying cursory attention to the shop windows. At one stage Poppy lost Jane, so after a few minutes she stood in the middle of the road, shifting out of the way of the occasional delivery van negotiating the small space.

'Making myself easy to find,' she explained when Jane tapped her on the shoulder, 'where did you get to?' Jane didn't answer, just led the way across the bridge to the pier on the other side. Fish, various sea-foods and chips, take-aways and restaurants lined the path, then the inevitable arcade of flashing lights, game machines, sirens and bangs. Poppy hurried past. Jane paused a moment, then matched her pace.

'That place was magic to me as a kid,' she said. 'It was much smaller then, more pinball than today's games, once a year on my birthday my father would take me and let me beat him sometimes…' Poppy smiled at her. 'I guess it's because I'm a New Zealander I just don't get amusement arcades at the beach.'

'Weather!' said Jane.

'What?'

'Rotten English summer weather, something indoors to do on your summer holidays.'

'Oh, oh yes, I hadn't thought of that. Look.' The stretch of almost-golden sand to the north had come into view. In the sunshine the water looked appealing and they scrambled down to the sand.

'Sticky sand, I had forgotten.' Poppy was trying to brush it off her feet after very briefly testing the water. They lay on dry sand for a while, enjoying the warmth of the sun, then Jane insisted they finish their walk to the end of the breakwater for the sensation of being surrounded by sea. By the time they made their way back to their room both were weary and they fell on the bed together. Jane jumped up again and searched for something in her jeans pocket, drawing out a bracelet of pieces of jet with links of silver.

'For you.' She held it out to Poppy, who put it on her arm.

'It's beautiful. Come here.' They lay in each others' arms, side by side, facing, eyes open.

Jane spoke first. 'Do you want…?'

'Not really. Lying here is good. Close. Sleepy.' Poppy ran her fingers gently over Jane's face, tracing the cheek-bones, nose, around her ears, across her lips. Then her eyelids closed, and Jane matched her regular, even breathing and lay very still until she too fell asleep.

Poppy woke to the feel of Jane's hand on her breast, her fingers kneading the nipple, and was instantly aroused. They were both perspiring in the warm room, slick in places, licking the warm saltiness of each other, exploring bodies with an intensity, fierceness even, that was different from their earlier languor. Jane, kneeling, her head flung back, moaning, Poppy burying her face, clasping, then biting kisses on her shoulders, unable to tell whose sounds she was hearing, wallowing, exalting, flying, falling, soaring again. Eventually they both fell back on the bed, hot and sweaty, arms and legs just touching.

'Mmmmnnnn,' came a throaty sound from Jane. 'Fan-bloody-tastic. How about you?'

'Mmmm-mmm,' Poppy was searching for words. Satisfied, no, satiated, and something else… then… oh, to hell with words she told herself and turned and nuzzled into Jane's breasts.

'Big nipples,' she murmured, 'not like my tiny ones.'

'Tiny and sensitive.'

'You noticed!'

'How could I not!'

They showered together, soaping each other and taking turns in the feeble water flow, and got dressed for the 'fish pie at the Duke of York' Jane insisted they experience, adding, 'We can have the famous Whitby fish and chips before we leave tomorrow.'

Chapter Eight

In the morning Poppy woke full of sadness for George and cried in the comfort of Jane's arms.

After a while she said, 'Talk to me about when your parents died. Not what happened, what it was like, how you coped emotionally.'

The hand that was stroking Poppy's back and shoulders tensed. 'I was angry when my father died because my mother had been ill so long and she was supposed to die first.'

'Was that all? Angry?'

'No, of course not! Look, I don't really want to talk about this. It was a long time ago and this is our time for us...' her hand was moving softly again, up and down and around Poppy's back, tantalisingly close to breasts and buttocks. Poppy moved away; she'd had a thought she wanted to say, even if it wasn't welcome.

'I wondered why you were so enraged when Héloise left before you could carry out your plan, maybe it was a bit the same...' Poppy said this tentatively and felt Jane's response as a stiffening of her whole body.

'Well, yes.' Jane's voice was dismissive and when she continued, resigned. 'And when my mother died nine long long years later it was more of a relief really, the emphysema was choking her, it was awful. So both were completely different from you and George.' Jane was lying quite still now.

'Yes, of course.' And it's still having a parent die, Poppy thought and didn't say; she didn't say, either, that she didn't feel like talking about George's dying now. And neither of them was attempting to talk about any time more than a day ahead, as though in silent agreement.

After a few moments Jane asked Poppy to reconsider seeing her at her own place now that Héloise had truly gone. She'd not continued with the bed-sit, it seemed silly to have no-one living in the house and H was even suggesting that she, Jane, should pay all the expenses and the mortgage until the house was sold.

'You need a lawyer.' It wasn't meant to sound as abrupt as it did, perhaps because Poppy drew away and sat up on the side of the bed as she said it. 'Really,' she went on, 'you need a lawyer for the property bits, it'll be much cleaner.' She knew she hadn't responded to the part about visiting at Jane's house.

'I know, I've been avoiding it, hoping we could work it out our-selves.' Poppy melted at the misery in Jane's voice and turned back to her. But the 'awayness' of the weekend had dissipated, so they started on an activity plan for the morning, and decided on a brief visit to the Captain Cook museum, a trawl through the shops, finding the kippers for George and Susanna, a late fish and chip lunch and an afternoon return drive along the coast.

'With a cliff walk.' Poppy wanted more open spaces.

Planning their day together brought them back into the same orbit and they made love again rather than get up in time for breakfast, searching for the powerful blending of the night before. As they lay spent, Jane said, 'I love you Poppy.'

'Me to,' she responded, very quietly.

While Poppy was in the shower Jane assembled leftover chicken and bread from Friday night into sandwiches, 'It's been in the chilly bin and it smells okay, I'm game if you are,' she said, offering one to a towel-wrapped Poppy who bit into it doubtfully at first, then hungrily.

'What about what's left?'

'Rubbish,' Jane was shoving all the remnants into a plastic bag.

Poppy got her walk, along Sandsend beach on their way out of Whitby. Jane had driven past the house she and her family had lived in, brick, in a street of identical dwellings, in the midst of several other streets much the same. None of the features of the town were visible from that street, not the castle, nor the church, the river nor the beach or sea. They'd had fish and chips on the pier from paper bundles, the batter light and crisp, the fish fresh and cooked just right, chips golden and crisp with soft insides, Jane's with vinegar, Poppy's without.

On the drive along the coast, past Saltburn-by-the-Sea where they had danced on the sand on the first night, Poppy raised the question of other lesbians, and lesbian groups around Middlesbrough again. Jane reiterated her lack of knowledge. She'd never heard of a lesbian group in Yorkshire, never mind Middlesbrough, except for a mixed lesbian and gay paper, *Shout!* that she thought came out of York and had seen once or twice.

'We used to socialise with another couple', she said, 'but they moved to Manchester a couple of years ago.' Then she added, defensively, 'we were both always busy with work, you know.'

'Sure.' Poppy could not imagine a life without lesbian friends. 'Wow! Look at that!' They had passed Redcar and a huge industrial estate was coming into view. Enormous concrete structures, towers, spheres with ladders curving up the side, cooling towers, high barbed-wire fences.

'Teesside. Industry. Chemicals.' said Jane. 'You remember, the lights the other night. You must have seen this in daylight before.'

'I suppose, but it's never struck me like this. And it goes on and on.'

'Yeah. Those of us who live here prefer to forget about it. Unless we work there I suppose, but I don't know anyone who does.' The traffic into Middlesbrough was heavy, so Jane kept most of her attention on the road. Poppy was thinking about George and liver cancer and information she'd got off the 'net; unusual to have primary liver cancer without cirrhosis, some chemicals could be a factor but she couldn't remember which ones, and she didn't know what happened here, but what about pollutants? She asked Jane.

'There was a big clean-up, oh, years ago. They boast that the air here is cleaner than in London now.' She went on to talk about the Teesside Corporation that had been formed to clean up the river as well.

'Uh huh,' Poppy said, 'and it won't help George to go looking for causes for his cancer will it?' Jane nodded agreement.

Just before the turn that would take them to George's, Jane pulled over. 'How about we see if Rachel is home, I'd love you to meet her and it's only ten minutes out of the way.'

'Yes, sure.' Poppy would be pleased to meet Rachel, who seemed to be Jane's only friend.

'Don't move then,' and Jane grabbed her bag, jumped out of the car and ran to a phone box on the footpath. Of course, people didn't drop in without ringing in these parts.

'She's got the jug on.' The traffic was even heavier now and it was a few minutes before Jane could pull out and then it took another twenty minutes to drive over the bridge, past more miles of industrial structures. Poppy wasn't sure that she had ever visited Billingham before.

'It's not somewhere you'd go for a Sunday drive,' Jane pointed out, 'chemical industries don't usually make it to the tourist brochures.' Waiting for a gap in the traffic so she could make a right turn into a side street, she added, 'There's the famous folk music festival in August if you're still around…'

Poppy met her apologetic glance with a smile. 'It's okay,' she said, 'you don't have to be careful what you say.'

Rachel was tall and thin with short grey hair She wore jeans and a hand-knitted jumper, and greeted Jane with a warm hug then held out a hand to Poppy for a firm handshake. The downstairs rooms of her terraced house had been opened into one space, suitable for someone like her, she explained to Poppy, who lived on her own and no doubt always would. The space was lined with shelves, some glass-covered, crowded with what Poppy soon learned were art deco ceramics, Rachel's passion. Her work as a radiologist at South Cleveland Hospital paid enough, she said, to 'support my collecting habit.' Poppy could not give her any idea of the chance of picking up a Clarice Cliff original in New Zealand at a reasonable price; she thought Katrina might know and offered to ask. Jane was making coffee for herself and tea for the other two in the kitchen-space where she was quite at home. 'I've already spotted one new piece since I was here last,' she called out, 'that small orange and yellow bowl.'

After half-an-hour of chat, during which Rachel was clearly sizing up Poppy, who didn't mind, Poppy said she'd like to get back, George would be expecting her about now. Their weekend together was over.

As they pulled up outside George's house, Poppy caught a glimpse of him at the front room window. She asked Jane to come in and was glad there were two of them to meet the questions which started as soon as they reached the door. They regaled him with tales of steps and walks and meals and beaches, Poppy producing the kippers with a flourish and a 'Tah dah!' When Susanna came in she promised to cook a 'real kipper breakfast' in the morning to start the week.

Jane turned down George's offer to stay for supper and insisted that no-one come further than the door, so she and Poppy fare-welled with a quick hand-clasp observed by George and Poppy wished she had walked out to the car with her.

Unpacking later, Poppy came across her notebook, and thought for a moment what she would write in it about the weekend, then scribbled: *To Whitby with Jane. Consummated.* And underlined <u>*don't take myself too seriously*</u> further up the page.

She thought of Jane, of the two of them making love, so tenderly then so feverishly, the sheer pleasure of it. And she thought of the halts in conversation, Jane's unwillingness to mull things over, tease them out, talk around and through to another understanding. What Poppy did with her friends. And had done with Kate. Surely. She couldn't remember in detail what she and Kate talking had been like, it had been, well, right, she was certain, easy exchanges on anything and everything. Of course.

There was no need to worry about Jane visiting here, everyone was at ease with that and soon, Poppy thought, soon, I will go to her place, and she became aware that at no time over the weekend had either of them attempted to suggest any forward plans. She put a tick by *go with the flow.*

Stefan had rung during the weekend, and Katrina, George reported, both sending love to Poppy; she was grateful to know that the rest of her family was being dependable. So far, there didn't seem much scope for finding local lesbian company, perhaps she would have to resign herself to a lack of it, apart of course, from Jane.

There was a tap on her door, George was on his way to bed.

'I missed you,' he said as they hugged goodnight, 'and I'm glad you had a good time.' Whether his smile was annoyingly knowing or not didn't matter Poppy told herself as she went downstairs to check her email.

Three new messages, two she deleted without opening and one from Martia with news of mutual friends – Alexa and Bessie were separating and both trying hard not to expect their friends to take sides – and reassurances about herself and Mrs Mudgely. Also,

> *went to a movie with joy, probably not the one you stood her up for*

> *she's struggling a bit with new big city new big job at public library*
> *ended a twenty year relationship with a woman and a longer one with the booze a couple of years ago*
> *and don't bother thinking what i think you're thinking*
> *she might be a new friend, but that's all.*

Not that it would be a bad thing if that wasn't all, Poppy thought, and set about writing her friend a long message.

Next morning the kippers, cooked under the grill and served with soft white bread by Susanna, were a great hit, even though George managed to eat only half of one. After breakfast they did a 'fridge-plan' for the coming week, which included, at George's suggestion, moving him to a downstairs bedroom. 'It's not so much the stairs,' he explained, 'but that it's not so comfortable sitting and I don't want to be lying down upstairs out of the way of everything all day.' Susanna was concerned that moving furniture would expose areas that hadn't been cleaned for a long time; Poppy thought she could deal with this with Mrs Madge's help on Tuesday and Friday. There was Susanna's cards on Wednesday afternoon, the doctor on Wednesday morning, afternoon tea for George at the Museum on Thursday, Poppy was meeting Sylvia for lunch on Tuesday and George wanted to help with the shopping today. Poppy put herself down for a long walk on Tuesday afternoon and booked Jock and two of his lads for furniture moving on Friday. No-one actually knew when the district nurse was coming again. The week looked full. Having Jane over for tea – she remembered to call it supper – one day was discussed but no day decided and Poppy was privately thinking that maybe she would spend a night with Jane, even at her house. Maybe.

Once the room-changing was done, she hoped, some sort of routine would evolve, a pattern in the days, something she could settle into.

Poppy wasn't sure she would recognise Sylvia, though they had met, at least at Christmas in 1991. As far as Poppy could remember they had hardly spoken to each other, she herself absorbed in her grief at Kate's death and Sylvia in her husband and his children. As Poppy was leaving she asked Susanna for some clues to pick Sylvia out by.

'Dowdy.' Susanna had been abrupt all morning. 'Skirt, blouse, white probably, sensible shoes, that kind of thing.' And she busied herself at the sink, shaking her head, whether at the thought of her daughter or because Poppy was going to meet her Poppy couldn't tell.

In the event Sylvia, who was already seated at a table, spotted her first, putting a sheaf of papers in a bag at her feet then standing, proffering a hand which Poppy shook. When they had sat down she couldn't think what to say. Sylvia was smarter than her mother's description had suggested, though skirt and white blouse were accurate; Poppy couldn't see her shoes but had noticed the jacket matching the skirt on the back of the chair.

'I thought…' she began and a waitress appeared beside them so they ordered. Sylvia asked for 'the lamb' and 'just water' without looking at a menu and Poppy went for chicken salad, the first item she saw, and water also.

'I thought…' she began again, 'um, that it would be good to meet and… well, actually I don't really know why, I just thought it would be a good idea. I'm going to be here for a while.'

'It probably is a good idea.' The smile helped. 'I'm sorry about George. And you might have worked it out, my mother and I don't exactly get on.' Barely a trace of Yorkshire accent, that was a surprise.

'Yes, kind of. She's not very well, you know, and…'

'You don't want to be saddled with looking after her as well as your father.' The smile was gone.

'No, well yes, look, I hadn't even thought about that I just thought that… well, probably I should have minded my own business, but I just thought that here we both are, in the same town with an ailing parent and maybe, I don't know…'

'You're lonely!' The smile was back.

'Well, it's true my family and friends aren't here, except for Ja...
well, never mind, oh dear, I'm sorry, I've probably just wasted your
time.' Poppy was disconcerted that Sylvia was so unlike the person
she had expected. The woman in front of her had the manner and
look of a lawyer more than the secretary she had expected. 'Stereo-
types!,' she chided herself.

'My mother,' Sylvia waved at the waitress to put the water on the
table, 'probably told you I was a clerk. Actually,' the smile was
almost a wicked grin, 'I'm deputy to the Council Chief Executive.
She can't believe that I've 'got on' you see.'

'Oh, I'm sorry.' Poppy plunged on, 'Would you mind, you know,
telling me some more.'

The other woman shrugged and poured water into two glasses. 'If
you like. She never liked me – and don't be sympathetic, I got over
it – and sent me off to boarding school even though they really
couldn't afford it and, of course, after a couple of years I didn't fit in
around here at all. And to cut a long story short, I came back here
because of a man – who is long gone – and I've stayed because I like
my job. A lot.' She took a long drink of water. 'Now it's your turn.'

'I had a happy childhood,' Poppy stopped herself apologising, and
gave a very short summary of her life to date, naming Kate as 'my
partner, who died,' and leaving out Jane altogether. Their food
arrived while she was talking and Sylvia began eating right away,
looking up at Poppy and nodding from time to time.

After what Poppy had feared was a disastrous beginning, things
were going rather well, so she asked about what really bothered her,
'Why don't you come around to the house?' and waited slightly
nervously.

'It doesn't work, the two of us together.' Sylvia was drawing circles
on the table top with her finger. 'She says something nasty and I
snarl and it's just unpleasant. I wish it wasn't, but there it is. I suspect
neither of us does sarcasm with anyone else like we do with each
other.' She looked up and met Poppy's gaze. 'So there you are.'

'Oh. Thank you. For telling me that is. I just couldn't understand.'

'I'm glad about her and George making a go of it. My father was… well, never mind, George has been a distinct improvement, I think she's even been happy. Do you want coffee?' She was waving the waitress over.

Over their coffees Sylvia asked Poppy about New Zealand and its clear air. She wanted to go there, she said, to see the stars of the southern hemisphere. Eight years ago, when her last relationship broke up, she had gotten into astrology in, she said, 'a probably desperate attempt to find out if she would ever find another man,' and it had gradually changed into a passion for 'the real thing,' astronomy. There had never been another man, and she was not bothered about that any more, she was having a love affair with the stars. She followed this with a slightly embarrassed laugh then went on to talk about the difficulties of seeing stars in the north England sky, because of a combination of the weather, air pollution and the amount of city lighting, so she went to Scotland quite often, and Ireland occasionally.

Her enthusiasm reminded Poppy of George and his lepidoptera and she felt a twinge of sadness at how easily he was letting that go.

'And next year,' Sylvia was saying, 'I'm going to Zambia, to see the solar eclipse.'

'Wow!' Poppy was liking this woman. She wished briefly that she had paid more attention nine years ago to her and her mother together. As they were leaving she asked her to think about visiting. 'George would like it. And so would I.' The answering laugh was more rueful than bitter.

'I just might do that,' and with a brief touch on Poppy's shoulder, Sylvia strode off. Poppy headed back to the car; she would have a walk on the moors before returning to what, for the moment, was home.

Chapter Nine

On this weekday afternoon the moors were blessedly empty of other people. Poppy knew enough about the boggy moors to seek out a well-formed path to stride off on at a brisk pace. She planned to walk fast until she tired, then turn back for the car at a slower pace. The moors had none of the drama of a New Zealand landscape, at least not away from the coast, but the low undulating hills and dull, moody colours on a grey afternoon had their own undemanding beauty. Poppy swung her arms as she strode, enjoying the physical sensations of her moving muscles, open air brushing across her face and the respite from troublesome thoughts and feelings. Out here she could simply be, a physical creature in a landscape that wanted nothing from her.

She was out longer than she intended and turned the car into George's street feeling guilty that she was later getting back than she had said. A strange car parked outside his house. Visitors, she thought, relieved, opening the front door, with a cheerful 'Hello-o.' However, she was brought to an abrupt halt by the sight of George lying on the floor, half in the kitchen half in the hallway, with the doctor, Jasmine Owens, leaning over him.

'Good, you're back,' said Doctor Jasmine over her shoulder to

Poppy. 'We must convince George that he should go to hospital for two or three days for tests and examinations so we can decide how best to keep him comfortable and to have a morphine pump put in.'

Poppy kneeled beside her. George gripped Poppy's hand. His pale face was beaded with perspiration but he managed a small smile.

'Please do it George,' she said. 'They won't give you treatment if you don't want it – will they?' The question was to Jasmine, who shook her head.

'The ambulance will be here soon,' she was speaking to George, 'you will go, won't you?'

He nodded. 'Come with me,' he said to his daughter.

'She should come a little later.' The doctor spoke again, to both of them this time, 'with a car,' then turned to Poppy. 'I would like have a talk with you first. Just for a few minutes,' she added at the look on George's face, 'your daughter will be at the hospital soon after you are.'

Poppy stood up and went to Susanna. 'Would you like to…?' Susanna was shaking her head. 'Are you all right?'

'I will be in a minute. It was such a shock, him falling like that.'

Poppy rang Glory next-door-but-one and asked if she would come and sit with Susanna for a while. 'Of course I will, pet.' Glory had put the phone down almost before she finished speaking and arrived at the door at the same time as the ambulance attendant.

When Poppy tried to involve Susanna in the conversation with the doctor she was waved away, so she left the two older women in the kitchen and took Jasmine to the front room.

It was possible, Dr Jasmine told her, that George had developed a brain tumour and that would account for his dizziness and today's fall; he had not told Poppy about his phone call to the doctor on Friday regarding the dizziness apparently for fear of spoiling Poppy's weekend away. And further, it was important for Poppy to know that when George had a set-back like this there could be no expectation of a recovery back to how he had been before. Nodding, gripping her own hands, Poppy concentrated on the doctor, needing to take it all in. It was likely George would be in hospital for two nights, come home with a morphine pump inserted, and have daily nursing visits from now on. She, the doctor, would come by every second day or more often if she was rung for.

Susanna and Glory broke off their conversation when Poppy entered the kitchen and both looked at her. She passed on the information from the doctor and gave Susanna Jock's phone number, asking if she would ring him and see if she could get him to come tomorrow, while George was in hospital, to move his bedroom, rather than wait until Friday. 'Offer him an extra fifty pounds if he'll change the day at short notice,' she suggested, as she went out the door, catching the shocked look on Glory's face when she turned back to ask Susanna if she would like to be rung from the hospital.

'If you can by nine-thirty, before I'm off to my bed, yes please dear.' Glory nodded approval, saying something about Susanna needing her rest as Poppy finally left. Finding the hospital, finding the ward and finding George took ages. His face brightened when he saw her.

'I got in a bit of a panic there,' he apologised, 'things like this bound to happen.' He took her hand and they sat quietly for a while, then George was saying how he knew he was at the beginning of the end, he knew he was dying and she mustn't worry about that, it really was all right, he was quite reconciled. For an hour or so they talked about death and dying, George reiterating that he really did not want to be in hospital again after this if they could get enough help to manage at home. Both of them wiped away her tears from time to time.

He promised not to die in the night if Poppy went home to sleep and she said, 'All right, I believe you,' kissed him and went, with an assurance that she would come back in the morning. On the drive home she thought about going to Jane's and then that the hospital didn't have Jane's number and Susanna might not get to the downstairs phone – or was there one in the bedroom? and it was too hard to figure out, so she gave up the idea.

When she got in and found Susanna had already gone to bed, she wished she had rung before she left the hospital, until Susanna called out as she passed the bedroom door.

'Turn the light on, dear.' Susanna's eyes were red. 'Sit down for a minute, bring that chair over.' Poppy told her about George being settled for the night and asked if she would like to come to the hospital in the morning.

'No, thank you dear for asking.' Tears welled. 'I'm not heartless, I do care for George, but it's the pain, for three years and more the pain, everywhere, all my joints, always the pain and it's got me so I can't think much about anything else, I get right narky with it.' She was pleading with Poppy to understand.

'What about – do you take – .'

'You name it, I've had it. Steroids now, they help a bit.'

'I'm sorry.'

'You can't be helping it. I just,' the older woman hesitated, 'I just don't want you to think ill of me, is all.'

'I don't.' Which was more true now than it had been earlier. 'I'm glad you told me. It must be awful.'

'Yes dear, it is, and we box on, what else is there, eh?' and she patted Poppy's hand and told her that she'd got that Jock and his lads organised for tomorrow afternoon and he'd agreed for twenty pounds extra. Then she added almost smiling, 'You sure set Glory off, with your offering him fifty pounds, said she'd do it herself if it came to that. With her back!' They said their goodnights on a friendly note. No phone in here, Poppy noted to herself, another thing to arrange, and went off to add to the list in her notebook and ring Jane.

A few minutes into the phone call it was obvious to Poppy that they both wanted to talk about their day more than they wanted to listen to the other's. When she hung up twenty minutes later, she felt edgy and alone, then rang Katrina, who insisted on ringing her back to take advantage of a special tolls deal from New Zealand. Her mother's practical briskness was a relief and her commendation of Poppy for how she was handling things very welcome.

'Of course I'll ring your brother, you sound exhausted and need to get some sleep,' Katrina had said and Poppy had not felt at all patronised. Sleep, however, was a long time coming, fitful and full of dire dreams when it did, so she was up early, dragging furniture in the the centre of the living room so Mrs Madge could clean around the edges and Susanna would be satisfied.

She was determined that by the time George came home he would be able to go straight to his new room and lie down. When the cleaning and shifting was finished, his bed had been set up with an armchair on either side and with two other easily-moved chairs in the room. The television set was angled for the bed and Poppy found, on a shopping expedition, a frame to hold up his pillows to make sitting up to watch it easier. There was also a tray on wheeled legs that went over the bed, and a lamp. Susanna had helped decide how the room would be arranged.

George's farewell at the museum had been cancelled; Poppy thought she probably minded that more than he did, but he was pleased when the chairman of the board came by with the present they had bought him, an elegant mantle clock.

'To watch the hours tick off,' George joked when the chairman had gone and seemed genuinely amused. Being in hospital, though, had been an ordeal he told Poppy and would she please shoot him rather than let him be taken back there.

Over the next days they did settle into a routine. The doctor came as she had promised, every second day; she would decide when nurses were needed. George could still get up and use the downstairs toilet and shower and even go for an occasional short drive. People dropped by, colleagues from the museum, people he and Susanna had socialised with over the years. George did not seem at all fazed to be in bed receiving visitors.

'It's a bit like holding court,' he said when one couple had left. 'I lie here and people come with offerings.' There were certainly many flowers in the room, and a regular supply of baked goods 'in case you need them,' from people to whom others' contributions were offered with the inevitable cups of tea. They'd set up a tea-making table in George's room – at Susanna's suggestion – so she, rather than Poppy, could make tea without having to carry it in. All Poppy had to do was fill the kettle as Susanna's hands were too weak to carry it full in from the kitchen, and Poppy was relieved to be able to avoid some of the tea and chat. The affection between her father and Susanna became apparent as she spent large parts of the day sitting by his bed, chatting, watching television with him. Sometimes they simply sat, hands touching on the bed-pane, one or both of them reading.

Poppy ran the household, did the washing, most of the shopping, talked to the doctor, and the nurses as they started coming in, sat with George who increasingly wanted to reminisce with her about the past, and tried to get time with Jane. They talked on the phone most days and saw each other when they could. Being away from the house overnight became easier for Poppy once she had managed to get telephones in both Susanna's and George's rooms. She did it by buying lengths of cord and taping it around doorways from existing phone jacks in the walls after spending a frustrating day on the phone trying to get the telephone company to come. So now there were three phones, two downstairs, and one and the computer modem connections upstairs. Then Poppy realised she could also have a phone in her room, dual-plugging from the end of the cord from the dual plug in the hallway that also led to Susanna's room. Susanna was doubtful, then amused, then delighted at the arrangement when she saw that it worked.

'George used to be like that,' she said to Poppy, 'wouldn't give up

until he'd figure'd out how to make something happen. I liked that.'
Once George could use the quick-dial option on his receiver for
Jane's phone number Poppy started spending a night every few days
at the Billingham house.

'I rearranged all the furniture in the bedroom and the living
room,' Jane said the first time she was there, 'so it would be different.' Once they had a meal at Rachel's but otherwise they hardly
ever went out together. Jane would call at George's house and visit
with them all every few days and Poppy would want to touch her,
and be touched; some days it was a hunger, an almost desperate
need for skin contact. So they would go upstairs to Poppy's room
and close the door, and it felt so teenage to Poppy, on her single bed,
hands under each others' clothes. Sometimes they got the giggles
and that was all right. Other times Poppy was overcome by a crush-
ing embarrassment that she couldn't explain and Jane didn't understand; after a while they stopped going upstairs.

Evenings at Jane's house in Billingham, occasional weekend
afternoons, these were the times they made love. If either of them
was tired – which would result in 'headache' jokes – they would
hold each other, skin to skin, without covers; there were hot days
that June. Poppy tried not to talk too much about George and illness and losing a parent, she did after all have other people to talk to
about that, even if they were on the other side of the world. She
appreciated Jane's efforts to limit herself to summaries of Héloïse's
outrageous demands ('That I should pay all the mortgage and the
rates and pay her rent!!') and cheered at the news that Jane had been
to a lawyer.

'I wish you'd stay.' Poppy had arrived early in the evening, crying
as she came in the door. This was the first day that George had not
got up and dressed, a nurse had come to wash him and Poppy had
seen his thin, thin legs and bloated, distorted belly.

'Shhh, darling, shh, it's all right…' Jane held her.

'No it's not!' came, muffled from her shoulder. Poppy stepped back. 'He knows he's dying, he knows it can only get worse, why does it have to go on?'

Jane held out her hands in a gesture of helplessness.

'That's what it's like,' Poppy mirrored the gesture, 'I run around and do what I can for him – for both of them really – and in the end it's useless.' She was pacing. Jane sat down on a kitchen chair and watched her silently.

'Except I want to – you know – do everything I can. And I know he likes it, and likes me there and that makes it better – a little bit –for him. Oh shit, I'm sorry, you don't need to hear all this, it's just that it's bloody hard. Bloody hard. If he was a cat it would be humane – huh!! – to have him put down.' Stunned at what she had just said she fell silent with a sharp intake of breath, hands over her mouth.

'But he's not…' Jane's shock was in her voice.

'A cat, I know, that was an awful thing to say, it's watching him suffer – and he isn't really suffering that much, he's – he's – diminishing – becoming less than himself, turning inwards, oh hell, it's just hellish!'

'Yes, yes, it is.' Jane did not say that for her watching a parent die slowly, much more slowly than George, reminded her of her mother's bitterness and her own resentment and grudging involvement. There had been none of the warmth that was between George and Poppy, none of the generosity, no concern for each other, no shared enjoyment at small things. And she couldn't tell Poppy any more about that, not just now.

Poppy looked across the table, wondering at the unhappiness on Jane's face, interpreting it as impatience, but really she couldn't just step out of the house and leave those feelings behind, she was living this every day and night, she had only one chance to do it right, or at least as right as she could manage.

Finally Jane spoke. 'Bad memories,' she said. 'Sorry, they took me away for a bit.' Poppy nodded, she knew a little of how Jane had hated her mother's lingering emphysema, how trapped she had felt. So different from her own wanting; wanting to do her best, wanting to ease things for George, and sometimes wanting desperately for it to be over for him. And over for her, but not because she wanted to be doing anything other than looking after him, rather because he should have, he deserved, the best he could have and that was, surely, an end to discomfort and pain and the intimate attentions of strangers. And yet he wasn't minding, so far, that she could tell, so why was she thinking like this? And here she was with Jane, in some of their rare time alone, sitting miserably at opposite sides of a kitchen table. She stretched her hand across and Jane's came out to meet it. 'Come on,' she said, and stood, pulling Jane up with her and taking them both to the sofa at the lounge end of the room, where they sat, still silent, but at least with their arms around each other.

'What are we?' Jane asked eventually. 'Lovers? Partners? Girlfriends?'

'Not partners,' came out more abruptly than Poppy wanted, 'not yet, anyway,' she added hastily, 'not enough shared lives, you know, friends, things we do together – except the obvious of course – that stuff.'

'Oh. I see, I think. Lovers or girlfriends then?'

'Dunno. Which do you fancy?'

'It's you I fancy, lover-girl.' Fingers around her ears and eyes and through her hair, a hand creeping under her t-shirt reminded Poppy who she fancied – a lot.

'I wonder,' Jane drew back her head, 'how we would be together if we didn't have our separate encumbrances?' Stiffening at George being turned into an encumbrance, desire stone dead, Poppy looked into Jane's eyes. They were shining, and tensed around the edges. Her smile came slightly too fast, too forced, too bright. She's trying really hard, Poppy realised, and the realisation softened her so she asked how Jane's 'encumbrance' was going.

They were now reduced to communicating through their lawyers, she learnt, and Jane's, a woman called Trudy, had suggested she change the locks on the house, at which Jane was shocked but Trudy had said that as she was paying all the expenses she was entitled to do this, as long as she let Héloise come at arranged times to collect anything that they agreed was hers. And Trudy thought they should put the house on the market right away, while it was still summer; Billingham was not the easiest place to sell at any time, not unless there was expansion going on at one of the chemical plants and right now there wasn't.

'So I could be homeless, any time. And jobless, I don't know how much longer I can stand the Cleveland, or at least the squabbling and stupidity.' The stupidity, Poppy gathered, continued to be that, after a flurry of interest about the material Jane had brought back from New Zealand, her ideas were increasingly marginalised as people fought for position and territory. By the time Jane wound down Poppy could barely keep her eyes open, she managed a final 'you poor thing, that's dreadful,' and pleaded to go to bed. 'And sleep,' she added apologetically. Jane was immediately contrite and made cocoa, bringing it to the bed and feeding the two soft soggy marshmallows on the top into Poppy's mouth with her fingers, rewarded with an appreciative and noisy suck. 'Yum. G'night.'

Poppy woke spooned against Jane's back, excited quickenings pulsing in her, guiding her fingers into swirling strokes on her lover's stomach. A slow langorous response heightened her desire so that by the time Jane turned to her she was grasping and gasping at her touch, and responded to the other with soaring intensity. Jane's final moan came from deep in her. Poppy's echo very soon after had them laughing, entwined, crying, nuzzling, kissing.

'Oh, golly-gosh.' Jane collapsed on top, their breasts squashing between them. 'Now *that's* a way to start the day,' and she blew in Poppy's ear and kissed her closed eyelids, 'and the best reason I know for being late for work.' She sat up, astride Poppy's stomach, trailing fingertips between her breasts. 'More, darling, more?' The other woman shook her head and opened her eyes.

'Enough, already.' She wanted her smile to be loving. 'To work, woman.' Jane hesitated for a moment, then slid down the bed, kissing an inside thigh as she went. Poppy heard the shower.

Driving away from the house she wondered at the feeling, the momentary feeling, of something like desperation, that had come over her at the height of their lovemaking, a second when she had absolutely wanted to be there *and* be a thousand miles away, both at the same moment.

Chapter Ten

The first time Sylvia came by the house, ostensibly to see George, Poppy saw Susanna making an effort. They were all sitting around in George's room and he asked Sylvia if she still saw the twins, to which she replied she hadn't heard from either of them in the past year or more; she thought one was in Australia and the other working in London, and had thought about contacting her ex-husband, their father, for news of them. 'They didn't need another mother,' she went on to explain to Poppy, 'but while Graham and I were married the children and I did get fond of each other.'

Susanna looked briefly as if she would make a comment, an unpleasant one by the expression on her face Poppy thought, then watched her stop herself, and say, 'They're nice boys.' Mother and daughter were stiffly polite with each other for the rest of the visit, and George told Poppy later, she'd 'done a good job there.'

'Don't be silly, I didn't do anything,' she said.

'What you did, my dear,' her father insisted, 'was be extremely kind to Susanna from the beginning, and then not take any notice of her nonsense about Sylvia. And, of course, I don't know what you said to Sylvia.' His look was enquiring. Nosy old bugger she thought, and pointed out that she herself had said nothing about

Poppy's Return

Susanna other than ask her daughter why she didn't visit. At this George smiled knowingly and Poppy let the subject drop while she was only slightly irritated.

Since that first visit Sylvia had begun to drop in at weekends and occasionally on her way home after work. She'd visit with George and, if Susanna was in the room, both of them. Poppy saw the beginnings of a spat when Susanna responded to something her daughter said about her work with, 'Clerking that is, nowt but clerking, nothing to give yourself airs about after that expensive education.'

'No, it's a lot more than that,' Sylvia replied, 'if you'd ever taken the…' then stopped herself with a short laugh. 'Okay, it'll always be clerking to you, but it suits me very well.'

She offered to show Poppy a local walk and while they were striding along a path by a tiny stream told her that she had made a decision to 'have another go' with her mother and do some things differently.

'Do you feel like telling me why?' Poppy was tentative.

'You and George actually.' Oh dear, Poppy thought, she thinks I'm digging for compliments.

'George getting sick, you coming over, and your brother and his wife, no fuss, no points to score, just doing it. And being decent to my mother. And you meeting up with me in spite of what my mother probably said. Get over it I thought, get over being the resentful one, you've got a life and she is my mother. That sort of thing. Don't snap back at her I told myself.' Then she turned and smiled at her companion, 'Well, actually my therapist told me to, you know, the "you can't change her but you can change the way you respond to her" line,' and waited for a response.

'Oh. I went to a therapist for a while, after something awful happened.'

'I know. When your partner died. I remember you that

101

Christmas, pale and extremely wan. You hardly spoke. George was beside himself about you.'

'Was he?' They were still walking at a brisk pace. 'I didn't notice I suppose, except I did get irritated with him a bit.'

'I'm glad to hear it!' They came to a bench and Poppy sat on it.

'Whew! You set a fair pace. What do you mean you're glad to hear it?'

Sylvia joined her on the bench. 'Just that a perfect parent-child relationship would be too much, I guess.' She pointed at a bird on a nearby tree. 'A robin, see the colours, a male.'

'You don't have to tell me – of course – but, well, what made you go to a therapist?'

'Breaking up with Graham.' She shrugged. 'The end of another rotten relationship, depressed at being on my own, depressed at the prospect of making another mess of a relationship, that sort of thing. Then she – the therapist – got me talking about my mother.' Sylvia had picked up a longish stick and was scratching in the ground with it. Poppy watched the stick. 'I resisted like mad for a while.' Sylvia tossed the stick aside and stood up, 'Shall we go on, this path doesn't go much further?'

The walk was one Poppy could do in forty minutes from the house without taking the car and she began to take it at some time most days, glad of an easy, quick break from the house. George hardly left his room – Poppy had given up any idea of getting him a wheelchair – the nurses came, the doctor came, visitors came; his downstairs room had turned into the centre of the house.

Poppy's idea that she would have to do any physical looking-after proved to be mistaken. It was more that she co-ordinated, organised, managed the household, though Susanna still did some of the cooking. The warm weather meant that Poppy could get the windows open at least for part of each day; she seemed to be the only one that noticed stuffiness. Getting out for a walk, occasionally a whole half-day on the moors, gave her a chance to clear her head. And she needed a clear head, to think about Jane.

Thinking about her and Jane made her uneasy and that in itself troubled her. At Jane's insistence that they needed to think of themselves as 'something, something that makes us an "us,"' they had settled on 'lovers' at least for the moment. They didn't feel like partners to Poppy because their 'encumbrances' – a word she still resented when it was applied to George – were so separate, they each failed the other in sharing their respective – no, she would not think of George as a 'burden'.

The truth of it was, neither of them could fully support the other in dealing with their present – there wasn't a right word – circumstances would have to do – so to Poppy they were not partners. She knew she became resentful too quickly when Jane was preoccupied with the details of separating financially, and emotionally, from Héloise. Even the name, Héloise, was becoming unreasonably irritating. She didn't exactly resent hearing about Jane's difficulties at the museum she just wasn't very interested, and found herself getting impatient with Jane for not being more outspoken to her colleagues about her concerns.

She knew, also, that Jane, while she was clearly fond of George and visited regularly, didn't want to hear very much or very often about Poppy's feelings, how she worried and tried to do her best and kept feeling she fell short. Jane didn't want to hear about that, and Poppy had pretty much stopped talking to her about it. She talked to her friends and family, who emailed and phoned from New Zealand regularly. Even people she didn't know emailed her, or sent cards. The woman Joy had sent a moving email about her own mother's death, Moana from school had sent messages from herself and all the staff. The support lines from the other side of the world were blessedly strong.

She had rung Cleveland Lesbian Line and listened to their answerphone message but hadn't followed up on anything; it seemed as though she already had all the connections there was time for. Sylvia was good company, Susanna she appreciated more as time went on, and the long slow hours with George were no less precious because there were times when she simply had to get away, get outside, walk fast taking large gulps of air.

If she didn't see Jane for a couple of days a longing would grow in her, a physical, almost desperate longing. Hearing Jane's voice on the phone would assuage it a little, seeing her melted it into desire. Poppy was uneasy, with this need, this desperation, that felt apart from her when it clearly was not. Lying awake in her small bed, the glow of the sleep light on the computer pulsing away in the corner, she thought of asking Sylvia for more information about her therapist. Jane, as much as her, avoided talking about what they would do after George had died; whether Poppy would stay on, when – whether – Jane would come to New Zealand again. How could they possibly become partners from opposite sides of the world? Why don't we talk about this? What future can we have if we can't talk about what is going on or not going on? These were Poppy's night thoughts, that often preceded troubled sleep full of dreams she woke from feeling anxious.

In the early hours of one morning, on a hot night, Poppy got out of bed, opened the window as wide as it would go and never mind Susanna's fears of what might fly in, and 'woke' the computer. She wrote it all to Martia, for over an hour, sending it off as soon as she had finished, without re-reading it. It still took her a long time to get to sleep but the night air drifting in was a relief, and Susanna didn't need to know what she did with her bedroom window!

When she next checked her email, after a morning sorting out a schedule for the Macmillan and district nurses so they didn't arrive at the same time and then leave a six hour gap with no-one, there was a reply from her friend.

> *wow! i'm flattered that you think me qualified to help, given my record. and before I forget, greetings from mrs mudgely.*

seriously though, here are a few comments
take or leave them
don't hate me, remember i am your best friend, aren't i?
hardest one first. seems like you are making jane the baddy. takes
two and all that, and you're usually so good at bringing up stuff.
gets me wondering – and i might be right off beam here – if your
idea of you and jane didn't assume a bit much. like that you
would both want the same thing from a relationship. remember
those conversations we've had about women who haven't had a
'lesbian adolescence'. just a hunch.
actually, this is all hard. you and kate. soul mates. no cracks. none
at all? i used to worry a bit about kate's drinking. you never
seemed to notice, so believing it wonderful that you carried all
before you. maybe you were right. forgive me if this is completely
out of line. you never believed there was anything wrong between
your parents until they split, eh?
last thing. remember when bessie was talking about when her
mother died? ages ago, when she was still married. how she
picked up a man in a bar and had sex with him twice a week
because she 'had to'. had to do something that reminded her she
was alive i think she said. might not be irrelevant but i thought
of it reading your message.

Poppy stared at the screen, stunned. A string of memories ran
through her mind like a newsreel. Her parents in the front of the
car, talking to them, the children in the back, not each other. Stefan
accusing her of a rosy, unrealistic view of their parent's marriage.
Kate holding a whisky glass up high, offering her one, she refusing
and cuddling up – to distract her from drinking? Never, not con-
sciously anyway. And that was Martia's point, wasn't it.

'I hate you Martia Roberts!' she said out loud, 'but only because
you just might be right,' and tapped out a short reply, reassuring and
thanking her friend and suggesting a phone call. There was a tap on
the door and Susanna's face peered round it.

'I'm sorry to interrupt,' she said, 'but if we're going to do the shopping this afternoon… George is awake and that tall nurse is here to wash him and do his nails.'

'Oh, sorry. I'll just send this and be with you in two minutes.' An hour-and-a-half had gone by. Something mundane like buying groceries seemed like an excellent idea. While they were out Jane rang and the message she left with George was that she was getting the five o'clock flight to London for something that had come up regarding work and would be back in two days. Poppy was startled, and then relieved, welcoming the opportunity to think some more about her exchange with Martia. It was some time before she realised that she really did not mind that she would not spend the coming night with Jane, a two day wait was okay. She hoped the something that had come up at the museum would progress the difficulties Jane was having; George had picked up allusions and speculations regarding the squabbles over spending the bequest in the *Evening Gazette*.

That evening Susanna went to bed early and Poppy sat with her father. He had a catheter now and had asked her to not enquire about his bowel functioning, 'the nurses have that under control.' Then he told her that he thought he would die soon, holding up a hand that was so thin it was almost transparent.

'I'm hardly eating,' he went on. 'Out of it quite a lot. Not drinking either.' He had been talking in short sentences for a couple of days, pausing between them for breath. 'No,' as she was about to pick up the water, 'it doesn't matter. Listen. I'll be unconscious soon. The lovely doctor Jasmine says…' he paused a moment, 'says I won't know anything after that. Be a few days.' He told her how he loved her, had always loved her and how glad he was to have had time with Stefan. 'To do repairs.'

'Don't talk any more, Dad. I'll stay here a while.' He smiled. 'Long time since you said "Dad".' She nodded. 'You have been the best of fathers, you know.' And they sat together, George propped up on his pillows, coughing occasionally, squeezing the morphine pump now and then. A shuddering snore brought Poppy out of a doze in a fright until he opened his eyes and squeezed her hand. She didn't go to bed, dozing in the arm-chair, waking when he coughed or moved.

'Not too many of those,' insisted Dr Jasmine next morning, 'you've got to get some real sleep. Time for a night nurse, I think. What do you think, George?'

'I don't know,' she said to Poppy's question on the way to her car about how long. 'My best guess is more than a week, less than a month, with less and shorter periods of consciousness. But I really don't know for certain.' She paused by the car. 'I'll come back this afternoon and make a point of talking to Susanna, I'm concerned about her, she's not looking at all well.'

'Thanks,' said Poppy, and they both knew it was for more than an uncertain piece of information.

Back in the house Poppy sat at the kitchen table and looked at the calendar on the wall beside her. For the first time she took notice of the picture – a photograph of bright red poppies, taken from down low against a green field and a blue sky. Smiling, she counted off the weeks. Five and a half since she arrived, a bit more since she found out George was so ill, about five since she and Jane became lovers.

When Jane rang from London she sounded excited.

'Good things happening there? I'm glad. You know the museum's in the paper again?'

'Yes, no, I didn't know and yes, good things, but not… I'll tell you tomorrow.'

'I could meet your flight.'

'That would be lovely, but I do have my car at the airport, how about meeting me at my place, say eight-thirty.'

Poppy hesitated. 'Okay, but I won't stay the night. I don't think I can any more, in case something happens here.'

'Oh. Didn't you say there was a night nurse now?'

'Yes. Yes there is. But I want to be here in case…'

'Oh. I see. Of course. Well, see you tomorrow night.' There was the sound of a kiss down the line and she was gone.

'Bye,' said Poppy to the dial tone.

The routine of the house quickly settled into its new shape; a nurse came at eleven and stayed until seven in the morning, and right away that was the way it was. Poppy had stayed up until the nurse arrived, to see what she required, and for a while after until George shooed her off to bed. She had introduced herself as Kitty and was short, solid and cheerful; George liked her right away. Not that she would come every night she explained, but two or three in a week and there would be others.

Poppy contemplated telling Jane she couldn't go to her place the next night, with a different, unknown, nurse to be on duty but Susanna said she would have a decent nap in the afternoon and stay up with George until the nurse came and was settled in and that was the end of it.

When Poppy pulled up at the Billingham house at eight-thirty Jane's car was in the driveway and there appeared to be lights on in every room. The door was flung open at her knock by a flustered Jane, whose flight had been delayed.

'I was going to have it all ready,' she explained, 'candles, champagne, soft lights…'

'What's the celebr…?'

'In a minute. Come inside, quick.' As soon as the door was closed they kissed, and as Poppy was warming to it, Jane rushed off and pulled curtains, grabbed glasses and what was indeed champagne from the fridge and summoned Poppy to the sofa.

'What…?'

Jane was perched on the edge of the seat. She sat back, stretched her arms over her head and assumed a more serious expression before she insisted on knowing how things were with George. So she can get that out of the way, thought Poppy, then felt mean-spirited and told her in more detail than she had planned.

'Now it's my turn to insist,' she said when she had finished, 'what *is* going on?'

'Have a guess.' Jane was wriggling with excitement. Like a child, thought Poppy and caught a glimpse of a disapproving Mrs Mudgely on the mantelpiece. 'Go away,' she said shaking her head to shift the image.

'Go aw…?' Jane's consternation was obvious.

'No, no. Just Mrs M.' And Poppy laughed, she didn't want to spoil Jane's news, whatever it was.

'Oh. Okay.' And the other woman's ebullience returned with a giggle. 'Go on then, guess.'

'Everyone at the museum has fallen in love with your plan.'

'As if. Nope. Try again.'

'The house is sold.'

'Nice one and no, it's not even properly on the market yet. Again.' Poppy thought gloomily that any moment now she would rain on Jane's parade.

'Okay and if it's not this one I give up! Héloise has suggested a really fair settlement over the house and everything else.'

'Nope. Do you really give up?'

'Yes, really.'

'We-eell.' Jane was savouring the moment. 'You know I've just been in London?'

'Yes, of course.'

'It wasn't about the museum, it was about me.' She paused. 'I've got a job! A job in London. At the Natural History Museum no less. Me!' Her voice was a high-pitched squeal. She jumped up, grabbing Poppy's hands and pulling her up, dancing them both around the room. Poppy finally couldn't help being caught up by her delight and excitement and they polka'd up and down then collapsed back on the sofa in each others' arms, laughing.

They toasted the job and each other and Jane talked about how she'd applied with little hope of success, though the job was to do with the sea birds she loved, and then got the last minute call for an interview. 'Some administrative mess-up they told me, I hope it's not a bad sign.' And at the end of the interview they asked her to come back in an hour, during which she later discovered they'd rung her referees, and then they offered her the job.

'So the chairman of the board at the Cleveland must have come across for me. I wondered; he tried to persuade me not to apply,' Jane concluded.

'Why didn't you tell me when you applied? I think I'm a bit hurt that you didn't.'

'On no! Please don't be. I really thought it wouldn't happen. And when I got the call to go, you know, I had to leave you a message. Don't be hurt!' She stroked the side of Poppy's face then pushed up the edges of her mouth until it turned into a proper smile.

'Okay, maybe I was just a bit miffed. Like my father, I like to know what's going on.' Damn. She didn't want to be thinking of George just then. 'Who else will you tell?'

'Rachel. My lawyer. Héloise at some point. That's it, really.'

So few, thought Poppy, so few people.

'And I'll have to resign at the Cleveland tomorrow.' The thought of that clearly pleased her. 'I hope they'll accept a month's notice, I don't remember what's in my contract.' Jane shook her head. 'Practical things tomorrow. Come to bed with me. Now. Please.'

Poppy held back. 'I've got to ask,' she said, 'what will this mean, you know, for you and me?' She was bewildered, finding it hard to believe that a move that would have so much impact on whatever it was between her and Jane was a done deal before she even knew it was a possibility.

'Adventure! Exhilaration! A lover with a pad in London! Come on, be thrilled for me, there'll be plenty of time to be practical!' Jane was pulling Poppy's hands, pulling her towards the bedroom and Poppy went, letting go of qualms, acquiescing to Jane's seductive excitement.

She was adamant about not staying, though, and while she was driving home, doubt and puzzlement returned; it was beyond her understanding that Jane would apply for a job in London without talking to her, no matter how low the odds for her application being successful. Making love had been without the desperation that had been bothering Poppy and she was not left with the clinging/aversion stomach-aching emotions that put her on edge. But it did appear that one troublesome circumstance had been changed for another. When she pulled up at the gate Poppy felt too tired to deal with anything or anyone, but she heard George's voice as soon as she opened the door. She met the night nurse, kissed George, and trudged upstairs to bed, wishing there was a warm and comforting Mrs Mudgely purring there in anticipation of her company.

Chapter Eleven

George died on July the eighteenth. Susanna and Poppy were with him, one on either side of his bed, sitting with him as they had since morning. For three days there had been nurses around the clock; he no longer drifted into consciousness.

When his hands began to twitch and his breathing stuttered the nurse made a quiet phone call. There were several periods of short, staccato breaths with long pauses between, a long shuddering breath and then a still quietness that Poppy recognised. She met Susanna's questioning eyes and nodded, and her father's wife held a hand to her lips and let out a long, shuddering sob, followed by another and another. Poppy made as though to go to her but sat down again at a small shake of the head from the nurse; she had not let go of George's hand.

When the doctor came in a few minutes later the tableau was unchanged. 'Four-past-seven,' the nurse said to her. Dr Jasmine looked at Poppy, 'Okay?' 'Uh huh,' Poppy nodded towards Susanna and the doctor nodded back and pulled up a chair beside the sobbing woman. I am okay, Poppy thought. Dear George, she smiled at his white face, you died without a fuss, just like you lived. I love you, she said, but not out loud, I'll miss you. And she put his hand gently on the bedcover, kissed his forehead and went to make phone calls.

Of course, George had had his say about funeral arrangements. And Sylvia had offered local knowledge and connections, so there was not a lot to arrange. Poppy rang Stefan first, and said, no, she didn't think he should come over for the funeral unless he wanted to for himself, and heard the relief in his voice. Coming when he had, he told her, had been the best thing, he'd been humbled by George's courage and finally learnt to respect his father. He said he would ring Katrina, and on the day of the funeral, whenever it was, they would get all together, at his place; May-Yun had suggested they all remember him together; his voice broke as he told her this.

Sylvia next. She said she would come right over, as soon as she had 'rung that brother of mine and put a rocket under him.' Once she had talked to him she would contact the undertaker, so the first thing to decide, she warned, would be the date of the funeral. Poppy thought sooner would be better as there was no-one coming from far away, and told Sylvia that her mother was taking George's death very hard.

It was when she was talking to Martia that Poppy cried, tears of real sadness. Her goodbyes with George had been ongoing and gentle, a tugging away of the father she loved, so this final separation had nothing in it of the wrenching and anguish of Kate's death.

It wasn't until she hung up from talking to Martia that she realised she hadn't told Jane. Jane had visited briefly in her lunch hour, sitting with them for a few minutes trying to contain her restlessness. Since she had disentangled her emotions involving George and his death from those towards Jane, Poppy didn't mind Jane's meagre sharing of this part of her life. Neither did she try so hard to attend to the details of Jane's separation from Héloise. As a result they were more relaxed with each other and Poppy could enjoy sharing her small knowledge of London with and joining in her enthusiasm for this new venture.

Jane had assumed that Poppy would spend time in London with her and so far Poppy had gone along with this; they both knew no details could be planned as long as Poppy needed to be with George.

Just as Poppy thought Jane's answer-phone was going to click in there was a breathless, 'Hullo?'

'Hi there, it's me.'

'Hello me. I was just sorting out the spare room with the radio on…'

'Jane. George is dead.'

'Oh. Oh, I'm sorry Poppy. How are you?'

'I'm okay actually, it's Susanna who's devastated.'

'What can I do? I'll come over, shall I?'

'There's no need, really.' And there wasn't. 'Sylvia is coming, the doctor is still here, I think, and I am fine. Sad, tired, and fine. He went so quietly, Jane, just a little ragged breathing and he was gone. Then Susanna broke down. And I'd better go and see how she is. Jane? Are you still there?'

'Yes, I'm still here. I feel bad that you don't want me to come.'

'Well, do then. That would be fine, too. It's just that it's fine if you don't.'

'Oh. Well, if you're sure, I have got to…' her voice trailed off.

'Yes, I'm sure. I'll ring again later.'

'Yes. Yes, please do. And Poppy…'

'Mmm?'

'I really am sorry, about George.'

'Yes, I know. Thanks. I'll talk to you again later.'

Susanna would not leave George. Sylvia came and they settled on Friday for the funeral. The doctor went, leaving behind a sedative for Susanna and emphasising that she really should get some sleep. As the door closed behind her Sylvia looked around the room. 'Is there a footstool or something? A couple of pillows, a blanket.' Poppy caught on. 'Give me a couple of minutes,' she said and went out. Susanna continued to cry, quietly now.

'Here you are.' Poppy had a picnic stool, cushions, pillows and blankets and together she and Sylvia arranged Susanna in her arm-chair alongside George. She agreed to take the sedative and soon nodded off.

'I'd kill for a cuppa,' Sylvia said, so she and Poppy went into the kitchen. Poppy didn't plan to go to bed either, not until the under-taker came for George in the morning. She would have liked him to come back, but went along with what Susanna wanted and Susanna wanted to be with him tonight and then no more. 'He'll be gone by the morning,' she had startled Poppy by announcing as they arranged the stool and cushions for her feet, 'there'll be nowt but a dead body by then, I'll not be wanting to see that.' I don't need to understand, Poppy thought and told herself to just let it be.

Over the tea Sylvia talked about herself and her mother and how, after nearly forty years of fighting and sniping, she could finally relate to her differently. 'Because I see her differently, I suppose. She's not the enemy any more.' Poppy was struggling with a wave of exhaustion but she wanted to hear this, so she nodded vigorously.

'Go on.'

'Well it's pretty odd. The therapist calls it "reframing". I call it growing up I suppose. You and George and the stars. Thank heavens for the stars!' And she laughed at herself.

'You'll have to explain.'

'Looking at stars, reading about them, it's a whole other dimen-sion – put things in perspective, showed up my mean-spiritedness to my mother. With the help of said therapist. And then you took no notice of our squabbling, you acted as though we were an ordin-ary mother and daughter.' She poured more tea for them both. 'Not that I think we'll ever be close like you and George, but it's much nicer being civil to each other. And I will look out for her, you know.'

'What about your brother, Oliver is it?'

'Selfish twit! Said he couldn't come to the funeral, he'd send his

115

wife. Not any more. You'll have noticed how our mother dotes on him.'

'Uh huh. He's only been once since I came.'

'Figures. She sees him when he wants something.'

'What about the other brother?'

Sylvia shrugged. 'Lost in America. Because he wants to be. I gave up.' Poppy did not understand how anyone could 'lose' a family or be lost by one, but was too tired to ask any more. Sylvia kissed her on the cheek as she left, promising to be back first thing in the morning with the undertaker. 'And I'm taking the rest of the week off work,' she added on her way to the door.

Jane sat with Poppy at the funeral. Rachel came. There were thirty-something people in all Sylvia said afterwards, including her brother and his wife. The chairman of the Cleveland Museum spoke, and Poppy for George's family, and the music was as George had ordered it. Susanna had to be supported on either side by her children leaving the chapel and did not move from her chair while people milled around at the house with cups of tea. She had requested only family back at the house, and Oliver had come, briefly. Sylvia offered to stay the weekend with her mother if Poppy wanted to 'do other things', so by nightfall she and Jane were back at Jane's house. As soon as they arrived Poppy knew she wanted to ring home, apologising at Jane's disappointed look, and promising to not be more than an hour.

As she embarked on a detailed description of the funeral, Katrina interrupted her. 'I know I'm not known as the motherly sort, but I'd rather know how you are,' she said. 'Where are you and how are you and what will you do now?' So Poppy explained about Sylvia staying with *her* mother, and a little of the background to that, and about Jane going to London in a week or so and said she didn't know what she would do next. There was a few moments' silence, and then Katrina spoke. 'You do sound okay. And I'm glad you're not being saddled with Susanna…'

'She's all right, you know,' it was Poppy's turn to interrupt, 'and she did really care for George, and he for her.'

'I dare say you're right dear, and I'm glad of it. And I don't actually have any advice for you about what to do next! Will you go to London? What about you and Jane, in the long term?'

'I don't know, Katrina, I just don't know.' Poppy was beginning to feel miserable. 'I think maybe I just want to come home, but there's Jane and I and... well, I really, really don't know!'

'Well, dear, I'm sure you will, know what you want to do that is, in a while. Maybe you're best not to try to decide for a day or two and maybe that wasn't a good question to ask you right now,' and Katrina steered the conversation back to the funeral. 'My greetings to Jane, and you take care of yourself my dear,' she said as she rang off.

May-Yun wanted to know how she was and hear about the funeral. Ivan had made a photo-board with pictures of George and members of the family over the years, and they'd keep that up until Poppy had seen it, she told Poppy, and they'd had Katrina around last night and toasted George.

'How is Stefan doing?' Her brother was at work.

'He's all right,' his wife reported, 'sad, I think, about lost opportunities over the years, but it makes him more understanding with his own boys.' That was the most May-Yun had ever said about her husband to Poppy.

'And Jane? She is well?' So Poppy told her about the London job too, and about her own ambivalence about what to do next.

'Perhaps you would like to see Jane in her new place before you come home.' May-Yun always made suggestions gently. 'And perhaps you would like some time on your own first to allow everything to settle a little before you make decisions.' May-Yun had done it again; got to where Poppy needed to go before Poppy herself did. Poppy thanked her, and sent love to the rest of the family. She sat back in the sofa and closed her eyes; tomorrow she needed to go off on her own, walking somewhere, maybe even stay away overnight, May-Yun had seen it, why hadn't she? She knew the answer as soon as she thought of the question. Because Jane had been waiting with as much patience as she could muster for the funeral to be over so she and Poppy could be – well, could be whatever they were, without a big chunk of Poppy's attention elsewhere. Jane's head appeared around the door.

'Finished? I meant to say to give my love to everyone. Damn. Anyway, I've got some soup…?'

'In a minute.' Poppy patted the sofa beside her and when Jane was sitting took both her hands.

'Tomorrow,' she said seriously, 'I have to go off, somewhere on my own, maybe even overnight and, I dunno, just, you, know, sort out for myself… there's been so much, so many feelings…' she tapered off at Jane's downcast expression. 'I know,' she struggled on, 'that's not what you want…'

'It's not what I want that matters right now.' Jane was looking directly at Poppy. 'Of course, I was hoping we would spend the weekend together – could we maybe go away together – no, that's not what you were saying,' she hastened on before Poppy had even shaken her head. 'Come here,' and she pulled Poppy into a hug. 'I can be very grown-up you know,' she said into her hair, 'and wait my turn.'

It's not about people being lined up waiting their turn, Poppy thought, and felt too tired to say so. They agreed that she would go back to George's in the morning and, if it was all right with Susanna, take his car and go off until Sunday. She refused to worry about finding a place to stay even though it would be a Saturday night in July but did agree to take Jane's mobile and leave it turned on from the late afternoon.

Jane dropped her off at Susanna's in the morning – George's will was quite explicit that the house would be hers – and she walked into the kitchen to find Susanna and Sylvia sitting in grim silence on opposite sides of the table. Her stomach sank. Taking a mug from the bench she sat down and poured herself some almost-hot tea from the pot in the middle. No-one had spoken.

'What's up?' Her voice sounded too loud. She didn't care.

Susanna remained silent, picking up a spoon and stirring her tea. Sylvia shrugged at Poppy.

'My mother wants my brother to be sitting here, not me, and I'm on the verge of giving up.' Her voice was flat. 'It's no good expecting Oliver to do anything that's not in his own interest, Ma, he never has and he's not likely to start now.' She glanced apologetically at Poppy. Susanna's head jerked up, her eyes bright with tears.

'You know I hate you calling me that,' she practically snarled, 'and you've never given Oliver a chance…' So far she had not acknowledged Poppy's presence in any way.

'Yes, I forgot, Mum.' Sylvia's voice was heavy with patience. 'And you have given Oliver enough chances for both of us, and when has he ever done anything just for you?'

Susanna's shoulders slumped. Poppy wanted desperately to be out of there; she had opened her mouth to ask about the car, when Susanna spoke.

'I know. I know.' Her voice was low and shaky this time. 'I can't stop hoping…' Then, 'Please don't go.' Poppy spotted the car keys by the phone, picked them up and waved them at Sylvia. 'Till tomorrow?' she mouthed at Sylvia, who nodded, yes. As she walked past Susanna, Poppy paused and put a hand briefly on her shoulder.

Too impatient to bother with a map, Poppy took the road she knew to Guisborough and drove on to a parking place at the moors. She locked the car carefully, then unlocked it for a nearly full water bottle on the back seat and strode off on the first path, pausing only to decide to stick to the well-formed way, straight on, left forks, so she was sure to find her way back to where she had started from. The day was grey, but did not look like rain; she had only a light jacket tied around her waist.

Walking fast, head back, she took great lungsful of air, concentrating on her surroundings, enjoying the beginning of the purple heather haze that would soon coat the whole landscape. Gradually she felt herself relax, taking in the calm of the enduring, uncaring moors, moors that were here long before she came, were untouched by her presence and had a longevity exceeding hers by millennia; given half a chance, she thought, then abandoned such considerations for the pleasure of being there. At the first fork she picked up a stone and put it in the left pocket of her shorts, her usual reminder to herself of which direction she was taking.

An hour later, the sun still not fully overhead, she stopped and took a long drink of the water, watching some nearby black-faced sheep as they grazed. She was hungry, so swapped the stone to her right pocket and headed back the way she had come, no longer fretting about decisions to be made, knowing she had twenty-four hours of undemanding time ahead of her.

There was an ice-cream van at the car-park so with the largest cone on offer taking the edge off her appetite she headed for the coast. South of Whitby and Robin Hood's Bay she thought, but not as far as Scarborough. She knew as soon as she drove into Ravenscar that she had found the place for the night; a room at a bed and breakfast on the cliff-top sealed it. Lunch was urgent again, so she found a tea-rooms. Fortified, she wandered until she came across a cliff-top path that took her away from the town, at a slower pace than in the morning, thinking about how the coast was and was not like parts of the coast at home in New Zealand.

The afternoon passed dreamily, Poppy largely oblivious to other holiday-makers, only occasionally required to respond to a greeting along the path. Every time her mind focused on Jane, or Susanna, or what next, she drew it away, making herself concentrate on a cloud, a plant or butterfly or passing bird. Crouching beside the path she examined a single branch of heather in detail, marvelling at the cluster of tiny flowers that would, later in the season, multiply across the moor into the famous purple heather haze. Of all the people she knew, she thought, George is – was – the one who would share moments like these with her. She looked quickly around then broke off a small tip of the plant, putting in her pocket. For George, she told herself and kept her hand in the pocket.

She ate a fish-and-chip supper on a bench among screaming sea-gulls, remembering to ring Jane's and tell her answer-phone where she was staying for the night. Then she turned the mobile-phone off and stowed it at the bottom of her day pack. 'I don't want to go to London,' she heard herself say to the cheekiest seagull, the one almost standing on her foot, stretching its neck up towards the paper packet on her lap. She threw a handful of chips as far as she could and the mob scurried after them.

Soon after dark she was in bed, sitting up with her notebook on her knees – the notebook she had not written in for several weeks. After half-an-hour all she had done was a series of doodles swirling down a page. She wrote *home,* then ~~London~~ with a line through it. More doodles. Surely she could come up with more than 'yes' to home and 'no' to London. She wrote *Jane* and looked at the word for a long time, remembering the woman who had arrived in Auckland eight months ago, sent to stay with Poppy by George – the late George. A tear fell on the page, Poppy doodled through it. Dear George, dying as he had lived – she went to add that to her earlier list of clichés, then didn't bother – quietly taking his own path. For the first time it occurred to Poppy that he could have tried to meet Katrina's expectations of him – ambition and matching income – but he had left that to her to do herself. He seemed truly to have had no regrets about his life; he took his portion and was satisfied. 'I love you George,' Poppy said to herself crying freely, easily, 'I love you and I'll miss you.'

Jane had come to New Zealand on a mission for the Cleveland Museum of Natural History and had fallen in love with Poppy, telling her so on what was generally accepted as the eve of the millennium. Poppy's emotions got engaged more slowly, or perhaps she took longer to acknowledge them, inhibited by the on-going presence of Héloise in Jane's life. She wondered whether, had George not got ill, had she come to England in December as planned, Jane perhaps already settled in London, would they have then worked out a way be together on one side of the world or the other, maybe even both?

Silly to wonder, she told herself, it hadn't been like that. Nor had Jane come home in January and said right away to Héloise how she felt about Poppy. It hadn't been like any of her romantic notions, getting on with her life in Auckland, taking no risks, waiting to see… She had come for George, for herself and George and the other had happened around that. Poor Jane, she thought for the first time, struggling to change her life in her own way with me suddenly thrust into the middle of it. And now, already, she didn't think of Jane with the same desire. Had George's death changed that? Or was it the trip to London without telling? Or both, or neither? Perhaps it was Jane, so keen, so excited at the chance to live in London, and she, Poppy, so anxious to go home, yes home, to the life she knew and loved, not a new life, not any new life. She and Jane, they had wanted each other so badly when she arrived. How had that changed so quickly? How was it that the eight year difference in their ages had begun to seem more like twenty?

Chapter Twelve

Poppy intended to tell Jane that she would not be going to London quietly and calmly after they had eaten, but within minutes of arriving at her house on Sunday, she blurted it out. Jane accused her of ruining everything and sent her away saying she never wanted to see her again. A couple of hours later Jane was at the door of the house Poppy still thought of as George's, tearful and regretful. Poppy wouldn't go back to Billingham with her, so they sat at the kitchen table while Susanna rested upstairs.

Poppy did her best to explain why she couldn't – wouldn't – go to London and Jane did her best to listen. 'Not even for a few days?' she asked once, and when Poppy shook her head, nodded.

'It's your adventure,' Poppy said, 'it's just not mine. All I can think about is going home. And if that makes me a boring old fogey...' She put out her hands in a gesture of helplessness. Jane took hold of them both and managed a smile. 'Not a fogey,' she said, 'and not old, either. Settled, maybe, wanting to hunker down in being settled. I can see that, even if I don't like it.' Poppy tightened her grip, grateful to be understood at least.

'I do wonder though what would have happened if...' Jane went on, but Poppy stopped her. 'No speculations,' she said firmly, not admitting to her own. There wasn't a lot more to say. They were sitting silently, still holding hands across the table, when Susanna came in. The three of them had a cup of tea together, Susanna responding to Jane's enquiry as to how she was doing in a tired voice. 'I'll be doing all right. It's times like this your good friends turn out for you.' Poppy nodded vigorously. 'And family, my daughter...' Her voice trailed off but Poppy was pleased to hear Sylvia acknowledged.

The museum, Jane told Poppy as she was leaving, had been almost insultingly eager to accept her resignation. In fact they offered to pay her for a month and let her go in less. 'Whenever it suits me best. I wish it didn't seem like "good riddance".' Poppy didn't have the energy to be reassuring, but Jane soon cheered herself with, 'Big smoke, here I come!'

'That's the spirit, dear,' offered Susanna.

Jane left for London on the morning of Poppy's last full day and they parted friends; Jane wanted to make love one last time and Poppy had said no. Her lawyer, she told Poppy, would take care of the house sale and could probably arrange for a stay on mortgage payments, which would mean less money when it was sold but less outgoings while she was setting up in London, and if Héloise didn't like that, too bad.

Poppy could more fully enjoy Jane's excitement about her new job and life in London once she was clear she would not be there. She advised against Brent Cross as a place to live, based on her experience in 1991. Although neither of them said so, Poppy was fairly certain that they both knew, by the time they made their farewells, that this was Jane's adventure and that it was right that she begin it on her own. They would keep in touch.

There had been a week of sorting in the house with Susanna; a carton of keepsakes, family photos and a few books was dispatched to New Zealand. Susanna moved into the downstairs bedroom, 'While I can and before I really have to,' she remarked. She was uncertain about staying on in the house on her own, discussing it at length with her friend Glory and others, including Sylvia, who was encouraging her to wait a while before she decided. Mother and daughter were rubbing along reasonably well as far as Poppy could tell. There was no sign of Oliver. She and Susanna shared some tearful moments going through papers and letters and promised to keep in touch with each other.

On 29 July Poppy was waiting for the taxi to take her to the station for the train to York and hence London. She would spend a night in a hotel near Heathrow and leave in the morning for Los Angeles and Auckland. Almost exactly two months from the day she had left home. The third semester had already started at school; she'd be putting Stephen the reliever out of work soon.

Early on Tuesday morning, after two twelve-hour flights separated by four hours in the middle of the (local) night, she arrived in Auckland and was met warmly by Martia, driving Poppy's car which she had collected from Katrina's garage. They'd had a bumpy descent with no view at all of the harbours and, outside the airport, it was cold and grey under thundery cloud.

'Welcome home!' said Martia as they ran the last few metres to the car in sudden heavy rain, 'and be glad this isn't hail! It has been up north.'

'I don't care, I'm just glad to be here.' The downpour was more than the windscreen wipers could deal with so they sat in the car, windows steaming up, and waited for it to stop.

'How are you, really?' Martia was looking closely at her friend.

'Apart from being wasted by the travelling, I'm pretty fine,' Poppy replied, 'but what a whirlwind of emotions!' As they talked the rain eased and as soon as the windscreen was de-misted Martia drove off.

Even running up the steps and into the house with one hand holding a coat over her head and the other her suitcase, Poppy could tell that her front garden was tidier than when she left it. Neat edges, and the ivy that fell down the stone wall at the front had been trimmed. Martia was close behind her. Poppy took hold of her friend's arm before she got the door unlocked, pointed out into the rain from the front verandah and said, 'What happened to my garden?'

'Joy.' Martia had the door open. And here was Mrs Mudgely walking calmly down the hall towards her. 'Joy is what happened to your garden. She likes to be busy and has a third floor flat down the other end of the road.' She half-heard what Martia was saying as she dropped everything in a pile in the hallway and scooped up the cat, nuzzling into her fur. 'How's my best cat then?' 'Sorry,' she looked up at Martia, 'what were you saying?' 'Just that Joy was a bit worried that you'd be offended, and was very careful not to move anything, just tidy.'

'Well, I just about was offended for a minute. I suppose it's all right. She didn't have to, I mean, I hardly know her.'

'I hope I wasn't wrong to let her…'

'No, not at all. I'm over it already.' Poppy was looking at Martia closely, still holding Mrs Mudgely, who was finally purring. 'Am I looking at a case of love among the weeds here?'

'No.' Firmly. 'I'll tell you about her later. Tea, toast and strawberry jam and I'll bet you'd love a shower while I make it.' The phone rang twice while Poppy was in the shower, so Martia reported to Katrina and Stefan that Poppy had arrived safely.

Poppy was both exhausted and hyperactive. She wanted to stay up until the end of the day if she could, to get herself re-synchronised with New Zealand time. Martia sat on Poppy's bed, the cat snuggled beside her, and they talked while she unpacked, made piles of washing and put other clothes away. 'Do you think she'll ever forgive me,' – gesturing at the feline – 'for being away so long?'

'I'm sure she will. She's just got a bit used to me.'

'What am I stopping you doing?' Poppy was examining a blue t-shirt for spots.

'Nothing. I'm at your disposal,' Martia said, and added hastily, 'If you want me around, that is.'

'Of course I do. I'd be miserable on my own today. Oh dear,' Poppy sniffed, 'I think I may be a bit leaky.' She dropped the clothes she had just picked up and sat down beside Martia on the bed. They talked and laughed and cried their way through the next couple of hours, Poppy filling in many of the details about George and Susanna and her family and how she had loved being with George in his last weeks and how easily he had died and how her love and respect for him had been strengthened. While she would miss him, she told Martia, there had been no anguish for her in his death; he was so accepting of the end of his life that he had made it possible for her to be almost the same.

It was still raining, so instead of walking as they had planned Martia drove them to the Konditorie in Mt Eden for lunch. 'Let's do a real lunch. On me,' said Poppy leading the way into the restaurant area at the back. Martia was laughing. 'I can either give up or fight to the end,' she said to Poppy's questioning look, 'paying for things. Actually I would like to pay for my own lunch today.'

'Okay.' Poppy grinned. 'Just to show I'm not at all like my mother!'

'By the way,' Martia said when they were settled, 'you've barely mentioned Jane. Is that because it's too sore?'

'No, not really,' Poppy replied, and over onion soup and crusty bread she talked about their leave-taking. 'It's strange, actually,' she said, stirring the coffee that had just replaced the empty soup plates, 'it was so intense for a bit, then "poof!" it was gone. The sexual stuff, that is. Now I'm back to the affection I always had for her.'

'What about Jane?'

'I think she was disappointed, devastated even, when I said I wouldn't go to London with her. Then she got over it, rather quickly, actually, which does leave me wondering what disaster would have befallen us if I had gone. Come on, old friend, what do you make of it?'

Martia met her gaze. 'Just what I wrote to you, really. You've done good, kiddo, with the whole shebang!' They grasped hands across the table, smiling appreciation at each other.

'"I got by with a little help from my friends,"' Poppy sang softly. She called a waitress over and ordered another coffee, 'Stay-wake measures.' Martia indicated no for herself.

'Now tell me about Joy-the-compulsive-gardener,' Poppy ordered. 'Did you ever meet her?'

'Yes, once, in the bookshop I think, she was with Alexa – and I want an update on her and Bessie before we're through – and we arranged that movie together then I didn't show.'

'So you know she's "five foot two, eyes of blue", which is how she describes herself?' Poppy nodded and Martia told her that Joy had moved to Auckland from Napier earlier in the year to a position at the public library as an electronic information specialist. Other details Martia knew were that she had been in a relationship for twenty-two years that ended two years ago, a year after she, Joy, had given up drinking.'

'She has such a different history from us,' Martia continued, 'in a drinking-and-smoking social group in a provincial city, very closeted during the week, weekend fishing trips, barbecues, landscaping their gardens.' Joy and her partner, Chris, had been the stable two in the group, while various of the others changed partners and moved in and out. Joy didn't like how much she was drinking and overnight she had stopped. A year later her relationship ended.

'That's a very short version,' Martia explained. 'I'm sure she wouldn't mind my telling you, she talks about it freely enough herself.'

'And you and her?'

'No spark,' Martia replied, 'but I like her a lot. She's found it hard to "break in" as she puts it, to an Auckland community, and was pretty lonely, so we got together for a couple of times and I've introduced her around and she came here and noticed the garden and practically begged to be able to tidy it.'

'I do love you, Martia, and your amazing capacity for…'

'Don't say "looking after people"!' her friend insisted, 'I'm giving that up and Joy is definitely not someone who needs looking after. She just needed to get started with knowing a few people.'

They split the bill and headed back to the car, Poppy enjoying the familiarity of her surroundings. 'What about Alexa and Bessie then? What happened there?'

'Nothing.'

'Eh?' They were at the car. It had stopped raining.

'Nothing happened. They decided to split. Now they're both miserable.'

'I don't get it.'

'You and everyone else. They've kind of gone to ground. Separately.'

'I got lovely a lovely message from each of them when George died. I haven't answered yet, I couldn't think what to say.'

'Well, good luck. Bessie's in their house still and I've got a phone number for Alexa, she's house-sitting for a friend of Rina's.'

When they got back to her house Poppy rang Moana and arranged to go back to school the following Monday. Then she collapsed into an armchair and Mrs Mudgely appeared and jumped on her lap, purring immediately and arching her back under Poppy's stroking. Martia checked that it really was all right for her to stay on for another four or five weeks until she moved to Northland, getting Poppy's reassurance that she would welcome the company. 'Okay,' Martia said, 'That's wonderful. I'd like to call over at Mum's for an hour, if you think you can keep yourself awake…'

Poppy stood up, holding the cat on her shoulder. 'Yep, we'll do a turn around the garden and I'll just muck around enjoying being home.' She was getting a folding garden chair and its cushions out of the shed when the phone rang; she ignored it and set up the chair outside the drip-line from the big magnolia tree. After a doubtful look at the clouds above her she sat back and let her heavy eyelids drop.

Spots of rain on her face woke her with a start.

'Hiya, sleeping beauty.' Bessie was in another chair a few feet away. As spits turned into a downpour they bundled the chairs back into the shed and raced to the house.

'How long had you been there?' said Poppy from inside their hug.

'Ten minutes maybe. And your front door was open.'

'Oops. I'm not very with it, the trip from London and all. Cuppa?'

'Yes please. I ran into Martia and her mother at the shops or I wouldn't have come round today.' Poppy was putting on the jug, assembling mugs and milk. 'I'm sorry about your Dad.'

'Thanks.' Poppy looked at her. 'And thanks for your messages and card, it made a real difference over there, hearing from home, even if I didn't get to answer everything. Here we go,' and she poured hot water on the tea-bag in each mug. Bessie picked up the milk and they went into the dining room.

'Now,' said Poppy when they were settled. 'What's the story with you and Alexa?'

Bessie shrugged. 'That's just like you, Poppy, straight to the point. Not that there's much of a story.' Her shoulders drooped as she told Poppy how they'd been 'kind of flat' with each other for several months.

'We talked about it, but that didn't help, I think it just made us both more depressed, at least it did me.' Bessie sighed. 'We tried making dates for dinners out and for sex, turning the telly off while we had dinner, all that. There was this great yawning gap opening up between us.'

'Oh Bessie, that must have been hard.'

'It was, kind of, but we were okay up to a point.' Bessie had supposed they would get over it, but when Alexa heard that Rina's friend Lynley was looking for a house-and-dog sitter while she went to Hawaii for three months on a post-doctoral fellowship, she announced she would take it.

'On her own. No contact. No discussion.' Bessie shrugged. Poppy tried to think of something to say. If only she wasn't so tired. So Alexa had gone to Lynley's house five weeks ago and Bessie supposed she should be doing something, showing she cared or something but it was all she could do to go to work each day.

'And another thing – and I haven't told this to anyone else...' There were tears in her eyes so she still must care, Poppy was thinking, 'she said we should both be open to anything that might happen with anyone else.' Then Bessie was openly crying. 'As if I wanted to... But I suppose she does or she wouldn't have suggested it.' She blew her nose. 'God knows why I'm telling you all this, sorry, after what you've been through...'

But Poppy was pleased to have someone else's emotions centre stage.

'What happens if you bump into each other somewhere?' she wanted to know.

'We're to say hello and leave it at that. Actually I've made sure it hasn't happened so far. I bolted once, before she saw me, at the bookshop.'

'It sounds awful.' Poppy moved her chair to beside her friend and put an arm around her shoulder. What was awful Bessie said, with pauses for blowing her nose and wiping her eyes, was that she felt that all their years together were slipping away and she wasn't doing anything to stop it.

'There's two of you in this,' Poppy reminded her.

'I used to think so. Now I think perhaps she just wants out and is doing it gradually. To let me down lightly!' This last with a snort. 'Drag out the agony more like!' Bessie stiffened. 'Oh shit. Forget that. We agreed that whatever else we wouldn't bad-mouth each other to our friends.'

'And when the house-sit finishes?'

'We have a date to meet – at the Domain tea-rooms for heaven's sake – ten days before.'

Poppy sat back, bewildered. She had thought A & B were solid, forever. They had been such a team, so staunch when Kate had died, running the ceremony, dealing with Kate's father, giving her so much practical and emotional support in those dreadful months afterwards. Yes, and that was ten years ago, she reminded herself, how much notice have you taken of what's been actually happening with them recently? Haven't you just assumed that they had gone on as they were then, as you wanted them to be? Again.

'Another thing,' Bessie went on, 'is that both our families are terribly upset. Which is kind of ironic, given some of their reactions when we set up house. But sweet, too. I just don't know what to say to any of them.'

'Um,' Poppy was struggling to find the right words, 'What's it going to be like for you if I see Alexa? Not that I'd repeat anything you've said,' she added hastily.

'All right. She's your friend too.' Apart from the tears, which she had allowed to happen without paying them much attention as far as Poppy could tell, Bessie was passive, lacking in any emotion. Flat was exactly the right word.

'Do you think you're depressed?' The words were out before she had given herself a chance to decide whether it was a good idea to ask.

Bessie shrugged. 'The doctor offered me pills, you know, Prozac or something. But I don't want pills.' Now Poppy was in well over her depth.

'What can I do?' she asked. Bessie shrugged again, and sighed. 'Put up with me a bit,' she said, 'interfere. Distract me. Any damn thing you feel like.' She visibly pulled herself together and stood up. 'Come on. Let's go get comfortable in the other room and you tell me all about everything in your life.'

When Martia came back from her mother's she joined them and eventually they ordered in pizza and she made a salad. When they had eaten Poppy gave up and went to bed. Seven o'clock was as good as she could do. 'It is *so* good to be home,' she said as she went. 'There is nothing in the world as wonderful as old friends.'

Lying in bed, with Mrs Mudgely, who seemed willing to return from the spare room she had been sharing with Martia, she thought about Jane and Héloise, living in Middlesbrough all those years without women – lesbian – friends. Except Rachel. Then she was asleep. Six hours later she was wide awake; one o'clock in the morning. It took her two hours to finish *Flight of the Swan*, a science fantasy story set in the twenty-third century when people lived in small units assigned at their birth and spent every second adult year working in food-growing hoppers, then she dozed on and off until daylight.

Over the rest of the week Poppy worked herself back into her own world. Friends and family came and she visited them telling and re-telling George's illness and death and the loop her relationship with Jane had taken, bringing them back to more or less where they had started, as warm friends. Alexa was elusive. At Martia's suggestion Joy was coming around for dinner on Friday.

Chapter Thirteen

Dear Poppy, Jane had written in her first email from London.

How are you? I wish you were here. The NHM, as I am learning to call it, is fantastic, so is London. Talk about a change of worlds. Apart from an occasional panic I am loving every bit of it, including the – seasonal I am told – hordes of young European tourists.

She would move into a flat – *well, bedsit really* – from the (modest) hotel the museum was paying for during her first few weeks, in a few days. And so it went on, a lot of detail about establishing herself in London, as well as what her lawyer said and what Héloise's lawyer said back. Poppy skimmed to the end and read,

We would be having so much fun if you were here! There is such a lot going on. I found the gay café and may even have made a friend (yes! just a friend!), a Yorkshire woman who works there. Averil comes from Hartlepool.

Please write soon, dear Poppy. I miss you. How about coming over in (your) summer as you had originally planned? Jane

Poppy sighed with relief that she was *not* in London, but exactly where she wanted to be. Going back to school after the weekend, would be a reality check; she'd spoken to Stephen, who said everything was fine in her class and she would be able to walk in and take back over. He was thrilled to have another relieving position at the school, for Amelia was moving south with her husband, to his new job in Wellington. Ah, Amelia, thought Poppy, remembering the carry-on nearly a year ago when Amelia had had an affair with Tony, another staff member.

Poppy wrote a quick reply to Jane, first saying she doubted she would come over again so soon, then changing it to say she definitely would not. She also read and answered a message from Sylvia; Susanna was low but managing, and she, Sylvia, was looking forward to *a star-gazing trip* to Scotland at Bank Holiday weekend.

Dinner on Friday had expanded to include Bessie. The day was cold and miserable so Poppy was making onion soup and Martia roasting a chicken.

Joy and Bessie arrived at the same time, introducing themselves, they assured Poppy, on their way up the stairs. Martia took their coats. 'Whew, it's good to be in the warm,' said Bessie, 'it's freezing out there.' Joy put out a hand to Poppy, who had been hugging Bessie, so she shook it while Joy checked that it had been all right for her to tidy Poppy's garden. 'I miss having an outside so much,' she explained, 'I think I'm going to have to change flats.' She refused the wine Martia was offering around and took a bottle of cranberry juice from her back-pack. 'I'm still trying to find something non-alcoholic that isn't too damn sweet,' she said, passing it to Martia who was offering to open it, 'and this is the best I've found so far.'

During the meal Joy did speak freely about what she called her 'past life' in Napier and her sudden decision to stop drinking. 'I never drank much during the week,' she explained, 'but at weekends Chris and I and our friends would start on Friday night and keep at it until Sunday afternoon.'

Bessie said that she had thought that heavy-drinking lifestyle had been a thing of the fifties and sixties.

'Some of us didn't get into either gay liberation or feminism, you know,' Joy pointed out. 'In fact we thought you made our lives more

135

dangerous with all that coming out, for us there was safety in the closet. Especially around keeping our jobs.'

'I think we – the ones you might have called "political" – rather took the moral high ground, but then without that revolutionary fervour…'

'Oh, absolutely!' interjected Joy, 'I'm describing, not criticising. Without gay liberation and feminism would we all be sitting around this table having this conversation? I don't think so.'

'Some of us were quite timid at the time,' said Poppy, 'like me for instance.'

As the conversation bounced around the table Poppy, adding a comment here and there, thought that this was what she had expected Jane's life to include, this companionship with people who shared a history, or as in Joy's case had a parallel one. She had been shocked, she realised, at the isolation of Jane and Héloise's life together, presumably an isolation they had chosen; there were bound to be lesbians like the four of them here tonight all over England, how had Jane not become part of that?

'Poppeeeey, Hellooooo.' Martia was waving across the table at her.

'Sorry. I was miles away for a minute.'

'In London with the lovely Jane, perhaps?' That was Bessie.

'No, well, kind of, but not really,' Poppy laughed, slightly embarrassed. 'I was just thinking that Jane didn't have many lesbians in her life and what a pity that was.'

'Amen to that. But Joy was asking if any of us knew anything about what's happening at Hero.' Poppy knew only what had been reported in the paper as money troubles and differences among the organisers, putting the annual gay festival and parade in doubt for the following February.

'What float would you most like to be on in a gay parade,' Joy asked, and was made to answer her own question first. 'A fairy float,' she said, to general laughter.

When they all agreed they had had far too much to eat Bessie and

Joy insisted on doing the dishes as the other two had cooked, so Martia and Poppy bustled about putting things away, Poppy making sure that a few chicken scraps made their way to Mrs Mudgely.

When the cleaning up was done and they were sitting around in the living room Joy asked if they would mind all doing a short history of their working lives. 'Call me nosy and refuse if you want,' she said, 'but I would like to hear.' Then she offered to go first and talked about being a library cataloguer – 'what I don't know about the Dewey decimal system isn't worth knowing and I can do Library of Congress as well' – who in the last three years had been applying those abilities to the various kinds of electronic information systems and was now 'a bit of a whiz on finding stuff on the internet.' Bessie at once started to ask her a technical question and Martia and Poppy groaned.

'Okay, I'll save that for later. Me and work.' And Bessie told the others how she had started as a wages clerk and ended up a chartered accountant, and was piloting an intraweb accounting system with two big clients at her firm.

Martia quickly owned up to being an internet-free zone and talked about her voluntary and paid work with Rape Crisis and various other jobs she had done to 'pay the bills'. They all looked at Poppy. 'Primary School teacher for,' she hesitated a moment, 'twenty-eight years. Yikes! And I still love it,' she ended slightly defensively.

Joy looked around at them all. 'Thanks,' she said. 'I've been finding the "getting to know you" thing a bit intimidating, haven't had to do it for a while, so I thought I'd try the direct approach.'

'Good on you,' said Martia, 'for the direct approach. I guess we've all know each other for ever and have lots of shared history. That must be hard to break into.' Joy was nodding, then blew her nose.

'Sorry, I'm not really the teary type, I guess it's been a bit hard and lonely, the last few months. I hadn't realised.' She sat up straight.

'Now don't go feeling sorry for me, or trying to "help" she went on. I'm a big girl and I'm starting to get the hang of the big city.'

Poppy smiled at her, liking her.

'I think Alexa and I have made it harder,' Bessie was saying, 'our friends have been laying low, not doing their usual winter round of shared meals, 'cos they don't know whether to invite one or both or neither and don't want to take sides.' Martia nodded. Poppy guessed she hadn't noticed on account of being away. Now Bessie was tearful.

'Whoa,' said Joy. 'Blame isn't in it. I'm the one who's learning how to meet new folks without a crutch.' She indicated the wine bottle.

Poppy was thinking of Jane again, on her own in London. Mind you, she has found a friend in the café, she reminded herself.

As they were milling about in the hallway, saying goodbyes, Joy and Bessie putting on coats and scarves against the cold night, Poppy surprised herself by saying to Joy, 'Would you like to come around some time over the weekend, and go over what you've done in the garden for me?'

Joy gave a small hop, grinning. 'Sure would. Tomorrow morning, latish suit you?'

'Yeah, that would be good.'

With a farewell gesture and a cheerful, 'Night all, and thanks for a great evening,' Joy bounded down the steps.

'I'm off too, see you guys.' Bessie's step had no bounce.

'I like the way Joy puts herself out to find out about us,' said Martia as she closed the door on the wintry night. 'What do you make of her?'

'I thought it was a bit much at one point, asking us for work histories, as though she was a career counsellor.' Poppy followed Martia into the living room. 'But it is true that we all know each other so well we take a lot for granted.'

Walking around the soggy garden in a cold mist the next morning, Poppy found Joy's enthusiasm stimulated her own interest. Up until now she had done nothing more than maintain her garden, not bothering to find out which plant was what, just pulling out what died, keeping what grew trimmed into some kind of order and dragging out honeysuckle wherever she saw it.

'That's one plant I do know the name of, except I think of it as bloodyhoneysuckle. It would take over given half a chance.'

'You need to eradicate it at the roots...' Joy started, then said, 'oops, you nearly got a lecture there.'

After an hour they agreed that in spring Joy would show Poppy some tricks and suggest some new plantings that would help keep the weeds down. Joy declined a coffee, saying she was off to meet up with a woman from the library and her husband who were looking for extra crew for their yacht for summer weekends. Poppy shuddered. She hadn't liked sailing before Kate's fatal accident on the harbour and she still felt menaced every time someone mentioned it. Joy didn't appear to noticed her reaction.

By the end of the weekend Poppy had thoroughly re-entered her life; she had had a meal with her brother and his family, Katrina had come by and on Sunday she spent several hours at school getting ready for the coming week. The reliever, Stephen, had done good enough plans so she could see what he had covered. There was little evidence of an active art programme in her absence, but that wouldn't be hard to pick up again, especially in the winter term. The school principal, Moana, was concerned about the effect of the new government's proposal to abandon bulk funding of schools; Poppy had never seen her so stressed. It was all a matter of the school board keeping on top of things, Moana explained, and she was not confident that the current chairperson had either the ability or the inclination to examine the small print and make sure the school didn't lose out, so she was doing it herself.

The weather carried on being typical for August, cold and wet with some fog, and extremes of snow and gales further south. Poppy received a letter from Susanna, who said she was 'managing' and several emails from Sylvia who said her mother was 'barely holding on' and Oliver, the beloved son was 'as big a prick as ever'. Messages from Jane decreased in number and got more frenetic in content; London was fabulous, she was out several nights a week, pubbing with the 'girls from work' which she loved. *'I've never done this before,'* she had written, *'just gone out to be out with people. I've developed a taste for vodka slammers.'*

Martia's move to set up the craft store in Maungawhai was set for the first week in September.

'I'm excited and scared at the same time,' she told Poppy. 'I've never sold anything. And Gloria and her friends will be depending on me selling their stuff.'

'It'll sell itself,' Poppy reassured her, 'and you will have everything wonderfully organised.'

'There'll be plenty of passing traffic at least. Note to self; make sure there's good signage. And hey! I am excited!' They both laughed for the pleasure of Martia's new beginning.

Poppy left home for her first day back at school in fog. Welcome back to an Auckland winter she said to herself, and then was touched by the warmth of her colleagues; she was glad of the few hours' preparation she had done the day before, as many of them stopped by her classroom before class to offer their sympathies and welcome her back. Even Amelia, who had in the end found Poppy 'heartless' regarding her affair with Tony and subsequent re-commital to her marriage, had stopped by. Amelia did manage to say how sorry she was about George before she went on in detail about her impending move south for her husband's new, important – of course – job.

The children, too, were pleased to have her back. Two of the boys tried 'Mr Cummings said we had to,' – or, 'let us' – but she soon stopped that. By the end of the day Poppy had some niggles about incomplete records and areas of disarray, though on the whole she was happy to report to Moana that Stephen Cummings had indeed done a good job during his two months in her class, and she saw every reason to have him back as a reliever when Amelia went.

Poppy drove home in a grey, bleak drizzle but was cheered by the thought of Martia being there when she got home, and Mrs Mudgely – 'Sorry Mrs M, I should have thought of you first,' she murmured to the furry frown over the rear-vision mirror. And the cat was just inside the front door when she opened it. She could hear Martia's voice on the phone so popped her head around the dining-room door and waved before she went into her bedroom, carrying the cat at her shoulder, to change out of her work clothes. Martia knocked and came in as she was pulling a faded, favourite woolly jumper over her head.

'Hi, how was your first day back?'

'Fine, though I'm tired now.'

'You will be, you know, for a while. Death, grief, loss, we get tired right through to our bones.'

'I know, I must remember. And that I probably won't like being in groups of people, especially if they don't know my father just died.' All three were sitting on the bed, the cat between the two women. 'Anyway, how was your day.'

'Okay, phone calls, arrangements, my stint at the local shop, and then in the last hour a call from Queer Line. They're looking for volunteers who've done the phone line training to go to Tauranga for a few days and help on their Gay Line. They've only got a couple of people and since that gay man was beaten up last week they're barely coping with the calls.'

'The one just after I got back? He died, didn't he?'

'Yeah. And I said no, but I found a gay man who'll go and a straight woman who's done Lifeline who will if they want her.'

'You're such a brick, you know.'

Martia reddened. 'And you're the president of my fan club,' she said back.

They sat for a few moments, not needing to voice their outrage and unease at the hatred that crimes like this reminded them was still out there. Neither mentioned, either, the violent deaths of two gay men in Fiji barely a day earlier. Then Poppy stood up, putting her hand on her friend's shoulder. 'Cuppa?'

'Please. I'm cooking. Martia's marinara, thanks to some fresh mussels from the village fish shop.'

'Yum.' And by turning their attention to satisfying everyday details of their lives they could bypass the sense of helplessness hanging in the air.

Cleaning up after the meal while Martia made much of sitting, 'with my feet up as they say', with a cup of herb tea, Poppy was happy. 'Tired, but happy,' she said, loudly so her friend in the next room could hear, then joined her with 'a cup of real tea, I can't be doing with those herbals.'

'I can't help saying it again, I'll miss you,' she said as she sat in an armchair. 'It's been so good having you here since I got back. I could really get used to us living together.' She settled into the chair, patting her lap for Mrs Mudgely, 'we could grow old together, best friends, and never mind the gossip.'

'Tempting.' Martia smiled at her. 'But for once in my life I have a plan, and I've a yen to carry it out. Don't feel old enough to settle. Even with my best friend.'

Poppy made a show of distraught tears, then laughed. 'Oh well, I suppose it would be giving up on romance, sex, all that. But I will confess to being a bit bothered about being on my own – well, almost on my own,' she responded to the cat's arched back with long strokes. 'Not that it's been a problem before.'

'And you've not had a parent die before… and there's the phone, I'll get it.' Martia was up before Poppy and Mrs Mudgely had moved.

'Alexa! Hullo! Yes, it's Martia.' Pause. 'Hang on, I'll check with Pops, she's pretty tired.' She held the phone against her shoulder.

'Alexa's driving almost past here on her way home and would like to drop in.' Poppy was nodding, she hadn't spoken to Alexa since her return. 'Tell her I'd love to see her, though I might fall asleep.'

'She'll forgive you if you nod off.' Martia was returning the phone to its cradle. 'She sounded odd actually, upset I think.'

Alexa was upset, though she tried not to show it at first, making an entrance with a partly-drunk bottle of wine and a tub of ice-cream. As soon as Poppy had her in a hug she was crying. She cried some more on Martia's shoulder while Poppy put the ice-cream in the freezer and got glasses.

'To George.' Alexa held up her glass. 'One of the nice men in the world. You must really miss him Poppy.'

'Yes, yes I do. It's knowing he's not there any more really. What about you, though, what's going on?'

'Oh Poppy, Martia, you're both such good friends and this is going to change everything, I know it is.' Alexa was hugging a cushion, rocking back and forward, looking from one to the other. 'I know I'm going to lose friends, wonderful friends I've had forever.'

'Come on then.' It was Poppy who spoke. 'You've got our undivided attention, for heaven's sake, out with it whatever it is.' She didn't mean to be abrupt, she had an idea she knew what she was about to hear and wanted it over with.

'Just say it, A,' Martia's tone was gentler.

'I've fallen in love with a man.' Alexa said it very fast and hid her face in the cushion. After a few moments silence she looked up.

'That doesn't mean we can't be friends.' Martia was definite. 'Though it must make a difference….' She looked at Poppy at the moment when Poppy said, 'No. You can't have. You're a lesbian.'

'But I have! So I suppose I am not – one – any more.' Alexa was looking from one to the other.

'A hasbian!' Poppy put her hand over her mouth. She hadn't meant to say it out loud. Alexa was crying. Martia took a tissue out of her pocket, checked it quickly, and passed it over. Alexa stood, putting the cushion carefully back in the corner of the sofa. 'I'll go.'

'No, please don't.' It was Martia who spoke. 'Sit down. Talk to us some more.'

Poppy sat silently while Alexa explained to Martia how she had taken the opportunity of the house-sit because she was feeling out of sorts in her whole life, including with Bessie and she needed some time to work it through. She had tried talking with Bessie but she couldn't explain, because she didn't know herself what was going on, just that everything felt wrong. Some time on her own, she thought, and she'd sort it out and she and Bessie…

'Then I met Ian.' Alexa looked at Poppy, who almost smiled, so she went on. She met Ian at a barbecue at the home of a colleague about a week after she started the house-sit. He was the brother of a different colleague. They had talked and met for coffee a few times and then she found she was thinking about him all the time and thinking about… she stopped, blushing.

Martia said, 'Does he…?'

Alexa nodded.

'So you're…?'

'Yes.' Alexa looked at the floor. There was a few moments' silence, before Poppy asked, 'Does Bessie know?'

Alexa shook her head. 'I'm seeing her tomorrow after work. I wanted to tell you two in case she wanted someone else to talk to. And to practice, to see if I could make it easier to tell her. I haven't. Do you never want to see me again?' This to Poppy.

'No. I mean, yes, oh, you know, you don't abandon old friends just because they do something you don't understand. And I don't, understand that is. But it can't be the same, can it?' Poppy brushed at tears with the back of her hand. 'It helps to have heard it from you,' she went on, and Martia nodded agreement.

Alexa didn't stay much longer. Martia and Poppy both forgot to offer her the ice-cream back. They sat side-by-side on the sofa when Alexa had gone and looked at each other. For once neither of them could think of anything to say.

Chapter Fourteen

Everyone was talking about Alexa. Poppy ended up defending her.

'Of course she's not a traitor,' she would say, or, 'I'm sure she hasn't done anything lightly,' or even, 'of course her friends matter to her and she knows what she's going to lose.' Including herself, Poppy thought, at least in the old, easy way. She knew they wouldn't see each other as often, Alexa's circle of friends would change over time, she'd socialise with other mixed couples, maybe even change the way she dressed, especially if the relationship with Ian lasted. Or if she really had had a complete change of sexual identity. That was what happened, Poppy knew, and she would be sad to lose Alexa as one of her closest friends, but they would remain friends, old friends, you didn't – couldn't – cancel all those years of closeness.

Naturally, it was hardest on Bessie.

'I screamed at her, right there on Ponsonby Rd, in the Turtle, and threatened to throw her clothes and books out the front door and hoped it was raining when I did. I can't believe myself now,' she told Poppy and Martia.

'What was it like at the time?' Poppy wanted to know.

'Exhilarating. I didn't care, I didn't care who saw or listened, I was so blazingly angry with her. I still am.' Except Bessie didn't sound angry, sitting at Poppy's dining table.

'And then,' she went on to her engrossed audience, 'I went home and cried all night, took the next day off work and had my hair cut short.' She ran her hands through what was almost a crew cut. Neither of her friends had commented on it. 'I haven't had it this short for twenty years.'

'It suits you,' said Martia. 'You look really dykey.'

Bessie screwed up her nose. 'I guess that was the idea.'

'What about your family, do they know?' Poppy asked.

'Yes, and they're really bewildered. They love Alexa.' Bessie faltered. 'Mum phoned Alexa who said she was sorry and then wouldn't talk any more.' Poppy and Martia looked at each other. Poppy knew one of them would be talking to Alexa about Bessie's family. The nephews and nieces would be terribly upset, surely Alexa would stay in touch with them.

'Omigod, your house, your wonderful house!' Poppy said suddenly with a sharp intake of breath. And immediately felt guilty as Bessie gave up trying not to cry.

'I don't know!' she sobbed. 'I can't even begin to think about that yet.'

Poppy made herself ring Alexa twice during the coming week but the conversations were awkward; Alexa wanted to bubble with excitement about Ian and knew Poppy didn't want to hear that. She asked questions about Bessie, how she was, anxious that Bessie should know that she, Alexa, cared a lot for her, of course… And Poppy didn't want to hear that, either, she wanted to talk about Alexa, when she first noticed a change, in herself and with Bessie, what she had thought it meant, whether Ian made the first approach to her, or her to him. Every time she asked a question Alexa got defensive. They were both unhappy in the conversations and neither managed to make this any different.

Martia spent a night at Bessie's, so did Rina and other friends. Eve and Shirley argued for several days over whether they should stop having anything to do with Alexa. Poppy was distressed by this, because she both feared *they* might separate over it and disagreed with the idea of deliberately shutting anyone out of their lives.

Each day Poppy drove home from work more tired than the day before. By Friday she could barely pay attention at the emergency staff meeting Moana had called after school to tell them that the worst of her fears about the proposed funding changes would probably not be realised but there was more work to do and she needed some help. Poppy was relieved when two others put themselves forward. She sent an apologetic smile to Moana, who came up to her afterwards, asking how she was. Poppy nearly answered by saying she was getting used to Alexa and Bessie splitting up, then felt bad that her father's death was being so quickly absorbed, so all she managed was, 'I'm okay, thanks Moana,' before she bolted. Even the harbour looked gloomy as she drove over the bridge, the water grey and torpid.

'Oh shit!' A line of stationery cars was banked up ahead, all the way down the bridge and snaking around the corner at the bottom. Both lanes. Joy was coming over with spring plant catalogues when she finished at the library at five and Poppy wanted to get to the supermarket for juice and nibbles. Leaning her arms on the steering wheel she closed her eyes for a moment, starting when the driver behind her blasted his horn – a lot of effort, she thought to advance a metre or two. Once the line started to creep forward it kept moving, too slowly for the speed to register on Poppy's dashboard, but moving.

Turning the corner into her street, she pulled up at the same time as the car in front. Joy jumped out, waved, and dived into the back seat, emerging with two supermarket bags. One proved to be full of an intimidating collection of nursery catalogues, the other the drinks and nibbles Poppy had not had time to stop for.

'It's a bit late for most of the bulbs, but there's still plenty of choice for spring flowers, and the new…' Joy stopped abruptly when she saw Poppy's face. 'You look exhausted.' She took the key from Poppy's hand and let them into the house. 'No Martia?'

'No, she's already started on a round of final dinners. She'll be gone in a couple of weeks.' Poppy leant down and scratched behind Mrs Mudgely's ears. Joy was already in the kitchen. 'Mind if I…?'

'Go right ahead. As you noticed, I'm completely bushed. Sorry.'

'Don't be. It's all right. The plants can wait. What would you like?'

'A… um,' she thought for a moment, 'cup of tea, actually.' She shivered. 'It's bloody cold in here,' she said and leant over to turn on an electric heater.

'Do you ever use that fireplace?' Joy had made tea in a teapot. Poppy hoped she had rinsed it first.

'Nah. It's okay though, I had it checked once.' Poppy warmed her hands on the teapot. 'I hardly use this, either.'

'Just as well I rinsed it then. Not that the dust gave me a clue! I hope you don't mind…'

She likes things, Poppy thought, things you can so something with like gardens and teapots.

'Yes. No. No, not at all, I just don't bother, you know, using it, teabags and all.'

The toaster popped and Joy went into the kitchen and came back with toast triangles and smoked fish roe. 'My favourite,' she said, 'I hope you don't mi…' Her hands were out, palms up. 'I can't help it, I just do stuff. Stop me if you mind.'

'It's fine,' said Poppy. 'I'm getting used to it.' She smiled. 'I'm just so tired I can't even think straight. This is lovely, I'd never have thought of it.' She smeared another piece of toast with roe and popped it in her mouth. 'The tea's good too,' she added, pouring more in her cup and holding up the teapot in a question. Joy shook her head. 'No thanks. Look, maybe I should push off and leave you to collapse, blob out in front of the telly or whatever.' Poppy was shaking her head. 'If you can bear with me, this' – she gestured at the food and drink – 'is helping, I may even be fit for human company in a moment.'

Deciding what to plant in her garden turned out to be more fun than Poppy had imagined possible. They sat back after an hour with an impressive list of possibles. Joy said she had to be off, she'd promised to help Bessie re-organise her bedroom. 'She wants to move Alexa's things to the spare room and re-arrange everything, says they've decided she'll stay there for now so she's going to make it hers,' she explained. After a pause, Joy went on, 'I'm not so good at talking, you know, chewing over what's happened, wondering why and so on, I'm better at practical things.' She shrugged. 'So I said I'd help. I've got a bunch of cartons in the car.' At the door she turned around. 'That was great,' she said, 'thanks. I'll see myself out.' The waving hand disappeared up the hall, Poppy called out, 'Thank you,' the front door opened and closed and the phone rang several times while Poppy contemplated not answering it.

'This is May-Yun, and Poppy, Chan and I have some exciting news.' Poppy heard, 'Go on, Mum, you tell her,' in the background.

'My son and I,' May-Yun was making an announcement of it, 'have enrolled together in a class to learn Cantonese. Spoken Cantonese. So when he goes to find my family he can talk. And we will practise with each other. Do you think I will be able to keep up with him?'

'That's great news, May-Yun.'

'It was Chan's idea.' She could hear the pride in May-Yun's voice. 'He is not embarrassed to go to school with his mother. Here, talk to him.'

'Hi Chan, what a terrific idea.'

'Yeah, I reckon. We asked Ivan too, but he's got soccer practice on Tuesdays. It's a night class.'

'What about your father?'

'He said he'd learn when we started talking to each other in Chi- ... Cantonese in front of him.'

'It'll be too late then.'

'Yeah. I'll put Mum back.'

'You know, Poppy, I was thinking I must start some new thing now my children are growing and Chan had this idea. I am very excited.'

'Wonderful!' Poppy was trying to summon the energy to tell her about Alexa and Bessie.

'Chan will join the Chinese Association too. I will wait and see what that is like. Annie with her talk of making a movie of my grandparents and Chan with wanting to go to where they came from, they are making me want to be more Chinese. I am lucky to have a good husband who encourages me.'

'And so he should!' He might not have once, Poppy thought, but my conservative brother has at least let his children widen his horizons. I might even have helped.

'Oh, I am sorry, I should have asked first, how are you Poppy dear? How was your first week back at work?'

'Tiring.' Poppy told her sister-in-law about the week, including her friends' break-up. 'I do miss George, but it's more the idea of him not being there, a kind of hole in the world, not something gone from my everyday life.'

'That is very good, Poppy. We all did the right thing, going to see him and you did the right thing staying.'

As soon as Poppy hung up the phone it rang again. This time she didn't answer, waiting a few minutes and checking for a message. It was Katrina, ringing to see how she was. 'In the morning, mother dear,' Poppy said out loud, turning the ring-tone off and heading for bed, Mrs Mudgely in attendance.

The weekend was as uneventful as Poppy needed it to be, with plenty of mooching about the house doing chores in a desultory way, chatting with Martia, phone calls, venturing out into the cold dampness only long enough to shop for groceries.

An email came from Jane, short, perfunctory even, Poppy thought, wondering herself at the speed with which their intense feelings for each other had dissipated. 'Burnt off in a flash,' she said to Mrs Mudgely, trying to think how to say it to Jane. 'It was real, Mrs M, it was more than a flash in a pan. We couldn't bring our lives together was all, we wanted different things.' The cat stopped rubbing her face against Poppy's leg and looked up at her. 'I know, clichés, but they must come from somewhere.' Poppy rolled her computer chair back so Mrs Mudgely could jump onto her lap. 'Now A and B have to *unpick* their lives. We might stick to you and me, eh, nice and simple.'

Sliding her legs carefully under the computer table so as to not disturb Mrs Mudgely, Poppy concentrated on replying to Jane. Never mind analysing what happened, she thought, and wrote briefly about the events of the week, remembering to pass on messages from Katrina and May-Yun. Her sister-in-law had not asked questions when Poppy announced that she and Jane were 'friends and that's all'. Stefan had said, 'it's your life, Sis,' with a smile.

If she resisted attempts to get her out and socialising Poppy found she had just enough energy for her work and keeping up with close friends and family. She didn't mind the short daylight hours, the winter damp, huddling into a warm room and staying put for the evenings was just what she needed. When she heard on the television news that the Labour Government had appointed the first openly gay cabinet minister in New Zealand, on impulse Poppy phoned and ordered the morning paper to be delivered; time to get back into the world out there she thought.

Suddenly it was the first of September and three days away from Martia's departure for what she was calling her 'northern adventure'.

'No farewell party,' she told Poppy. 'I've seen everyone I think I should as well as everyone I want to, and I'd really like a quiet weekend with the two of us. There's packing my car and a final visit to Mum on Sunday, which I am *not* looking forward to, and that's all I want to do.'

Over the weekend it rained and rained and rained. Bessie came round and told them she and Alexa were selling their house.

'It's too hard staying there on my own,' she said.

'But it's only…'

'I know, but I hate it too much. And,' Bessie paused for effect, 'I've been offered a big project in Wellington for nine months, great money, accommodation provided in a downtown furnished apartment.' She paused for effect. 'As well as that,' she added, 'I don't mind a bit that Alexa will have to deal with agents and all the final messy bits.'

'Are you sure? It's so fast…'

'Thanks for your concern, Poppy, and yes, I am sure.' Bessie's leg jiggled while she spoke. 'It feels better, easier,' she said, 'to take this opportunity, take my shattered self right away, lose myself in some challenging work in a strange place.'

'What about friends, people to talk to, your support networks?' Poppy's anxiety showed on her face.

'I know.' Bessie stood up. Sat down again. 'I figure,' she paused then took a big breath and went on, quickly, 'that I could cry and talk and wonder why and examine every little thing over the past few years, and talk to Alexa, try to understand. Or I can go. It's done, no amount of talking and crying is going to change what has happened, and I've got this great chance to prove how good I am at my work. What would you choose?' she ended defiantly.

Friends and family, thought Poppy but didn't say so.

'Go girl!' said Martia, and Poppy added, 'Right on, Bessie!' as enthusiastically as she could manage then couldn't stop herself adding, 'but what about all your things? Your books, your wonderful wall hangings… Oh.' She put her hand over her mouth as she realised she had no idea which one of her friends they belonged to.

'Cut them in half!' said Bessie, making a slashing movement in the air, then laughing at the look on Poppy's face. 'Joke!'

'Sorry.' Poppy was wiping tears. 'It's selfish but I can't help thinking about George dying, and Jane living it up in London and Martia going North and Alexa off with a chap and now you going to Wellington.' She tried to laugh. 'Everything's changing. I wanted to come home to my nice, predictable life here, and here I am and now everyone is changing and abandoning me.' She pulled a face at the almost-whine in her voice.

'Abandoned you are not,' insisted Bessie. 'Imagine a cheap flight to Wellington for a weekend of fun and debauchery with me in the capital.' She grabbed Poppy's hands, pulled her to her feet and swung them both around. Poppy joined in the laughter. 'Anyway, I don't go for another month. Sep-tem-ber-twen-ty-nine, she chanted.' Letting go Poppy's hands, she flopped into an armchair. 'Seriously though, it will be a lot easier not to be wondering whether I'll bump into Alexa and her chap. You know, she wanted me to meet him. Fat chance!'

'I didn't want to be a wet blanket, but really, all that talk about having a good time, makes me feel gloomy,' Poppy confessed to Martia later. 'I'm turning into an anti-social curmudgeon, I just don't want to do that stuff that everyone calls "fun", you know, parties, loud music, late nights.'

'Me neither,' her friend replied. 'The difference is that I don't mind.'

The rain was unrelenting. By Sunday morning there were reports of flooding in Northland and, after an anxious phone call, Martia thought about delaying her departure, then decided she couldn't bear to string it out. The phone rang constantly for her on Sunday afternoon and evening and people dropped in, including Katrina.

'Just about a party!' Martia said, easing herself onto the sofa between Poppy and Mrs Mudgely at the end of a phone call from Rina. She putting her arm around Poppy's shoulders. 'Thank you,' she said. 'And that is absolutely inadequate for so many years of friendship.'

'With many more to come, I trust!' Poppy turned the gesture into a full hug.

'We-ell. There is the matter of where I might stay when I come down – just to see Mum, of course – every month.'

Poppy screwed her face into a thoughtful pose. 'With her, of course!'

'Spare me, please, my old and dear friend, not that, not that!!'

'Okay. You can stay here then.'

Neither of them wanted to make the first move. When Mrs Mudgely jumped down and marched towards Poppy's bedroom, her tail straight up in the air they hugged one more time, then Martia ran off to her room.

Chapter Fifteen

'Well, that gave your credit card a bit of a workout.' Joy was helping Poppy load a huge trolley full of plants into her car. Martia had been gone nearly a week, and Poppy was touched by all the ways her friends were finding for keeping in touch. Her second week back at school had been easier.

'Uh huh.' Poppy was packing the boot in one tight layer of small plastic trays, reading the labels, wanting to be able to tell them apart. 'I haven't enjoyed shopping so much for years. It helps to have an expert along.' Joy, fitting taller specimens into the space in front of the back seat, grinned through the back window.

'I wouldn't make too much of the "expert",' she said. 'These might all curl up and die.'

Poppy grinned back. 'They certainly will, if they're left to my brown fingers. I'm relying on your continued involvement in this project.' She wedged a tray of impatiens into the last space and stood up with a grunt of satisfaction. 'There, all done,' she announced and stepped back into a nodding tree just behind her.

'Sor —.' She jumped away. 'Oh,' when she realised it was not a person. Joy appeared on the other side. 'Allow me to introduce,' she said, 'Ms Variegated Hoheria, ready and waiting to grace your garden.' She proffered a branch and Poppy shook it gently. 'Pleased to meet you, I'm sure,' she said. 'Please excuse me a moment while I figure out how the hell we're going to fit you in the car.' Both women were laughing, oblivious to the glances of other shoppers.

'No worries.' Joy bent down and tied the plastic bag around the base of the trunk, gently folded the top half back and slid the young tree onto the back seat. 'There, won't spill a speck of dirt.' She closed the door gently and made a thumbs up to Poppy.

Driving carefully along Mt Eden Rd, Poppy slowed to let a van out of a parking space almost outside the The Top Café and eased into it. 'A park right here on a Saturday is a definite sign we should stop for lunch. On me.'

'It's different, this Auckland life,' Joy said as they moved to a table being vacated by an older couple.

'What do you mean?' The menu was in a standing plastic holder on the table. Joy looked at it briefly and passed it across to Poppy.

'In Napier, we'd go to the supermarket on Saturday morning and "do lunch" – as they say – at home. Since we stopped playing hockey, anyway.'

A waitress appeared at their table and they both ordered kumara and bacon soup with bread.

'Tell me more about living in Napier – if you want to, that is.' Poppy knew the soup would be good and that it would be at least ten minutes before it arrived.

Joy wrinkled her nose. 'That's a past life now. I'd rather talk about your garden.' Poppy opened her mouth to apologise for asking. 'But then,' Joy went on before she could say anything, 'I have been asking a lot of questions myself. So here goes. Have you been there?'

Poppy nodded. 'Jane and I spent a couple of nights there in January.' It felt like years ago, not the less than eight months it was.

'You'll have noticed, then. A town and some suburbs. Flasher on the hill. Low buildings, since the thirty-one earthquake. Lots of sun, lots of narrow-minded people. Not all, of course. My lot, we lived

157

on or around the wrong – read cheaper – side of Hospital Hill. Mostly we owned, mostly in couples. Led to some interesting – to say the least – breakups.'

'That doesn't sound so different.'

'Then I'm not describing it very well. Okay, a typical week, then.' Poppy shook her head, to say it was all right, Joy didn't have to try harder, but Joy carried on, concentrating. 'Monday to Friday, *very* respectable girls, very responsible, nurses, accountants, probation officers, white-ware salespeople, bus drivers, and of course a librarian. Good citizens. Closet, goes without saying, at least until the last few years and even then we "don't know why people have to keep talking about it".'

Poppy was nodding, uncomfortable that perhaps she had been too curious. 'Now that's different!' Joy went on. 'Look at the way y'all are talking about Alexa and Bessie. We would have let the waters close quickly over that and Bessie would have been out of the loop. Except perhaps for one or two who would see her on her own; she'd certainly drop out of the weekend round pretty fast.'

A waitress arrived with the soup. 'Weekends in a later instalment.' Joy picked up her spoon. 'I'm ravenous.' Conversation over the soup was desultory, Poppy waving at a couple of people who came in, brushing rain off their shoulders. 'Work colleagues,' she explained. 'We're going to get wet unloading.'

'Looks like. It sure rains a lot in this big town. If I miss anything it's the Hawkes Bay sunshine.'

Poppy tried unsuccessfully to pay for them both. 'I get at least as much out of your garden as you do. I suspect more.' Joy insisted, 'I should be paying.'

'We'll pay separately,' said Poppy firmly to the young man at the counter.

The rain was steady when they pulled up at her gate. Joy wouldn't have an umbrella for relaying plants up the steps, but did accept the loan of a hooded jacket. She rolled up the sleeves until her hands appeared without comment and Poppy turned her head away to hide her amusement. It's not funny if someone is short, she told herself and tried to keep up with Joy's cracking pace up and down the steps.

When they had finished unloading they stood in the shelter of the front verandah looking down on the collection of annuals, shrubs and small trees.

'Wonderful,' said Joy.

'Intimidating,' said Poppy.

'Well! That's a sight I never expected to see!' Katrina appeared under a huge golf umbrella. She bustled onto the porch and shook it briskly, struggling for a moment to get it closed. Joy, moving forward to help, noticed Katrina's expression and changed her gesture to a proffered hand. 'Hello,' she said, 'I'm Joy.'

'And a blessing to this garden by the look of things.' Katrina shook the hand firmly. 'Katrina Lancaster, Poppy's mother, please call me Katrina.' She kissed at Poppy's cheek. 'Hello dear, just passing, dropped in to see how you are.'

'Hello, Katrina.' She and her mother didn't hug, so she touched Katrina's arm. 'I'm fine, thank you. Joy's helping me with the garden.'

'Indeed.'

You never ever mention my garden, so don't be disapproving, Poppy said to herself. 'Come on in,' she said out loud, 'I'll put the jug on.'

Joy moved to leave.

'Only if you must,' said Katrina. 'We haven't properly met yet. Tell me what you do.'

'Yes, do stay,' Poppy encouraged. Then, silently, my mother doesn't really vet my friends, she just likes to know people. Poppy left them chatting and went into the kitchen. 'Katrina doesn't usually annoy me this much this quickly,' she muttered to Mrs Mudgely as she got out mugs and put biscuits on a plate, 'there's a definite air about her today, she's come for something more than checking up on me.'

Of course Katrina knew all about the politics within the City Council regarding the library; she was telling a fascinated Joy when Poppy brought in the tea.

'Thanks for that, it explains heaps.' Joy added sugar to her tea.

'You're most welcome, dear,' said Katrina, turning to Poppy.

'I've something to tell you.' There was a slight pause. Surely she wasn't blushing? Poppy wanted to get whatever it was over quickly.

'Yes? I'm all ears.'

'You know I've been, well, on my own since I tossed that dreadful Don – he's left town, by the way, too many people after his tail. Anyway…'

Poppy smiled encouragingly. It was all right, Katrina had found another man to take her to the opera and the orchestra.

'It's very convenient, really, Horace lives right next door.' Katrina turned to Joy, 'You get past moving in with people.' Joy was clearly enjoying the conversation but didn't say anything. Katrina looked back at Poppy.

'Dreadful name,' she said, 'but he's a real gentleman.' Poppy was about to say she was pleased for Katrina but didn't get a chance. 'I didn't encourage him for a while, not once he'd told me he had problems – how do you say it these days – "getting it up" – without the help of those pills. But then, I thought, what does it matter, we need assistance to do all sorts of things as we get older, I don't even try to clean my inside windows myself any more.' She wriggled her shoulders.

Joy was spluttering.

'You may laugh.' Katrina was brisk. 'Oh for heaven's sake!' she said at the look on Poppy's face, 'You don't really think I've given all that up do you?'

Poppy looked at her mother, then at Joy whose face was contorted in an attempt to stop laughing, Poppy suspected, at her. I'm poised, she thought, between laughing and crying. If she cried it would be for a little girl who couldn't bear to have a wrong idea. A hoot of laughter exploded from her and they were all laughing, Katrina as loudly as anyone.

'I'll spare you more detail,' Katrina was almost apologetic, 'but I do want you to know I enjoy having a man again, and not just to partner me to civic functions. Is there more tea?'

Poppy had used the teapot. She noticed Joy noticing and poured some more tea for her mother.

'Are you really all right? You must miss Martia.' Katrina was clearly drawing a line.

'Yes and yes. I miss Martia and I am all right.' Poppy went on to tell her mother about Alexa and Bessie.

'Well, you have surprised me, I would never have picked that. Who's the man?'

No-one else had asked that question. 'Ian someone.' Poppy looked at Joy who shook her head. 'That's all I know.'

'Oh well.' Katrina stood up. 'I'll be off then. Give my best to them both. No, don't get up, I'll see myself out.' She nodded a farewell to Joy and patted Poppy on the shoulder on her way past. 'I'll arrange for you to meet Horace soon.' And she was gone, the front door closing with a click behind her.

'Whew!' Poppy let out a long breath. 'That's my mother!'

'Fan-bloody-tastic!' Poppy was used to her friends admiring Katrina.

'How old is she?'

'Seventy – um – three, seventy-four in November.'

'Impressive. I've got no idea when my mother stopped "doing it" and I surely would never have asked.' Joy shuddered a little. 'She kind of – went to seed. After a very hard life,' she added quickly and jumped up. 'I've got to go, I'm expecting my ex, Chris, she's in town for a grand-niece's christening – it wouldn't do to be out when she arrives.'

'Hey, thanks for…'

'It's been a real pleasure, *all* of it. Don't get up.' And she too was gone.

Poppy looked around for Mrs Mudgely – she didn't actually remember seeing her since they got back with the plants, that was unusual. 'Here, puss,' she called and Mrs Mudgely sauntered in, tail up, walked right past her as though she wasn't there, then turned and made a graceful leap onto her lap. 'Mrs M, you weren't sulking were you?' The cat kneaded, just twice, and subsided elegantly into a ball, with her tail covering her nose. No purr.

'Oh dear, I quite forgot about you.' She moved the cat onto her shoulder and nuzzled its fur. 'I don't do that often, there's a lot going on around your person at the moment…' she murmured on and was finally rewarded by the gentle rumbling that preceded a full-blown purr. Fancy Katrina having a new fellow called Horace, she mused, not to mention sex, her droopy eyelids suddenly shot up. 'Horace Dowling,' she said aloud, 'the new deputy mayor!' Oh well, subsiding again, soothing both herself and Mrs Mudgely by stroking the cat's back, at least she didn't tell me that about him first.

She woke with a start some time later, cold. 'Hot shower,' she announced, placing the cat on the chair. 'Then off to bro's.' Annie was home from Sydney for a few days; she was looking forward to seeing her niece.

What had induced her to buy so many plants she wondered as she left the house. Blue eyes, she reminded herself, blue eyes and winning enthusiasm. She cast a grateful glance at the big phoenix palm in the corner, standing guard over the house and the street without any help from her or anyone. 'Keep up the good work,' she said at it, then told herself talking to her cat was one thing, to a tree quite another. '*I talk to the trees, but they don't listen to me,*' she hummed on her way down the steps and into the car. This is your life Poppy Sinclair and a jolly good life it is.

Stefan was carrying in an armload of split pine for the woodburner when she arrived. 'Good timing,' he said, 'we're just going to look at some pieces of film Annie has been working on in her course. Actually,' he said as she followed him into the house, 'it's video, the animation's done digitally, with software that can enlarge parts of the image on-screen so you can see every pixel…' His next words were lost in the clunking of the wood into the woodbox, but it didn't matter. Her brother, Poppy realised, had got interested in his daughter's career choice through its technical detail.

'Good thinking Annie,' she muttered into the top of her niece's head as she returned a fierce hug.

'Pardon?'

'Never mind. It's *so* good to see you.'

Annie was proud of her work at a Sydney advertising agency, which was supporting her film study. Animation was still her passion, 'not special effects,' she told them, 'animation, where you start from a blank screen.' The short pieces she had to show them represented weeks of work for her course, they were assessment pieces. The first, about three minutes long, showed a mother and a small child – it wasn't clear whether the child was a boy or a girl – tussling over getting the child into outdoor clothing and how the mother helped the child, at the same time allowing the child a sense of accomplishing the task unaided. Poppy was very moved by the triumphant smiles from them both at the end. The mother, she had realised in the first seconds, was May-Yun. The figure did not look exactly like May-Yun but the gestures and movements were hers. There was no dialogue, but quiet, evocative music followed the surprisingly – to Poppy – strong emotional movement of the piece.

Ivan broke the silence. 'Cool,' he said, 'am I the kid?'

'You could be.' Annie was serious. 'It's a kind of every-child.'

'I am flattered to be the "every-mother".' May-Yun didn't often make a joke. Everyone laughed. If Annie was wanting to reassure her mother that she would handle family history matters carefully, she was doing well, Poppy thought, adding her congratulations to the others'.

The second piece was harsher in both style and content, involving drugs and a night-club scene. 'We had to use two different styles,' Annie explained, 'that one's modelled on the Japanese style of animation.' Poppy remembered going with Annie to an animated movie called Princess-something, from Japan, with the scariest creatures, morphed from trees, she had ever seen. And a woman who rescued girls from the city streets and gave them work... she was going to ask Annie the name of the film, but her niece was explaining, with the same seriousness she had showed with Ivan, to her mother about why she had chosen to portray drug users. 'Don't worry, Mum, it's not based on personal experience,' she began. On the button again, thought Poppy.

Even Chan, the middle child was enthusiastic about Annie's work. He wanted to know if she was going to branch into pure fantasy, 'you know, whole invented worlds with different rules.'

'Probably not, I'll leave that to you,' she said, referring to his passion for reading science fiction novels, 'there's plenty in this world for me to work on. I like the challenge.'

'The technical aspects?' asked Stefan.

'Partly, Dad. And partly the challenge of saying something worth-while about the real world in the stylised medium of animation.' She laughed. 'As my theory lecturer says.'

As always, Poppy enjoyed being with her brother's family – my family, she reminded herself. As they were finishing dinner, Annie asked Poppy if she could stay the night at her place the following Tuesday. 'Mum needs her car for Cantonese class, and I've got some people to see in town, it would be easier... And I'd love to!'

May-Yun demurred, and looked at her husband, clearly wanting to offer his car, but Annie insisted, and Poppy welcomed the idea. She was a little startled, Annie had never suggested this before, but she was pleased at the thought of it and dismissed the idea that

Annie might be wanting to talk to her about whether she herself was a lesbian. Now if it were Chan, wondering if he was gay…

'Hul-lo-o.' Ivan was waving his hand in front of her face. 'If Grand-dad were here, he'd say, "earth to Poppy",' he said, and stopped abruptly, looking at his father, who smiled as he said, 'It's okay, son, we still talk about Grand-dad.'

Chan had be at work by ten – he was working Saturday nights at a bakery in Otahuhu – so Poppy offered him a ride. She asked him how he was getting on with his father; she was entitled to ask, she thought, as she had intervened in a way that had turned out to be helpful the previous year.

'Okay. Better, even,' he said. 'We've sort of mellowed a bit towards each other. I guess in my case it's called growing up.'

'I'm glad.'

'When he and Mum got back from England, they were chuffed that Ivan and I had done okay. Not that we told them *everything*.'

'Don't tell me, either then,' said Poppy quickly, 'I hate secrets.'

'Oh. Okay. It's nothing really bad…'

'I don't care, I don't want to know!' They both laughed and went on to talk about his plans to save enough money to go to China, to the southern province his mother's grandparents had emigrated from.

Chapter Sixteen

Mrs Mudgely was snuggled under the bed covers. Poppy could hear rain. The radio by her bed was telling her about snow to low levels in the south island. And gales. Then more on the Sydney Olympics. They haven't even started yet she thought crossly and turned the radio off.

'Maybe we won't get up at all today, Mrs M.' She thought glumly of the array of plants huddled in the cold rain near her front door. 'Whatever induced me to spend nearly two hundred dollars on garden plants I don't know the names of?' she asked the cat. 'Joy,' she answered herself, cheering up at the memory of her cheerful enthusiasm, and wondering how the visit from her ex had gone.

'Damn!' Gingerly she inched a hand out into the cold air to get the phone.

'Martia! Hi! It's good to hear you!' Apart from an answer-phone message on Monday to say she had arrived in spite of the rain, it was the first time she had heard from her friend since she left six days ago. 'How is it all going?'

'Okay. Wet. I hope it isn't too early to ring…'

'… of course not…'

'But I've got an hour before I open the shop – well, stall really.

Nothing is quite as organised as I expected, and the weather's keeping people away in droves.' She sounded despondent. 'But Gloria has found me a job at the local fruit shop on Mondays and Tuesdays. I think it was her job really, and she's embarrassed that things aren't ready for me. So it's a bit awkward.

'Oh Martia, I am sorry. What will you do?'

'Give it a month or six weeks. I feel better for having told some-one. And I'm okay really, my health is fine and I'm enjoying the practical work. What about you?'

In the end Martia had to rush from the phone to open up. Poppy wriggled back under the bed-covers and decided she'd go up for the long weekend at the end of October and see for herself. And Martia would be down at the end of this month, she thought, and they could talk on the phone often. She really wanted this venture to be a success for her friend, though if the alternative were for her to come back to Auckland, back to stay even… 'We could be best friends growing old together,' she suggested to Mrs Mudgely, who was on her way out of the bedroom, letting her know it was more than time for cat breakfast.

Poppy swung her legs out of bed, groping with her toes for slippers and pulling on a dressing-gown as she stood. There was school preparation to do, household chores, and possibly something with those green growing things, though planting looked out of the question. She rang Joy.

'How did it go last night, with your ex?' She hadn't meant to ask that first.

'Uh, okay. She's still here, actually, she stayed over.'

'Oh.' Maybe she wasn't an ex any more. Or they just did it for 'old time's sake'. Or the ex slept on the sofa. Or Joy had a spare room, Poppy didn't know, she'd never been to Joy's flat.

'Are you there?'

'Sorry! Yes. I – uh – missed what you said.'

'Not much of a day for planting, I said.'

'Yeah. What now?'

'Hope for better weather next weekend.'

'Will they be all right for that long?'

'Oh sure. The biggest risk is having them dry out and there's not much chance of that.'

'No,' Poppy laughed, sort of. 'Well, thanks, I'll let you get on.'

'Sure. And, hey, I had such a good time yesterday, I hope you didn't buy too much more than you wanted.'

'No. Really. I enjoyed myself too.'

Poppy didn't even go out for the Sunday paper. She had tea and toast at the kitchen bench and got warm vacuuming through the whole house, something she seldom did. Lunch was a can of soup and more toast, then she settled at the dining-room table with the heater on and her planning for the coming week's teaching.

When Annie arrived she was packing up and thinking about walking to the shop for a paper to get outside for a few minutes while the rain had eased. Annie had ice-creams.

'I know, terribly unseasonable, but there's always the freezer if you don't fancy one.' Annie was talking, fast, while she fumbled with the umbrella, dropping it in the porch open in the end, pushing it out of the way with her foot and stepping inside.

'Hi Poppy,' she said brightly, too brightly. 'I've just come from lunch with an old school friend and popped in on my way home.' She held out an ice-cream, soft in its wrapping. Poppy took it, opened the top carefully and started eating.

'And to tell me what's wrong?' The question was out before she had even thought of it.

'Not wrong exactly. Difficult. Will you help?'

'Of course.' Maybe she *is* a lesbian. Or thinking she might be.

Annie pulled a face. 'The thing is,' she said, 'it involves a secret and I know you hate secrets.'

'You're right there. Do you mean a secret from your parents?' They had both sat down at the dining table.

'Uh huh. I'm afraid so. I've thought and thought and there isn't any other way. If you really can't bear it, I'll go without saying any more.' Poppy couldn't remember ever seeing Annie look so miserable. And felt miserable herself. It wasn't being a lesbian, that wouldn't be a secret. Drugs? There was that film. An unsuitable boyfriend? She put her hand across the table and Annie gripped it, hard. 'Really,' the young woman said, 'I don't want to make problems for you with my parents, but I suddenly got... scared.' She held herself upright. 'But I won't change my mind.'

Nothing could matter more than doing the best she could by Annie, Poppy told herself. 'Tell me,' she said.

Annie took a big breath and said, very quickly, 'I'm pregnant and I'm having an abortion and I can't tell my parents.'

'Ouch. Why didn't I think of that?'

'Why should you. You think I'm sensible. And I am. But not sensible enough, obviously.'

'Just give me a minute to get my head around this.' They sat there silently, hands still touching. Every time Poppy looked up Annie held her gaze.

Finally Poppy said, 'Anything more to tell?'

'Not really. I knew at the time the condom hadn't worked, I sent him away and douched and jumped up and down. Panicked. He hasn't been back, which doesn't matter, but this does.' She gestured at her stomach. 'I can't do it.' For the first time her voice faltered. 'I can't have a child. I thought I could do the abortion on my own, I got scared, I'm sorry, you don't have to...'

'Yes I do. You'll have to get...'

'I've done all that, it's booked for four o'clock Tuesday.'

'Oh, I see.' Poppy knew her voice had gone stiff, just as her body had.

'No, you probably don't actually. I wasn't going to tell anyone when I booked it. And Friday night I had this kind of nightmare with blood everywhere, that's when I got frightened. When you were there on Saturday, it just popped out that I should come here afterwards and then I thought of the story. I didn't plan to get you involved, honestly, it's my mess I can…' Her voice was firm, her eyes pleading. Poppy moved her chair and put an arm around her niece's shoulder. She thought, briefly, of Jane.

'I'm sure you could manage on your own, and you don't have to. I'm glad you told me.' Poppy wasn't sure about that. 'But tell me, why can't you talk to your parents?'

'Because they will want me to have the baby! Mum will offer to look after it. I don't want them to know, ever.' Finally, she was crying.

Oh boy, thought Poppy, a lifetime secret from May-Yun.

'I can't have a baby,' Annie said again, 'I have other things to do with my life, and anyway it isn't even a baby yet, it's just a – thing. I'm only nine weeks.'

'Had you thought – no, I'm not going to try and talk you out of this, but I have to ask, had you thought that not telling them will make a barrier between you.'

'Sort of. But Poppy, in a few days it will be done and I'll go back to Sydney on Thursday and it will be all over. For good. I should have had it done in Sydney but I wanted to come home…'

'Go on.'

'I thought there was a chance I could tell them so I came to see. But when I was there, I knew I couldn't, it would all get so big, it would be a huge deal and Mum would never get over it.' Poppy wasn't sure she agreed, and wasn't sure enough that she disagreed to put up an argument; she had become part of a secret from her sister-in-law, who would certainly never forgive her if she ever discovered it. Odd, she thought, I would have expected to feel a lot worse about this than I do.

They arranged for Poppy to pick Annie up from the abortion clinic on Tuesday at four-thirty and bring her home for the night. Annie was sure she didn't want her to be there earlier. 'I need to do that bit on my own,' she said. 'Mum has insisted that she will be in the area and will pick me up from here on Wednesday morning. She told me I should have a sleep-in, I was looking a bit peaky,' Annie was bashful. 'And she said she's getting used to the idea that I won't always want to stay at home all the time I am in Auckland now, I have my own life.'

'I would like to talk to Martia, just Martia, about it.' Poppy said, as the implications of knowing something about May-Yun's daughter that May-Yun did not sank in. 'I'm sure you can trust her to keep it to herself.' Annie nodded. 'Thanks,' she said. 'Thanks, Aunty.'

Poppy told her niece about taking women to the airport for abortions in Sydney before they were legal in New Zealand, then they talked about other, ordinary, things until Annie left in the car her mother had lent her for the day.

Poppy picked up the phone to ring Martia, then realised she would be still working. She put the handset down but not in its cradle; she did not want to risk answering the phone to May-Yun. Outside, that was the thing, she needed to get out of the house, go for a walk. It would be light for another hour at least. So she put on shoes and a hooded jacket and set off on the road up Maungawhau, the volcanic hill a block behind her house. It wasn't actually raining, but the trees over-hanging the footpath were letting go heavy drips, so she walked along the edge of the road, pausing at the street that led off to the block of flats where Joy lived, then moving resolutely on. It took a couple of minutes before there was a break in the traffic so she could cross Mt Eden Rd. Walking steadily up the narrow road that wound to the top of the hill, sticking to the outside so she could step out of the way of any cars, she looked across the familiar, sprawling city. Way over to the east Annie would be home by now. Maybe she would change her mind and talk to her parents. And maybe – likely – not.

Poppy was surprised that she was not more disturbed at having information about their daughter that Stefan and May-Yun did not.

It didn't even seem like holding a secret. Annie was twenty-three after all, she was entitled to her own life, some privacy from them if she wanted. It would be different if she were seventeen, Poppy told herself, a child still. She walked fast, enjoying the fresh air, the expansive view and ignoring the few other people and their dogs out walking on a winter Sunday afternoon. The path around the crater was muddy and she had to watch her footing. Where were the cows, she wondered, where did they shelter? Suddenly it was raining, heavy rain that had her hair wet before she could get the hood up. People ran for their cars. Poppy cut across the grass to the road and headed downhill.

By the time she reached the shelter of her own front porch she was soaked to the skin. She unlocked the front door, stripped to her underwear and rushed to the shower, leaving the pile of wet clothes at the doorstep. She heated leftovers from the fridge, stirred through a couple of eggs and ate the result watching the Sunday mystery on television. Then it was too late to ring Martia, so she went to bed. In spite of her earlier conversation with herself, Poppy expected to lie awake and worry about keeping a secret from May-Yun but instead her mind was full of Joy and her ex-partner Chris and whether the 'ex' still applied.

One way and another, it was Wednesday evening before she got to phone Martia, who listened without comment while Poppy told her about Sunday's visit from Annie, and picking her up from the abortion clinic on Tuesday afternoon.

'How was she on Tuesday?' was Martia's first question.

'Good. A bit subdued at first, but clearly relieved. She made me a little speech about being grateful that I had met her at the clinic, she would have felt very lonely leaving by herself, and now it was done and behind her and could we please talk about other things, and she was looking forward to an evening with just her and me.'

'And…'

'We had a nice evening, looking at some old photos, me and

Stefan and George and Katrina and she wanted to hear about Stefan as a boy. She clearly admires Katrina and said she doesn't feel she really knew George, which she didn't, so it was a good chance for me to talk about him to an interested audience.'

'And about not telling May-Yun?'

'You know, that's surprisingly okay. It feels like this is something Annie can be private about if she wants, and choose who knows, and I'm kind of pleased she chose me.'

'Wow! Are you sure? Knowing how you are about...'

'Secrets. Yes, I know. For Annie, telling her parents would have made the whole thing much bigger than she wanted it to be and I think I understand that, and I think she's entitled to – I don't know – decide that for herself. And she took a chance that I wouldn't insist on blowing it up...'

'Way to go! Women's right to choose and all that.'

'I certainly wasn't thinking about the...'

'Politics. I know you weren't, you were as always doing your best to do your best. And you get ten out of ten from me.'

'Thanks.' Poppy swallowed. 'That's the first time I've felt emotional about the whole episode. Now tell me how things are going up there in the winterless north.'

'Huh! It may not be cold, but it's certainly wet...'

'... Here too...'

'... And it's going better, I think I just panicked a bit the first few days.' They settled in to a long conversation that Poppy told her friend as they were saying their goodbyes was, 'almost as good as you being here,' and they agreed that capped-price off-peak toll calls were an extremely good idea.

Poppy had told an interested Martia about shopping with Joy for plants and the visit of Chris but did not quite manage to let herself acknowledge how much she wanted to know what had transpired, so that didn't get mentioned.

Too late to ring Joy? Nine-thirty. Yes for some people, no for others. Poppy picked up the handset and heard the pips that told her a message had been left while she talked to Martia. It was from Joy.

'Hi there. I'd love to chat. Any time before ten-thirty. Cheers. Oh. it's Joy.'

'Hi, it's Poppy. I was on the phone to Martia. We talk for ages.'

'Good friends, huh. And hello to you. How's your week going?'

'Fine. Good really. I'm not so tired. And yours?'

'A bit down and a bit up…'

'… Do you want to …?'

'… Shall I tell you about it?'

'Yes.' Forcefully. 'Please do.' Warmly.

'Twenty-four hours in Chris's company and I wonder how I put up with her for all those years. No, not fair. I wonder why I stayed so long in that relationship. Have I changed so much? Don't try to answer that, I will, and I have. Changed that is. Being sober, you see a different world and the not-sober one looks like shit. But I liked it when I was in there. Sorry, I'm babbling…'

'That's okay. I've never been much of a drinker so I can't say I know what you mean.'

'It's more I needed to say it, I guess. How did the evening with your niece go?'

'Uh,' Poppy was disconcerted by the change of subject, 'It was good actually, she –,' remembering just in time that she wasn't to talk about Annie's abortion – 'looked at some old family photos with me. It was good to talk about my father.'

'Aunty stuff, eh? I'm good at that, too.'

'I don't know anything about your family,' said Poppy, 'how many brothers and sisters have you got.' There was a pause.

'I walked into that, didn't I?'

Poppy was miffed, 'You don't have to say if…'

'No, no, it's just – well, there's family stuff,' Poppy heard Joy take a deep breath. 'Four brothers,' she said, 'Andy, Si, Fred and Walter

in descending order. And me smack in the middle. Ni…' Another
pause. 'No, ten nieces and nephews.'

'Whew! I'd never remember their…'

'Birthdays? Yeah, I've been pretty bad at that. But I was always
good for a note or two when I saw them.'

'A note…?'

'Yeah, money.'

'Oh, of course.' Poppy wanted to say tell me about your family, all
of them and what it was like growing up with four brothers and do
you get on with them now…? She had lots of questions and didn't
ask them because Joy seemed reluctant… If the conversation ended
now, she thought, she would feel miserable, but this was the longest
pause yet.

'What are you doing tomorrow?' she asked. 'After work.'

'Nothing special.'

'Come round and I'll cook – something.' She ploughed on. 'A
thank you for, for – your help in my garden.'

'There's still a ways to go, I seem to remember a gathering of
plants by your steps. And yes, I'd love to come to dinner. What
time?'

Chapter Seventeen

Poppy thawed pumpkin soup and planned a stir-fry with vegetables and chicken to follow; she had lit the open fire. Joy insisted on helping to chop vegetables and Poppy could see the two of them, side-by-side at the kitchen bench, reflected in the window against the dark outside.

Over dinner they chatted about their work, and Bessie's plans, and how Martia was doing and Rina's latest bulletin from the bookstore. When they settled back in front of the fire, replete, Poppy said, she hoped lightly, 'I'm on a promise to hear about how your lesbian crowd spent weekends in Napier,' and quickly went on, 'and I'd love to hear more about growing up with four brothers. You choose.'

'I think I've pretty much given you the picture of lesbian life – well, the one I had – in Napier. Growing up was Havelock North – do you know…'

Poppy nodded. 'I know where it is,' she said, 'near Napier. I never went there, though, maybe drove through.'

'My Dad worked for National Tobacco in Napier, which became Rothmans. He – there's a whole history about that, which I'll spare you for now.' Joy looked at Poppy. 'Is this …?' Poppy nodded again. 'Mum stayed home and cooked and cleaned and made our clothes and let us do pretty much as we liked. Me and my four brothers. I come bang smack in the middle. We had a horse, a dog, chooks, a vegetable garden, chores to do and what seemed then like endless sunny days rushing about outside.' She paused. 'Is this just too boring?'

'Not at all.' Poppy was vehement. 'The only thing that could get boring is…'

'Me going on about being boring. Okay. We went on picnics, mostly to the beach. Dad taught us all to swim, he said so we'd be safe, Mum said we were already too confident by half in the water and he really wanted to see if at least one of us would take to it like he had and then he could be our trainer. He swam in competitions when he was young, there was a shelf of championship cups. I suppose he was disappointed, but he never said so.'

'Mmm. Parents,' said Poppy. 'Would you like coffee or anything?'

'I'm fine thanks.'

'Go on, then, tell me more.' Poppy smiled. 'Just think of me as incurably nosy.'

'I guess I can't complain about that.' Joy smiled back. 'Well, the three older ones took to rugby. Walter – the baby – and I played hockey. I'd have preferred rugby, but being a girl … in the sixties… never mind of small stature.' She squared her shoulders and sat tall. 'Though I always thought of myself as big, and ex-treme-ly strong.' Poppy laughed at her puffed out chest and grim expression.

'All up though, the word had to be "idyllic", at least until I was twelve.' Joy let out a big breath and sank back into her chair.

'What happened then?'

'I had my first period and started to grow breasts. I didn't want either. I was very angry and my mother said I might as well get used to it, being a woman was all about getting used to it. I had no idea what "it" was but I knew it involved having breasts and getting periods.'

'I'm sorry.'

'What for?' The question was clearly genuine.

'For it being awful,' Poppy said.

Joy shrugged. 'No worse than a lot and better than some. I dealt with it by playing sport. Hockey in winter and tennis in summer. Fiercely. I was better at hockey and made the A team at Napier Girls when I was fourteen.'

She was a good goalie she told Poppy, but longed to play at centre, she loved to run around the field, and finally got a chance in her last year at high school.

'Then I blew it.' Poppy waited.

'Sixteen, I got pregnant. To a friend of my brother's. Who took off when he found out.' Her voice was unusually flat. Poppy waited again, held Joy's glance for a moment when she looked up from drawing circles on her knee with her finger. Joy finally continued in the same expressionless voice.

'My father hit me for the first and only time and talked about *his* shame. My mother endured, as always. My brothers?' She shrugged. 'They didn't seem to take much notice, except Andy who was twenty and marrying Penny, his pregnant girlfriend. Andy wanted to beat him up, maybe that's why he scarpered. I think Penny's father did hit Andy once.'

'What happened?' That person would be in his? her? thirties now, Poppy was thinking.

'I dropped out of the sixth form and hockey when I started to show, helped Mum around the house, nearly went mad with boredom and not *doing* anything, read lots of rubbishy books. Everyone else decided the baby would go up for adoption. I didn't have any other idea. Mum said she couldn't "start again" with babies. Nobody, including me, ever suggested I might keep it.' Joy's words were getting choppier, faster. She wants to get to the end of this, Poppy was thinking.

'Anyway, Andy and Penny's baby was stillborn and they adopted Diane. It was Penny's idea. I would have agreed to anything, so it was decided to tell Diane she was adopted but not that I was her mother. Until she was eighteen. So I was a not-very-attentive aunty. Still am, though she knows now.'

The phone was ringing. Poppy waved it away, saying, 'answer-phone,' and gesturing to Joy to continue. 'What do you mean?'

'Penny's her mother, Andy her Dad. She wasn't that interested, really, when she found out I was – am– her birth mother. Now she's married herself, with a couple of daughters who also call me aunty. I don't know if they know or not.'

'That is so sad.'

'Is it? They were – are – good parents. Andy's the only one of all of us who's stayed with the same partner all through. I think they're even happy. Childhood sweethearts who made it work.'

'Did you ever, you know, try to get closer to your daughter?' Poppy hoped that wasn't a thoughtless question.

'Not really. She knows I'm lesbian, doesn't really approve, doesn't want to rock the boat, wants an "ordinary" family and I don't have the right to disturb that.'

Poppy wanted to ask more, but couldn't think what.

'You look disapproving.'

'Sorry, no, not disapproving, more disconcerted.' She would love to talk about colluding with Annie in her abortion, but she'd promised, only Martia. 'Do you see her – Diane?'

'Family gatherings – not that there've been any since Mum died. She sends a Christmas card, I send money for the kids to spend like I do all of them 'til they're grown-up.'

'What happened after the ba – Diane had gone to your brother?' This is too many questions, Poppy thought, but I really want to know.

Joy smiled, briefly. 'Get it all over with, eh,' she said. Poppy wanted to demur, it wasn't like that, she wanted to hear it all, she wanted to know how Joy had felt, how she felt now… So she smiled back and nodded.

179

Mrs Mudgely got up from in front of the fireplace and stretched. Poppy and Joy both noticed the dying fire, both stood up; Joy was nearer the woodbox, so Poppy sat down again while the other woman carefully placed some smaller pieces on the embers with two logs balanced across them. 'Hello Mrs Cat,' she said, 'thanks for the reminder,' as Mrs M recurled herself in the prime spot.

'Where was I,' Joy said as she returned to her chair. 'Oh yes, post parturition. Are you sure you want to hear – ?'

'Yes,' Poppy was definite, 'I do.' She had watched Joy, concentrated for those few moments on the fire, placing the fuel deliberately, standing almost into a stretch. Strong, tidy movements, she thought, attractive. Am I –? Joy was talking.

'I got a job in the library. With hindsight I think that's surprising and I wonder if one of my parents... Anyway, to work, back to hockey and there I found sex with girls.' She grinned at Poppy and did a thumbs up. 'And after-match drinking. Then eventually Chris, and a house in the 'burbs and the hockey stopped and the drinking didn't.' She was looking off into the distance. 'I played for the club and Hawkes Bay for two years, and once was up for national selection but didn't make the team.'

Poppy opened her mouth to speak. She thought she might say, 'Can I kiss you?'

But Joy held up a hand. 'Enough already, no more questions. I don't usually talk about myself so much,' she said and quickly followed it with, 'you know one of our women's hockey players in Sydney is the daughter of a woman I played with in the Hawkes Bay team.' Poppy had been ignoring the Olympics as much as she could, apart from seizing the opportunity for some geography with her class. She barely registered Joy's words. Entranced by the other woman's enthusiasm, which became more and more apparent, she found herself thinking she could at least take a look at the opening ceremony.

They cleared up the remnants of dinner together, Poppy drying and putting the dishes away. No, she wasn't bothered about not having a dishwasher, she said, she rather liked doing dishes. 'But I'd like to kiss you more,' she added, and felt herself blushing. Joy turned, flicking soap suds off her hands and a glob landed on Poppy's nose and slid down her face making her splutter. Neither of them laughed. Poppy didn't remember ever feeling so embarrassed.

'No.' Joy said eventually, then, 'Oh shit.' Poppy took a step back to stop herself taking a step forward; she could barely believe she'd been told 'No'.

'Oh shit,' Joy said again. She leaned forward to take the tea towel from Poppy, dried her hands on it, and kept drying them, looking down while she said, 'Please don't get me wrong, it's just that I have to – I promised myself a year, a year on my own in the big city, a year without any – you know – and it's only six months!' she ended.

They looked at each other. 'I didn't say I wanted to get married, just that I wanted to kiss you,' Poppy managed. 'No big deal,' she added, and wished she hadn't. 'Well, a medium-sized deal. But look, not a single bruise.' She held her arms out from her body and twirled around. 'Okay,' she said when she was facing Joy again, 'rewind and let's finish the dishes.'

'All right…'

'Don't you *dare* apologise,' taking back the tea-towel, 'and please don't abandon me and the plants.'

'Saturday morning, barring only a storm. I'll bring my gumboots and a spade, you haven't got one.' Of course, she knew what tools Poppy had from her earlier efforts in the garden. Her voice was more or less normal.

As soon as they finished Joy said she'd go. 'Thanks for a great meal and evening,' she said at the door, with a bit of a smile.

'Me too,' said Poppy. 'And I'm not sorry…'

'Me either,' and Joy touched her briefly on the arm and was off down the steps.

'And I'm *not* at all sorry.' This to Mrs Mudgely as she held the door open waiting for the cat to move her tail from the gap.

'Though there was a bad moment there. Come on, let's you and me have the rest of the fire.'

'I don't want to shock you Mrs M, so soon after Jane, but I definitely fancy that woman.' The cat kept both eyes closed. 'I don't think you like her as much as you did Jane, she doesn't suck up to you, you old sucker-cat.' Still no response. 'Well I may have to give up any ideas about her if you don't approve.' Nothing. 'I'll take that as a "do as you like" then,' and she flicked on the television news to a panel speculating on New Zealand's medal prospects, and flicked it off again.

At school the next day everyone, staff and pupils alike, seemed to be buzzing about the Olympic opening ceremony that night. It would be late of course, with the time difference between Australia and New Zealand. Some children in her class, Poppy discovered, would be 'camping out' with sleeping bags in their living rooms in front of the television. She declined an invitation to join a group of colleagues at a sports bar with a big TV screen; it was harder to not ring Joy at the library at lunch time to – well, check out gardening arrangements for the morning. Asking if she wanted to watch the games opening together was definitely not on, she thought, not after such a definite 'no'. Intimate twosomes were out in the meantime, unless they were initiated by Joy.

Poppy did not understand why she didn't feel miserable. It was true that she understood Joy's reason, wanting to keep faith with something she had undertaken to do, but still, she had been firmly rejected; she had expected that in itself to give her a stomach ache and it didn't. She didn't want to try and analyse her feelings and after all, lack of anxiety was hardly something to worry about. What she was noticing, she decided, was that she was 'falling in love' whatever that meant – falling was accurate, but she was falling gently, pleasurably, and believed that whatever the outcome, and so far she had only a clear refusal, she would have a soft landing, or at least one that would leave her on her feet and intact in her life. What about the anguish that went with 'in love', at least in the early, uncertain stages? Did it's lack mean that 'in love' didn't apply. Obsession was missing, too; she certainly thought of Joy a lot, remembering her small, compact body, her energy, expansive gestures and whole-heartedness about whatever she was doing. Joy's image would appear in Poppy's mind and she would be smiling and Poppy would smile back.

'I'm glad someone's enjoying this.' Poppy started and became conscious of the staff meeting she was in. Yet another emergency staff meeting on a Friday afternoon. Everyone had been speculating about it all day. 'That was a beatific smile,' Tracy, year-two teacher, whispered, 'it can't have been pleasure at being here.' Poppy willed herself to not blush, unsuccessfully, she thought from Tracy's knowing smile. The deputy principal, Ian Brownley, had called the meeting; Moana was on sick leave for the second week, and Ian was dotting 'i's and crossing 't's in areas where he had previously made it clear he thought Moana gave too little attention. She's a big-picture, education-focused leader, he's a get-the-details-right-and-the-rest-will-follow manager, she was thinking when raised voices got her attention. I have the concentration of a flea this afternoon, she chided herself. Apparently Ian had proposed a roster of teachers to patrol the grounds for fifteen minutes after school ended each day. He was being asked, forcefully, for justification of this new measure.

'Two schools in this area have problems with after-school bully-ing, and on the basis that prevention is...'

'And both those schools are run by bullies.' That was Hugh, year-six teacher, who hardly ever spoke at all in the staff-room. 'Bullying doesn't even get started here,' he went on, 'we've already got much better prevention than policing the playground would ever give us.'

'Go Hugh!' said someone.

'Sorry, kids to pick up,' said someone else, and left.

Ian put the proposal to the vote and lost and was clearly miffed. He left the staff-room quickly.

'Anyone know how Moana is doing?' someone asked as they were leaving, and Poppy felt bad that she hadn't.

'Better,' said someone else, 'her 'flu ended up being bronchitis. She's been ordered to stay off until Monday.'

Poppy resolved to ring her when she got home.

Later, checking her email, she sat and stared at the only two new messages in her inbox. blaikiej was Jane's email name now. And immediately below it one from joy.sanderson. For a moment she couldn't decide which one to open first, then settled on order of arrival.

Jane was out most evenings, loving not having a house and garden needing attention, the job was okay, she was much lower down the food chain than she had been at the Cleveland. It was more expensive even than she had imagined living in London, '*but hey, I'm 40 this year and thankful every day that I won't be 40 in Billingham with a baby in the house! Which reminds me, Héloïse is pregnant, just, so there won't actually be a baby by November, but I'm sure you get the idea.* There was a lot of detail about the women Jane went out with, mostly in a group it seemed, though a couple of references to (different) women staying overnight were ambiguous. Jane seemed so much younger than she had in New Zealand nine months ago. 'Oh my, what a year this is!' Poppy remarked to the cat at her feet and opened the next message.

> *Dear Poppy*, she read,
> *I want to explain. Not on email. Is nine too early for planting to begin on Saturday? I know it's winter but how about one of my famous (you didn't know?) picnic lunches afterwards. Mystery destination. Weather forecast precludes rain.*
> *Cheers, Joy.*

Poppy hit 'reply' and wrote:

> *No, not too early.*
> *Yes to picnic.*
> *Cheers,*
> *Poppy*

She was tempted to add something about watching the Olympic opening ceremony together but thought no, waited for the computer to shut down and was happy. Happy *and* restless. After a couple of turns up and down the hallway she picked up the phone and dialled. May-Yun answered and Poppy asked if Annie had gotten away okay and then if they were watching…

'Yes, indeed we are. I've promised Ivan he can stay up until the end. Chan is working.'

'Can I come and watch it with you?'

'Indeed you can, Poppy. I would have asked you if I had thought you would…'

'Be interested. Well, you're no more surprised than I am. I seem to have been caught up in it by everyone else.' Well, maybe not everyone, she thought. 'After all,' she said to the cat, 'we do have a women's hockey team competing.'

It wasn't raining but it was very cold. 'If this wasn't Auckland I'd expect a frost,' she remarked to Mrs Mudgely who passed her on the steps as she was leaving. The only answer was the clunk of the cat door.

'My Annie is very grown-up these days.' May-Yun and Poppy talked in the ad breaks. 'She is very self-contained, don't you think?' Poppy could detect no trace of irony in her sister-in-law's tone.

'Yes,' she agreed, 'she certainly is in charge of her life.' Then she moved on with, 'we had a lovely time together looking at some old family photographs, she wanted to know about you when young, Stefan,' and the moment when Poppy might have floundered was past.

Chapter Eighteen

There was a knock on Poppy's front door at exactly nine o'clock. Four bags of Zoodoo, a bag of slow-release fertiliser, a shovel, a spade and a pair of gumboots had joined the array of plants. Joy's gleeful smile sent Poppy's stomach plummeting straight to her knees.

'Hi,' she said. 'Spending more of my money, I see.' That wasn't what she meant to say! 'Nice to see you,' would have been a better start. Joy was unruffled.

'Not at all,' she said, 'a contribution from me. And the shovel, spade and gumboots are mine.'

'Oh. Yes. I didn't me…'

'I know you didn't. Shall we get started?'

'Sure. What goes where?'

'I thought you'd want to talk about that first. Over a coffee?'

'Oh, all right, your car or…'

'Actually, I meant here…'

'Of course. Yes. I'll go…' Poppy gestured back into the house.

'Okay.' Joy was so cheerful and Poppy felt so stupid. 'I'll organise these,' waving at the plants 'into groups and we can have our coffee here –' indicating the steps – 'and decide where to put them.'

'Sure. Very sensible.' Put a good face on it, Poppy told herself. 'I'll bring out the coffee.'

'Milk, no sugar for me.' Plants were being re-arranged as Joy spoke.

Poppy got out a tray, found a cloth for it and put milk in a jug while the kettle boiled. 'I can so be orderly and sensible,' she announced to Mrs Mudgely, 'and don't you ever think otherwise.' She found some ground coffee and went on talking to the cat. 'This is not the morning for instant coffee. Now where is that damned plunger? Is it too early for biscuits do you think?'

'Not a bit.' Poppy jumped. Joy was at the kitchen door. 'We could just take mugs… no, this looks splendid. May I?' And she picked up the tray and left Poppy to fill and bring the coffee maker. In spite of herself, Poppy was smiling as she carried it down the hallway.

Her beloved phoenix palm would get a ground-level collar of red and white impatiens, sure to bloom in its shade, she was told.

'I like having flowers to look at from my kitchen window.' That was the only preference she could think of, otherwise she went along with Joy's suggestion. By summer, she was assured, her kitchen window would frame two blooming fuschias and and an abundance of multi-coloured petunias.

Then there were the lessons in planting, first annuals, then the shrubs. Joy worked quickly, muttering occasionally about the water-logged soil, commending Poppy for buying a place high enough to 'at least have some natural drainage'.

As the sun, albeit still a wintry one, rose in the sky, and the digging got more vigorous for the larger bushes, Poppy peeled off layers until she was down to a t-shirt, jeans and gumboots. The morning went surprisingly fast and the sense of accomplishment as they gathered up their tools and the empty pots and bags was gratifying. Spread around the garden, what had seemed like a huge number of plants had melded into insignificance.

'Maybe I could get to enjoy this.' Poppy was pulling off her gumboots.

'I love it. Gives you something to show for your efforts.' Joy looked at her watch. 'I'll be off home for a shower,' she said, 'and back to collect you for the promised picnic in – an hour?'

'Great,' said Poppy, a grey jumper half over her head, 'where are we going?'

'Wait and see. Not far, I'll tell you that much.'

'Thanks. Thanks a lot – you know, for the gardening.' Poppy called after the woman disappearing down the steps.

If she says an hour, she means an hour, said Poppy to herself when she heard 'hel-lo-o', from the open front door. She had showered and changed into jeans with a red sweatshirt.

'Come in,' she called.

'Snap,' she said, laughing, as soon as she saw Joy in jeans and a red sweatshirt.

'Golly-gosh.' Joy was laughing too.

'I could cha…'

'Nah. Unless you want to.' They shrugged in unison and Joy said, 'Let's go then.'

In the ten minutes or so it took Joy to drive to the domain they didn't talk. She parked on a road leading up to the museum. 'That's where Jane worked,' Poppy said.

'Uh-huh.' Joy was out of the car and opening the boot. 'Here, take these would you.' She handed Poppy two stools and a table, all folded into one neat carrying package.

'That solves the wet grass problem,' said Poppy.

'I guess, but we're not sitting on grass.' And Joy led the way, carrying a picnic basket and a small backpack to the band rotunda. 'Not…'

'Yep. I've wanted to have a picnic here since I first saw it.' Joy had the table and stools set up in a flash and with the flourish of a small tablecloth began setting out the meal. Asparagus quiche. 'Still

188

warm,' she said proudly, 'but I did buy it frozen.' Soup in a thermos. 'Chicken barley.' A loaf of kibbled wheat bread appeared, plates, cutlery, and, from the bottom of the chilly bin, two cans of beer.

'I thought you didn't…?' Poppy began.

'I don't, at least not like I used to. I'm trying one or two drinks a weekend, one or two through the week. I've been a habit drinker more than a real alcoholic…' Joy looked at Poppy uncertainly. 'I never know with you politicos whether it's okay to… what's so funny?'

'Me being described as a politico, that's funny.'

'In that case I'm *really* confused.'

'That makes two of us, no-one's ever called me "political". Quite the reverse.'

'Well, you and your friends, you're all, I dunno, so sure about what's right and what's not…'

'Honestly,' Poppy responded, 'I've always been a bit of a wimp about big ideas.' She was standing back, watching Joy arranging the food. 'No "passionate commitment" I've been told, only bothered about the small picture in front of me, not the big picture.' Joy gestured to her to sit in one of the chairs. Poppy was pleased to let that line of conversation drop. She watched a few cars driving by less than thirty metres away and felt self-conscious when someone hooted and Joy waved. No-one else had come near their picnic spot, not yet anyway. People generally were staying in their cars.

'When I was drinking – serious drinking –,' Joy said, as she cut the quiche, 'it was Saturday afternoon 'til Sunday evening, wine, beer, spirits, anything. Not getting really drunk, just holding a level of – well, now I'd say numbness, then I would have said something about having a good time. We all did.'

'We?'

'The crowd. Ex-hockey players and others who came in over the years. Couples. We helped each other a lot, it wasn't all bad. In fact, it was very good in some ways, good mates, some relationships went on for twenty years and more. We'd meet in each others' houses help each other with painting, gardens, have some beers, a barbecue, a party. Sometime a group of us would go to Australia – Sydney or Brisbane – for a week or ten days. Chris and I became a kind of core couple.' Joy stopped. 'This we should eat before it gets stone cold,' she said, sliding a knife under a generous slice of quiche. Poppy held out a plate. They had the soup with it, and thick slices of bread, watching the cars go by, both waving now, especially at children who waved first.

'Mmm.' Poppy sat back, wiping her mouth with a blue paper napkin. 'Divine,' she said.

'Not quite finished.' Looking pleased with herself, Joy leaned over and with a flourish produced a second thermos. 'Coffee,' she said, groping around in her pack until she found two mugs and a small bottle of milk wrapped in a tea-towel. 'Do you want this?' She pointed at the unopened cans of beer.

'I'd rather have the coffee,' said Poppy. The beer went back in the picnic basket.

'Right-ho.' Joy sat back. 'Rest of story. Short version. Imagine a couple of years that include a bad car crash involving two of the group, a death from cancer, two women who were both partners with someone else in the group running off together.' Poppy poured the last of the coffee into each of their cups. There was little heat in the sun, she was glad of her jacket.

'There was a Saturday at our place, our mates giving us a hand to replace a rotten fence. Two years ago last February. We got in the beer as usual, and we always had plenty of other drinks, wine and spirits and stuff. It rained, so we all ended up inside playing cards. There was an argument. One of the couples. They really lost it, screaming at each other and they got up and started to scuffle and when some of us tried to intervene, Val gave Andy a shove and she fell through through the glass door. Cut her shoulder and leg. Blood everywhere. Chris called an ambulance and the police came, but they believed our story that it was an accident.' Poppy was hugging herself to keep warm.

'How about we walk?' she suggested.

'Sure. This isn't more than you wanted to know…'

'No. Not at all. I want to hear it. Really.'

They packed up together and stowed everything in the boot of Joy's car before setting off on a circuit around the domain. Joy might be short but she walks at a fair pace, Poppy thought. 'What happened afterwards?' she asked.

'It's the aftermath that really upset me. Everyone dropped Val and Andy after that, including me, some said they'd "spoiled everything." There was talk about people's jobs and how awful it would be if it got in the papers. What was to get in the papers, for heavens sake?' They were passing the tropical house, and looked at each other, shaking their heads at the same time and kept on walking.

'It affected me, you know, we were supposed to all be mates and no-one cared about Val and Andy, just that something had been spoiled, and we might be outed or something. No-one would talk about it, not even Chris. So I said I was giving up drinking and everyone laughed, but I did it.' She took a few strides in silence, then slowed and turned to look at Poppy. 'You know, being around people who are drinking a lot when you aren't is… odd.' Without waiting for a response she increased her speed again. Poppy matched it. 'You notice things you hadn't noticed before, liking people being snarky with each other, and how banal a lot of the conversation is. Chris and I started arguing, and I felt stuck and when the Auckland job came up I tried really hard to get it and I did!' She strode on.

'Thank you for telling me.' Poppy wanted to remind her that she had promised to explain her 'no' in the kitchen two nights ago. 'Now I see what you mean about a different life, I think.'

'Living in Napier is a bit like living in that movie, "The Truman Show", everything has to be sweetness and light. Pretty lives in a

191

pretty town.' The bitterness in Joy's voice was new. 'I really don't know why I stayed so long.'

'Because it was what you knew, maybe.'

'Yeah, whatever. Now it's your turn, tell me something about your past.'

Poppy had expected that they would mull over Joy's experience for a bit; she expected to seek out detail, discover more about Joy feeling stuck and what it was like leaving a relationship after more than twenty years, find out about moving to a strange city at forty-something – or was she fifty?

Joy had stopped walking and was facing her. 'Fair's fair,' she said, 'your turn.'

'Uh, sure, I was just wondering about…'

'Don't wonder. Talk.' Joy stopped and put a hand on her arm. 'I'm not very used to talking about myself,' she said, 'it's a lot easier if you do it too.'

Poppy's hand covered the other woman's. She lifted it a fraction of a second before Joy pulled hers out. 'Jane or Kate, then?'

'The most recent. That would be Jane?'

For the rest of the walk Poppy told of Jane and their trip around the country and her having to go to England because of George and Jane and Héloise not being sorted out and how they had some good times and times when they were kind of desperate together and suddenly Jane was going to London and Poppy knew she wanted to come home. 'It all happened so fast, and changed so fast, the way I felt changed so fast. I can usually keep track of my feelings and they kind of ran away from me. It all got mixed up with George dying.' And suddenly they were back at the car. Joy had said little while Poppy was talking. She didn't say anything now, except, 'Roller-coaster feelings go with people dying I reckon,' and unlocked the car.

'You haven't exp…' Poppy began as she was doing up her seat-belt.

'Explained that "no"? I know. There's not much to explain, I just need to do what I promised myself and not, you know, get involved yet.'

'I see.' She didn't but couldn't think of anything else to say, and gave up and said nothing for the drive home. When Joy pulled up outside her house she touched her arm briefly and said, 'Thanks for the picnic, it was wonderful. And the garden. Come back soon and – um – see how it's going.'

'I will.' And there wasn't anything left for Poppy to do but get out of the car and go up the steps into her house. She heard the car turn and head back down the street to the block of flats where Joy lived.

'We both know no means no,' Poppy said to Mrs Mudgely as she shoved the damp washing she had brought in off the line into the dryer, 'so we're stuck with fancying Ms Sanderson like mad and not doing anything about it – aren't we?' The cat turned her back. 'I see. Either there's no "we" or you don't give a damn that my heart might be breaking.' Which Poppy knew it was not in danger of, not at that moment; she was feeling stubborn and determined, but not at all anxious. 'Is this how stalkers are born?' she asked an unresponsive feline. 'Oh well, if you won't help, I might as well…' she was contemplating the last towel and a full dryer… 'answer the phone.'

It was Katrina, wondering if Poppy would like to come over to her place, she was cooking a meal, Horace would be there and it really was time they met.

'Do I have a right of veto?'

'Of course not!' Katrina was at her most brisk. 'Whether that's a joke or not, it's in extremely bad taste. I *never* attempted to veto your – friends.'

'True enough. Sorry. Yes, I'll come. What time?'

'Six thirty for seven – oh, and Poppy dear, it would be nice if you were not wearing jeans.'

Poppy didn't know whether she would have worn jeans; she did know she was irritated at being given instructions. 'Not instructions, dear, just a preference,' she could hear her mother saying, and knew she wouldn't try to make an issue of it. She settled on black trousers and a dark green silk shirt, adding a scarf in bright swirly greens, yellows and pinks at the last moment.

'If that's not good enough for you, mother dear,' she said to the mirror, 'then too bad. Actually,' she said in the direction of the cat on the bed, turning to get different views of herself, 'I would be impressed if I saw me at government house, and Mr Deputy Mayor had better appreciate that.'

Katrina opened the door looking slightly flushed, wearing an apron. 'I forget how hot cooking can be,' she said as she kissed Poppy's cheek. 'Come in dear and taste this soup, I can't decide whether it needs more salt.' Then she stood back, looked at Poppy and nodded approvingly. 'Well done, dear. I think I gave you that scarf.' Poppy didn't remember, but she probably had.

Horace would be here in a few minutes, and Katrina had been delayed by a call from May-Yun wanting to know how she could check the credentials of the Chinese language teacher taking the class she and Ivan were attending. 'She's discovered he's not actually on the school staff, and I suspect she doesn't like some of his politics.' Katrina was stirring sauce, checking the rack of lamb in the oven, washing broccoli, passing a home-made dressing to Poppy to 'drizzle on the salad if you would, not too much.'

At the moment Katrina was removing the apron with a sigh of satisfaction the doorbell went.

'We've time for a drink while the lamb rests,' she said over her shoulder to Poppy, 'could you open the bottle of white in the bottom of the fridge?' She turned to meet Horace with a smile, which almost turned to a giggle when she saw him, short, shorter than Katrina, dapper, bow-tied, bald. She shook his hand and turned quickly back to the half-opened bottle.

The meal was delicious. Horace turned out to be funny in a dry kind of way, and gave the person he was speaking to his full attention. Katrina could learn from that, Poppy thought. She liked the way Horace was with her mother, almost gallant, and Katrina stopped just short of coy. Over coffee and liqueurs they disagreed over ideas for Auckland's transport tangle and Poppy enjoyed watching them tussle, both firm in their opinions and articulate in expressing them. Her contribution was to describe what it was like going against the flow of traffic across the Harbour Bridge in the mornings.

Poppy's offer to help clean up was firmly refused by them both; it was Horace who said they would do it together in the morning. Telling Horace, truthfully, that it had been a pleasure to meet him, she took herself off soon after nine.

'Thank you, my dear,' said Katrina at the door, with a mischievous smile, 'I do prefer my family to approve of my choices.' A reference no doubt to the unwelcome Don Smart, and to the pointlessness of pretending.

'And your "choices" to approve of your family?' she couldn't resist asking.

'Of course, that is best. Good night dear, drive home safely.'

Her route home went past that block of flats again. No point in stopping, Poppy thought, even if it is a bad idea, I don't even know which flat she is in. Somehow, she had pulled up in front of the building and noticed a row of carports one of which contained a car that looked like Joy's. She couldn't be sure of the colour in the dim light, so got out and walked across the driveway; sure enough it was Joy's car and the number over the carport was 4a.

'Can I help you with anything?'

'Ah!' she jumped and squealed. 'You shouldn't go around scaring people like that.' He was big and tall, was all she could tell, halo'ed by the street light behind him.

'I've got your licence plate number and unless you can tell me what you're doing around these cars I'll be ringing it in.' Then she saw the security guard patch on his shoulder.

'Oh shit,' she said.

He actually folded his arms across his chest, and waited.

'Look,' she began, sounding guilty to herself, 'my friend lives in this block but I don't know which flat, and I saw her car and came to see if there was a number. 4a,' she added, feeling foolish and unconvincing, pointing to the number.

'Let's take a visit to 4a then, and see your friend.' He didn't move. 'Unless you'd rather I rang the police…' She shook her head, embarrassed and miserable, and started to walk towards the entrance with him following closely behind. Briefly, she thought of making a run for it, but there was the matter of him identifying her car. And his ability to run faster she realised when they got into the light; he would be no more than twenty, big and no doubt fit. She looked around helplessly, 'I don't know where…'

He pointed to the lift. The doors opened immediately he touched the up button and he waved her in but she noticed his foot was in the gap.

'It'll be level four, don't you think?'

'I guess.' Should she be trying to make conversation? There didn't seem to be anything to say. I'll bet Katrina would be finding out who his parents are by now, was all she had time to think before the lift doors opened and there was number 4a directly in from of them.

'Do you have some ID?' At last, something sensible. He showed her a card with a photograph and the logo of the security firm; it looked real enough.

'Okay?' he finally asked. She nodded. He stepped over and pressed the doorbell at 4a.

'Do you have any idea what ti…? Joy said through the crack allowed by the security chain. Then she spotted Poppy, said, 'hang on' and closed the door and opened it fully.

'I'm sorry to disturb you miss. Do you know this lady?' Joy was wearing blue pyjamas with white spots and a darker blue dressing gown.

'Yes, I know her.' Her eyes were wide, she looked at Poppy.

'She was hanging around the cars downstairs miss, suspiciously I thought.'

'Oh no! I'm sure there's some mistake. She lives just down the road, she's a friend.'

The security guard wanted to see both of their driver's licences, then he went. Poppy stood in the corridor, looking at Joy's left shoulder, wishing the ground would swallow her up.

'You'd better come inside,' Joy said. She sounded as though she was about to laugh. If she does, I'll kill her, Poppy thought. 'Come on, I'll put the jug on, and it's definitely your turn to explain.'

'I'm so embarrassed,' was all Poppy could manage.

'I can see that. But no-one ever actually died of embarrassment you know.' She held the door open wider and stood back. Poppy resisted an urge to run away and walked in.

Chapter Nineteen

Perched on the edge of an armchair, clutching a mug of hot cocoa and looking at a spot on the carpet, Poppy blurted out everything that had happened since she stopped on her way home from Katrina's. Her voice faded out when she got to the security guard knocking on Joy's door. She looked up slowly and met Joy's eyes.

'You didn't laugh,' she said.

'Nearly, when I first saw you, dressed up flash and looking like a naughty child,' Joy said, seriously.

'I'm glad you didn't laugh.'

'It is funny, though.' Joy sipped cocoa. Her eyes, over the top of the mug, were shining bright blue.

'Is it? It feels incredibly stupid and soooooooo embarrassing. I mean, I don't think I was going to come up or anything, I just saw your car and wondered what number your flat was.' Poppy faltered, then desperately carried on. 'I wish security was that good in my street, my car's been broken into twice and the aerial bent once…' her voice trailed off again and she sat silently looking at the floor.

'I think there's been some vandalism, I got a notice from the landlord,' Joy looked around vaguely. 'Anyway, I guess he arranged something.'

'I don't know what you must think of me…' Poppy was looking a the floor again.

'I think you're rather cool, actually. And, sorry, but…' Joy spluttered, spraying a mouthful of milky brown liquid across the room, collapsing into a fit of laughing and choking.

After a moment of horrified paralysis, Poppy went over and thumped her on the back. A huge intake of breath later, Joy was wiping her face and laughing helplessly.

'Your face… that huge young man… Sorry… I can't help… you – so proper…' Joy was incoherent. Poppy didn't know why she started crying, standing there, rooted to the spot, tears running down her face. They could have been tears of laughter but she wasn't laughing; humiliation was more like it, standing beside an armchair in which a person she was probably in love with was hooting with laughter at her stupidity. There was Mrs Mudgely, hovering over the door jamb, shaking her head. It felt like days since she had been standing in front of her own mirror feeling pleased with herself and the way she looked.

'I'll be off, then,' she managed, lifting a foot heavy as a stone.

Joy was wiping her face with a sleeve. 'No,' she said, 'don't go. Sit down, please.' Poppy sat. Now Joy was studying the inside of her mug.

'I was in awe of you…' she began.

'Awe?' Poppy interrupted in disbelief.

'Yes, awe. Please be quiet and listen You do – did – everything right, even not knowing stuff, you listen and take notice…'

'You mean the garden?'

'Yes. Now stop interrupting.' Poppy sat back. 'You have a perfect life,' Joy went on, 'a good job you like, a house you love, family you get on with, heaps of friends, you're relaxed about being a lesbian, you know all the feminist stuff… you're bloody intimidating in fact.'

'Me? Intimid…'

'Yes.' Firmly. 'I'm not talking about what you feel like, I'm talking about how I've felt around you.'

'Oh.' Joy was serious now and Poppy was wanting to laugh at the very idea of being intimidating. 'Um, I don't know what to say, I certainly don't mean…'

'I know. And you are – or were. I'll tell you something else.' Joy stood up and walked around the room. As she spoke, Poppy watched her walk backwards and forwards, from time to time catching a glance, briefly.

Joy talked about how closetted she and Chris and their friends had been. 'We didn't talk about being lesbians,' she said, 'to each other let alone anyone else.' They got along with their neighbours without getting friendly enough to visit each others' houses and generally, Joy explained, didn't question anything. She herself saw little of her family, she didn't know how to be around her daughter, it was easy to get in the habit of thinking of her as a niece.

'When the feminists came along they ruined everything – well, that was what we thought at the time. Gay liberation was bad enough, but the feminists were worse.'

'I don't understand.' Poppy concentrated, hoping her stomach would unknot if she gave it no attention.

'They blew our cover. Outed us. Oh, not personally, but people began to notice us in ways they hadn't bothered about before. So we dug deeper into our closets, we were scared of losing our jobs, scared of being attacked and vilified, just plain damn scared. We hardly talked about that either, just pulled our little heads in. A few started going out with gay boys now and then, you know, cover for both. Some even got married to straight guys, others went to the big city, Auckland. Or Sydney.

'It was around then that Chris and I got serious together and bought our house. We let the real estate agent think we were sisters and had conversations in front of him about who would have what bedroom. There's lots more, but that'll do for now.' Joy had sat down and was turning her mug round and round and Poppy was watching her hands.

'It was a secret life in all sorts of ways and I stayed there *all that time*, I never left, I never changed, until a couple of years ago. I *envy* you, for heaven's sake and I don't see how I can ever measure up.'

'Measure up to wh…? No, I think I get a glimmer of what you're saying…'

'So you making a complete idiot of yourself was, well, kind of equalising…' She grinned. 'And bloody funny.'

Poppy could not have said what she was feeling. 'I guess,' she managed, and then, 'do you think I'm smug?'

'No, not really, just a bit earnest sometimes,' said Joy, with the slightest twitch of an eyebrow.

'Oh.' So forthright! All right then. She could match that.

'I still want to kiss you. Oh, do I want to kiss you!'

'All right.' Joy's face flushed, her voice was small.

They met between the chairs. Poppy had to stoop. Both were tentative at first, but not for long. Joy's hands were in her hair, down her back, someone was moaning and they were together on the sofa, eyes locked, touching each others' faces. Poppy slid a hand down the other woman's neck, under the blue and white collar onto a breast, mirroring the movements of the hand moving under her shirt. She wanted this, wanted this surging in her body, wanted this woman.

'Whoa. Just a minute.' Joy jumped up. The tears in her eyes were not from laughter now. Poppy watched her, silently. 'The thing is,' Joy went on, 'I haven't done this without a drink for more years than I care to remember. I need to tell you that.' Before Poppy could reply, Joy took a big breath and reached out to grab Poppy's hand, leading her to a surprisingly white and cream bedroom with a brilliantly blue cover on the large bed. 'I'm over it,' she said, as she flung the cover back and pulled Poppy down onto the bed with her, flinging away the multi-coloured scarf and sliding both hands up under the silky shirt.

'Skin is best,' she murmured, with a sharp intake of breath when she encountered a soft breast with a rigid nipple. They explored each other's body with great attention and mutual satisfaction until they fell into a shared exhausted sleep, spooned, with a tangle of legs.

It was still dark when Poppy woke. She lay still on her back, wondering at the past day… year, even.

'I meant what I said, you know.' She could feel the other woman's breath on her cheek and turned her head to meet it with a kiss.

'Mmmmm.' Joy pulled back and repeated, 'I meant what I said.'

'Which bit.' Poppy tickled naked ribs as she spoke.

'All of it. Stop that.' A light smack to her hand. 'I have to have a whole year living by myself. I made a promise.'

'All right. Who did you promise?'

'Me. I told you before.'

Poppy hadn't got up to thinking about consequences of the night's happenings. 'Okay, we won't move in together on the second date.' On the whole that was a relief. Unless it meant… she turned, running her hand up Joy's thigh, and over the next while was thoroughly reassured that their love-making the night before had indeed been a beginning.

Afterwards, they slept again, waking to a cold, grey, dry morning. Poppy borrowed a robe that barely covered her buttocks and they had breakfast together – toast, jam and coffee – in Joy's tiny kitchen. For the first time Poppy noticed the flat; it was small compared to her house, tidy, decorated in blue and cream with red cushions and rich, bottle-green curtains. Very deliberate. A contrast to her own comfortable hodge podge.

'Did you…?'

'Yes. Kept me busy the first few lonely weeks. Still a bit too 'designer' but I like the colours.'

Poppy wanted to talk about what had happened, was happening. She put a hand across the table and grasped Joy's. 'I want to say "I love you",' she said, 'and I'm shy.'

'Me too. To both.' Joy's grip tightened. 'I'm scared I'll be a disappointment to you.'

Poppy swallowed the laugh that bubbled, remembering what Joy had been saying the night before.

'How about,' she said, 'we agree that if I'm disappointed I'll tell you, and you don't worry about it unless I say. And I'll do the same. If you see what I mean.'

'I don't believe it can be that si…'

'Simple. Right. But we can have a go.'

'Uh-huh.' They sat and smiled at each other.

'Go away!' Poppy said to a serious Mrs Mudgely hovering over the doorframe, and then was embarrassed and confused explaining that she talked to her cat, even when she wasn't really there. She ended up explaining the whole Mrs Mudgely phenomenon. 'It's different,' she said, 'Mrs M was besotted with Jane and she doesn't seem so keen…'

'On me? No. I have my own way with animals. We'll work it out. What about Jane? What if this is just a rebounder? Now that would *really* bother me.'

'It isn't, really.' Poppy was serious. 'I think Jane was an interlude – a something – to nudge me out of – something – and I certainly was for her.'

Poppy declined an invitation to join Bessie and Joy for the lunch they had planned together in the city and the movie they would go to afterwards. 'Preparation for school,' she explained. And a chance to mull over… things… 'Do you mind if I tell Martia –?'

'That we became an item? We did, didn't we?' Poppy nodded. 'Not if,' said Joy smiling wickedly, 'I can tell Bessie. How long do you reckon?'

'Before the world knows? I dunno, a week maybe.'

'I give it two days.' Joy made a phone of her hand. 'Have you heard about Poppy and the new blonde in town?' she said in a silly voice. They laughed, and hugged, and kissed. Joy drew back first, and pushed Poppy towards the door. 'Go, woman, and mull. Let's talk tonight…' she made the phone motion again.

Poppy stood for a moment on the landing, then ran down the stairs, faintly surprised to find her car exactly where she had left it a long night ago. Mrs Mudgely met her at the bottom of her steps within seconds of her pulling in to the curb.

'Grumpy, are you?' Poppy picked her up. 'Sorry. And you might have to get used to this. I'll leave out more biscuits next time, promise.' The cat refused to purr until Poppy was scooping food, one-handed, into her dish, holding the cat on her shoulder with the other.

There was no point in ringing Martia until after five, so Poppy did a load of washing, optimistically pegged it outside, tidied, sorted clothes for the coming week. Happily, she thought, I'm happily cleaning and tidying my house. She thought, too, about being called 'intimidating' and decided that was for talking with Martia about. As she moved her familiar pieces of furniture – or a least, some of them – to run the vacuum cleaner over the floor underneath, it came to her that when Joy's year of living alone was up – if she and Joy were still, in Joy's words, 'an item,' – oh, please let that be! – there were implications. Oh yes, she thought, implications about where they would live. She turned the cleaner off and sat in a misplaced arm chair, fondly patting its shabby arm.

'I can't expect her to just move in here,' she said to Mrs Mudgely, whose head had appeared around the door. She patted her knee and the cat jumped up. 'It might mean getting a new house together, I'd better start thinking about that.' She knew she didn't want to think about that. Mrs Mudgely kneaded in her lap. 'And even if she does want to live here, it'll mean changing things.' She stroked the chair arm, then the cat, expecting a sinking feeling that didn't arrive.

At five o'clock she rang Martia and had to wait for her to ring back when she had finished a planning session with Gloria about what stock they would need for the summer trade. When she finally

had an attentive Martia on the phone and was making a joke of her
encounter with the security guard her friend interrupted.

'What exactly *were* you doing hovering about the car parks at Joy's
flats, Poppy?' Martia asked.

'Trying to find out her flat number so I could… Oh, I don't know,
Martia…' and at last she was telling her friend about being told 'no'
in her kitchen when she wanted to kiss Joy, and everything that had
happened since. Martia said very little, other than to encourage her
to continue. When she had told it all Poppy waited for a response.
After a few second's silence, Martia said,

'Well, that's a turn-up. I didn't pick it, not in the least.'

'Me neither. You don't sound very pleased.'

'Oh. No. Sorry. I think I'm just getting used to a little hiccup in
my back-up plan, you know, us as best friends growing old together,
if up here doesn't work out. Sorry, that's selfish. Actually,' and
Martia's voiced changed, 'I am used to it, and it's terrific. You and
Joy, of course, I predict you'll do splendidly together.'

'Oh, Martia, for a minute there I thought you were going to
disapprove. Of course you could always come and stay, you know
that.'

'Yes, I know that…'

'… and it doesn't stop us being best friends…'

'Of course not. And, hey, what now?'

'She doesn't want us to live together for a bit.' By the time she had
explained Joy's reasons, and they had talked about Katrina's Horace,
Poppy was ravenous. 'No, it's not a secret,' she said as they were
saying their goodbyes, 'but I do feel a bit shy about it, especially so
soon after Jane…'

'… well, it's not that I see anyone to gossip with up here. And I
am truly really, really happy for you both. I wish I could give you a
hug.'

'Me too. And you'll be down in a couple of weeks – you will stay
with me, won't you?'

'I'm counting on it – as long as I won't be intruding…'

'Dear Martia, you could never intrude…'

Finally she was in the kitchen, cheese and tomatoes grilling on toast while she put out food for an insistent Mrs Mudgely, who had finished eating by the time Poppy's food was done. They sat side by side on the living room sofa, heater on full, the cat eating tiny pieces of bread and cheese off the edge of the tray on Poppy's lap.

'You're not infallible, you know,' Poppy told her, 'you with your Jane-can-do-no-wrong and Joy-who's-she?' There was no response except the licking of a paw. 'Maybe I don't need your advice any more,' she went on, then added hastily, 'but I'll always treasure your company.' They both started at the sound of the doorbell.

Joy was on the doorstep, overnight bag in one hand, brandishing a toothbrush in the other.

OTHER BOOKS FROM SPINIFEX PRESS

Poppy's Progress
Pat Rosier

An evocative look at life and love, *Poppy's Progress* is a delightful story of a woman coming to terms with loss, and discovering that you can be surprised, even by those you are closest to.

ISBN: 1-876756-28-4

All That False Instruction
Kerryn Higgs

Passionate, funny and heartbreaking, this remarkable novel traces a young woman's turbulent coming of age.

"An explosive mix of raw sanity and wicked humour – a bombshell of a book."

–Robert Dessaix

"a feminist classic."

–Debra Adelaide, *Sydney Morning Herald*

ISBN: 1-876756-14-4

Goja
Suniti Namjoshi

Sunit Namjoshi grew up between the rich and the poor, between the ruling house of the Ranisaheb and the servant woman, Goja, between the East of experience and the West of the English language.

Part autobiography, part elegy. A celebration of the quest for love.

"Suniti Namjoshi is an inspired fabulist."

–Marina Warner

ISBN: 1-875559-97-3

Figments of a Murder
Gillian Hanscombe

Babes is about lust. Babes is about power. But what else is she up to? Set in London *Figments of a Murder* is passionate and satirical, probing images of self, sex, stardom and sisterhood.

"A rich and robust satire of feminist politics combined with a murder mystery. May scandalise the sisters, but some wonderful writing."

–Anne Coombs, The Australian Year's Best Books

ISBN: 1-875559-43-4

Parachute Silk: A Novel in Letters
Gina Mercer

Molly and Finn have been passionate friends for over twenty years. In their feisty letters Finn describes her previous love affairs, and past secrets come to the surface.

"a must for any woman who has cherished the written word in the form of a letter."

–Michelle Grant, Lesbiana

ISBN: 1-876756-11-X

Rumours of Dreams
Sandi Hall

Beginning in a South Pacific future and stretching back to a Mediterranean past, Sandi Hall's new and startling novel explores a friendship that could affect the history of the world.

"Move over, Matthew, Mark, Luke and John: this is a Gospel for the new millennium."

–Denis Welch, NZ Listener

ISBN: 1-875559-75-2

Still Murder
Finola Moorhead

Why has Senior Detective Constable Margot Gorman been assigned to watch over a raving woman in an asylum? And what is she raving about? Does it have anything to do with the dead body discovered in the park?

"I delighted in Moorhead's intricate and lucid manoeuvres through the genre. *Still Murder* is an elaborate jigsaw of rival perspectives and rival documentations, and yet unfolds with deceptive ease."

–Helen Daniel, *Australian Book Review*

ISBN: 1-876756-33-0

Darkness More Visible
Finola Moorhead

Margot Gorman is now a free agent, a triathlete and a connoisseur of good wine. When she finds a body in the women's toilets a tangle of mysteries opens up.

"Wry, sardonic, cool and spirited, its themes of subversion and survival are exciting and marvellous ... a contemporary classic."

–Debra Adelaide, *The Sydney Morning Herald*

ISBN: 1-875559-60-4

The Falling Woman
Susan Hawthorne

A vivid desert odyssey; the falling woman traverses a haunting landscape of memory, myth and mental maps.

"A remarkable, lyrical first novel."

–Robin Morgan, *Ms Magazine*

ISBN: 1-876756-36-5

If you would like to know more about Spinifex Press
write for a free catalogue or visit our website

SPINIFEX PRESS
PO Box 212 North Melbourne
Victoria 3051 Australia
<http://www.spinifexress.com.au>